D1713848

Southside Gothic

J. E. Staab

Cover art by Tyler Spicher and Julie Milliman
ISBN-13: 9798555345790

DEDICATION

Many, many thanks to the family and friends who have encouraged me, especially my husband, Bob. This book is dedicated to my mother, Donna, who loved a good mystery or crime novel as much as anybody.

CHAPTER ONE

Jordan Bell stepped out of his apartment, locked the door behind him, and stumped down the worn wooden steps, three flights of them, into the early summer evening. His back ached from the move; he could feel the grittiness of dust and dried sweat under his tee-shirt. In the middle of unpacking a box, his tiny apartment had abruptly seemed stifling; he had to get out. A trip to the grocery store seemed as good an excuse as any.

He slung his body into the driver's seat of his car and glanced in the rearview mirror at his face, then ran a hand through dark hair that was frosted with dust and started his vehicle. It wasn't much; a ten-year-old Impala acquired a week ago from a small, seedy-looking used car dealership in New Jersey; it had over one hundred thousand miles on it, and the gray paint was fading. He hadn't needed a vehicle in New York City, but the Impala was an unfortunate necessity in Pittsburgh. When it started to get colder, he would need to get tires for it; the balding rubber on it would never handle the steep, snowy western Pennsylvania hills. He started it up, opening the windows to let out the August heat until the impotent air-conditioning kicked in.

The nearest grocery store was across the Birmingham Bridge, in Southside. He stopped there and got a few staples to stock the pantry. Protein bars, coffee, sandwich fixings, ramen noodles; he wasn't a cook, and frankly, he hadn't had much of an appetite lately. He'd lost at least five pounds in the last three weeks, pounds that he could ill afford to give up. By the time he was back in his car, it was nearly seven, and this time when he opened the windows, he left the air-conditioning off.

It was the kind of summer evening that Pittsburghers dreamed of all winter long. The air was balmy; the sun, low in the sky, sent a hazy golden glow over the city. Trees, full-leaved and green, softened the banks of the rivers and the steep rocky hills above them. Instead of heading back to his apartment, Jordan drove away from the bridge, heading along East Carson Street to Arlington and up, up the nearly vertical slope to Mount Washington.

Mount Washington sat on the south bank of the Monongahela River, and from its height, offered a magnificent view of downtown. Jordan pulled his car into a parking spot on Grandview near the overlook and took in the scene from the open window. The perfume of a honey locust tree drifted in on the breeze. The last time he'd been up there, he'd been wearing an expensive suit, riding in a Mercedes, on his way to an upscale restaurant.

The sun had sunk to the horizon, turning the west sides of the skyscrapers orange, the U.S. Steel Tower rising above them. He could hear the muted hum and bustle of a big metropolis, but the softness of the evening lent an air of serenity. Jordan had the sense that the city had moved on without him in the two years he'd been away; it looked the same but somehow didn't seem the same. Familiar, yet it felt foreign. Home, but it didn't feel like home. He was twenty-three, and although people who knew him called him an old soul, there were times when he felt his youth and inexperience. Tonight, for instance. For that matter, for all of the last few weeks.

He sat there until the sun had set and darkness began to take over, and with the night came the vaguely unsettled feeling that had dogged his waking hours ever since the incident at the warehouse in Brooklyn. He turned the key in the ignition and headed for his apartment. There, he carefully locked the door, made himself a sandwich, and showered. A dress shirt and some pants, wrinkled from their journey in boxes, went under the iron. He plugged his cell phone into its charger and fell into bed.

The panic attack took him by surprise. He'd gotten up at six the next morning and had been up for a half-hour, had a shower, coffee, and a shave. Although his anxiety level was high that morning, the surge of fear was completely unexpected. Jordan had closed his eyes as he tilted his head back to adjust the knot of his tie, and without warning, he was back in the warehouse, with a heavy hand on the back of his neck and the sound of gunshots, the smell of blood and fear and death. He opened his eyes and stared at his face in the bathroom mirror: pale, eyes dark, pupils dilated, beads of sweat on his brow.

He opened the medicine cabinet, rummaged through it, and pulled out a prescription bottle. He could hear the dry rattle of pills inside as his hand tightened around it. He held it for a moment while his breath evened out, then let his hand relax and put it away. The container's plastic bottom hit the shelf again with a solid click, and the cabinet door creaked shut.

Taking a deep breath, he stood with his arms propped on the sink and let his head drop, and stared at the ring of rust around the sink drain. Then he cleared his throat and gave a small shake of his head, and straightened his back. The panic attack had been an anomaly, the result of first-day jitters and the unusual sense of pressure on the back of his neck; that was all. It wouldn't happen again. And even if it did, he knew he could act his way through it. Every encounter with others was role-playing of one kind or another, and he was good at that.

The Pennsylvania Department of Investigation was in downtown Pittsburgh, situated in a corner of the same building that housed the Pittsburgh Bureau of Police headquarters. Jordan found the place quickly enough; the big yellow brick building spanned the better part of a block on Western Avenue on Pittsburgh's North Side. He got there early and made his way through the building to the PDI office. There, he met briefly with the PDI West head, John Morrissey, who seemed to be a busy man. He gave Jordan a few facts about the organization, then plunked him in a chair at an empty desk and told him that a man named Mike DeLuca would be in shortly, walked into his office, and shut the door. There were others in the office seated at desks in the bullpen, three men and a woman, but Morrissey made no introductions, so Jordan sat there in awkward silence and tried to ignore the glances sent his way when they thought that he wasn't looking.

Eventually, another man strode into the office. He was good-looking and tall, with brown hair and eyes and an air of authority. He threw a briefcase on a desk set off from the rest of the bullpen by cubicle walls and, with barely a pause in his stride, walked into Morrissey's office. Through the office windows, Jordan could see Morrissey talking, could see the skepticism on the other man's face as he turned to study him. It didn't bother Jordan; it wouldn't be the first time someone had underestimated him based on first impressions. He was young, and he knew he looked even younger than he was. His appearance probably didn't help much; he was aware that he was attractive, with his dark hair and eyes, but in an androgynous sense, the pretty-boy look favored by teenagers. At five-nine and on the slight side, he wasn't what one would consider beefy.

Eventually, the man snagged the file from the desk and stepped out into the office, closing Morrissey's door behind him. He walked up to Jordan, who rose from the chair as he approached. "Jordan Bell? Mike DeLuca," said the man, and he held out his hand.

Jordan said, "Good to meet you," and gave his hand a solid shake.

DeLuca said, "Welcome to the PDI. I'm the team leader and your partner, at least for the time being. You'll be working with me as you train. Let me introduce you to the rest of the group."

His manner was abrupt, gruff. He led Jordan over to two desks near the far windows, and Jordan shot a glance at him as they went, trying to get a read on the reason for the dour face. The rest of the team included four agents. Jen Sandberg, a blonde from Iowa, was wearing a no-nonsense gray pantsuit and making it look good. She was partnered with her sartorial opposite, a lean, sharply-dressed man named Devon Young, from Chicago. He sported a lilac shirt and an expensive tie, and a sleek jacket hung from the back of his chair. The other two agents were Pittsburgh natives: Marty Beran, a rumpled, big, impressively bearded man nicknamed Bear, and Milt Walecki, a thin, wiry man with a face that bore the premature lines of a smoker, who wore a suit that looked to be vintage 1950. All of them, including Mike, were at least in their early thirties. Experienced, seasoned agents. They were friendly enough, but their eyes were sharp. Jordan knew what they were thinking - that he was too young to be here.

Introductions complete, they walked over to Mike's office, a small piece of carpet with a desk and a table on the far side of the room, surrounded by six-foot-high beige cubicle walls. The cubicle's entryway had no door, and looked out into the room. The one empty desk in the bullpen was closest to that office, right across the aisle. Jordan would be within eyesight of DeLuca at all times, like an insect in a jar.

DeLuca motioned, and Jordan stepped into the cubicle and took one of the chairs facing his desk. "Jordan Alonzo Bell. You know anything about the PDI?" DeLuca asked as he settled into his chair. He leaned back and squared his shoulders as he asked the question.

That was easy enough, simple regurgitation of what Morrissey had told him. "It's a state agency, with heads appointed by the governor," said Jordan. "There is an East division located in Philadelphia and a West division located in Pittsburgh. We're the West Division, and Morrissey is the West Division head." He paused. DeLuca kept his mouth shut, so Jordan went on. "The PDI shares some resources with the Pittsburgh Bureau of Police, such as the Mobile Crime Unit, which does their forensics, and you use some of their administrative resources. Sometimes you do joint investigations with them or with the FBI, and sometimes you work with agencies across the state borders in Ohio or West Virginia."

DeLuca sat there a moment longer, studying him. Jordan fought the urge to fidget and returned his gaze impassively. DeLuca finally spoke. "So, NYPD, huh? Two years. Pretty tough to get in there right off the bat. And you were, what? Twenty-one?"

"Yes, sir. I started work on my twenty-first birthday – I tried to apply earlier, but NYPD won't take anyone younger than twenty-one."

"Graduated first in your class in high school at age sixteen -," DeLuca paused and looked down, scanning paperwork. "Pre-law degree from Pitt at age nineteen. Fluent in Spanish."

"Yes, sir. My mother is from Bolivia."

DeLuca nodded, pursed his lips. "You think you're pretty sharp."

Jordan met his gaze directly. "Yes."

"So, why'd you leave New York?"

"That was classified, sir, and it's an ongoing investigation. I'm not supposed to discuss it."

"Did you get canned?"

Jordan's jaw tightened. "No."

"Morrissey told me that your dad is head of neurosurgery here at UPMC and that he and the governor are friends. Maybe pulled a few strings to get you in here?"

"My move here had nothing to do with my father." That came out more curtly than Jordan intended.

DeLuca cocked his head, studying him again. "Okay. We've got a lot of stuff to get through today. You're going to fill out this paperwork. We're going to get you a badge, a computer, and a gun, in that order. Then we'll head down to the gun range to test your shooting skills, and we'll finish up with your physical test. We use a version of the Cooper test, and we'll be using the PBP facilities. Did you bring workout gear?"

"Yes, sir."

"Let's move, then. And do me a favor and drop the 'sir.' It's 'Mike.'

Later that afternoon, Jordan pulled his Impala around the back of his Oakland apartment building and into the parking lot. He stepped out of the vehicle and grabbed his backpack; the car door groaned and creaked as he slammed it shut.

The worn, discolored red brick on the building radiated summer heat. Jordan unlocked the outer door and pulled it open. Smell assailed him, a conglomeration of mustiness, takeout Chinese food, pizza, and grease, along with the odor of curry that always came from an apartment on the second floor. Today, it was all laced with the scent of pot, also coming from the second floor, along with the muffled sound of pounding music; most of the apartments were leased to students who attended the University of Pittsburgh. Jordan pulled off his aviator sunglasses and trudged up the third flight of steps to the top floor. He was technically a student himself; he had signed up for an evening class starting in the fall – this time around, computer classes. Probably what he should have taken as an undergrad. Professor Latimore, head of the Computer Science department at Pitt, had tried to talk him into changing his major when he was there studying law and was happy to see him again.

The day hadn't gone too badly, he thought, as he unlocked his apartment door – first the regular lock and then the secure deadbolt he had added. No further panic attacks. He'd passed his tests, which had not been a foregone conclusion. His shooting skills were marginal but had been good enough, and his upper body strength was average, at best. But he'd done well on the speed, endurance, and agility testing and had aced the written exams.

DeLuca was something of a disappointment. He'd been oddly confrontational; Jordan suspected that the man was trying to test his self-control. He didn't seem very excited to have a new partner, but Jordan had complied with his peremptory orders and had shrugged off the jabs. He hadn't given the man any inkling that he'd noticed. He'd learned long ago never to show emotion.

He locked the door behind him, slung his backpack on his sofa, and put his sunglasses on the cheap paste-wood coffee table in front of it. He walked into his bedroom and laid his newly-assigned Glock in a drawer in the chipped wooden nightstand next to his bed. He would be issued a department cell phone, but he didn't have it yet. He unloaded his pockets - personal cell phone, wallet, and keys went on the top of the nightstand pausing only to study his new badge. He stood for a moment; a shaft of sunlight was filtering through the cloudy glass of his bedroom window, and he watched tiny particles of dust shimmer and float in the pale yellow light and thought about New York.

Later, in the new hours of the next morning, Poppy Jankovic sat in a chair in the dark and watched her life drip away.

The night had started at her favorite hangout, a bar called Harry's, in Pittsburgh's Southside neighborhood. She traveled there from Ohio because it was hard to find Goth hangouts anymore, at least in the Youngstown area. She would get out of work at the nail salon, run back to the house she shared with Cassie and Tara, her roommates, and don her pale makeup, touch up her black eyeliner and put on her black clothes and her piercings. Then she would get in her ratty old Ford and start the eighty-minute drive to Pittsburgh.

She hated Cassie and Tara – they were mean and catty and as thick as thieves. She knew they looked down on her because of her Goth interests, and she spent as little time with them as possible. She only lived there out of necessity because she couldn't afford a place of her own, and she refused to live at home. So, a night out at Harry's was a true escape from her sorry life, a chance to spend time with a group of people who thought as she did.

The evening at Harry's had started as it always did; she'd hung out in the corner of the bar where the Goth crowd collected. Contrary to popular belief, many Goths did not get into the drug scene, and a lot of them didn't even drink, at least not any more than the general population did. Poppy didn't do drugs, but she did like a drink or two, and she'd had a couple that night. Maybe more than she had thought because she must have passed out. She dimly remembered going outside to the parking lot for air, and then, well, she'd woken up here – wherever here was.

Her head was still fuzzy, and the room was spinning. There was a soft golden light coming from behind her, like a candle or a lamp, and she could make out the dark interior of a small corrugated metal building that must have been old because the metal was rusting and coming apart in spots. She was having a hard time getting air, and when she tried to move her jaw, it was stuck – she understood, with a sudden surge of fear, that her mouth had been taped shut.

She was sitting, her arms tied to a heavy wooden chair at the elbows, taped at the wrists. The inside of her forearms faced up, and she realized they had been cut, slit from elbow to wrist with something thin, like a razor. Blood, black in the faint light, was spilling over them, dripping onto the concrete floor and pooling in a drain beneath her chair. She could hear a quiet gurgling noise as her life ran down into the old pipes.

She could sense someone behind her, watching, and as terror spiked through her, she moaned and cried through the tape. Then the voice started, taunting her, talking, talking, through the almost painful thirst that began to consume her, through the dull ache in her head, through the pounding of her heart, through the screaming and crying and writhing against her bonds until she grew weaker and weaker and all of it faded away, as she slipped into the soft gray of unconsciousness.

And then there was only Death and Darkness. Darkness let out a breath and said, "Damn. That was intense."

Death hovered over the body, in silent ecstasy.

CHAPTER TWO

The buzzing of his cell phone on his nightstand made Jordan sit upright, and he groped for it, frowning, blinking blearily at the time. 5:36 a.m. The caller was unknown, but it was a Pittsburgh number, and he punched at the phone to answer, to be greeted by Mike DeLuca's voice, brisk and business-like. "Bell? Hey, we're gonna need you in here early today. We just caught a case. We need to get out to the scene."

"Yeah, okay. I'll be right in." Jordan's voice was rusty with sleep; he'd been up late surfing the Web the night before. He hung up and sat propped on his elbow for a moment, rubbing his face, trying to clear the cobwebs from his head, and then pecked at his phone, attaching DeLuca's name to the unknown number and adding it to his contacts. Then he shuffled into his tiny kitchen and started the coffee before he headed for the shower. He felt anxiety nibbling at the back of his mind, but not as prevalent as the day before.

He dressed in a suit – that seemed to be correct office-wear – and decided that he would need to get more of them. Gun, badge, phone, coffee, notebook, and a protein bar; he collected them and was out of the door, drinking his coffee on the way and pulling into the police headquarters lot by twenty after six. The August heat hadn't kicked in yet, and it was still cool at that hour, although humidity hung in the air. As he got out of his car, he saw DeLuca heading toward him across the lot, waving. "This way," he called. "Come on; I'm driving."

Jordan got into the vehicle, the same shiny black Ford Explorer he remembered from yesterday, and shot DeLuca a glance. "What's up?"

DeLuca put the vehicle into gear, not bothering to look at him. "We've got a body. An early morning jogger spotted it on the tracks near the Hazelwood Trail, near the Hot Metal Bridge. Young woman, her ID was on her. Her wrists were slit." He swung the Ford out of the parking lot.

Jordan frowned. "It sounds like suicide."

DeLuca nodded. "It would, except that there was very little blood at the site. The PBP officer who got there first thinks someone must have moved her from wherever she was when she died. They've got a medical examiner and forensic team already there."

"Why do they need us?"

"Because she's from Ohio. They usually call us in on cases that may cross state lines."

Jordan pondered that as DeLuca crossed the Fort Duquesne Bridge and maneuvered onto Interstate 376. The early morning sunshine glinted off of the river and the vehicles of early commuters, illuminating one side of the downtown buildings and leaving blue shadows on the other. Jordan squinted into the light and slipped on his aviator sunglasses. He knew they made him look like a rock star. DeLuca finally glanced sideways at him and lifted an eyebrow, and Jordan stifled a grin.

Pittsburgh was a city of bridges; it sat at the confluence of three rivers; the Allegheny, which they had just crossed, and the Monongahela, both of which emptied into the Ohio River. The Hazelwood Trail was a tree-lined section of bike and jogging trail that ran along the Monongahela; as an avid cyclist, Jordan had been on it many times himself. The portion of the path near the Hot Metal Bridge was just south of Oakland, where he lived. The body had been found roughly a mile from his apartment, maybe less.

They arrived, tires grating on gritty asphalt as DeLuca pulled into a parking lot next to the bridge, behind a collection of cars in the corner of the lot. They stepped out and headed toward a group that milled around on the trail itself. Beyond it, across a small grassy area wet with morning dew, the body lay on a gravel area that ran along the railroad track. In the background, Jordan could glimpse the river through stands of trees. The ME was already there, lifting a cover to examine the corpse. A forensics team member strolled around the site, studying the ground, stopping once to take a picture. DeLuca walked up to a fit-looking man with gray sideburns standing on the trail and stuck out his hand. "Will." He indicated Jordan with a jerk of his head. "This is Jordan Bell, my new partner. Jordan, this is Detective Will Lacke, with the Pittsburgh Bureau of Police." Jordan shook hands and murmured hello as the rest of the group, mostly PBP cops, shot glances at him, some pretending disinterest, some openly curious. Jordan gave them a look, face flinty under his Hollywood sunglasses. DeLuca said, "What do we have?"

Will said, "Deceased is a young woman, Poppy Jankovic, aged 26, according to her driver's license, which we found in her back pocket. She was discovered lying on her back, fully clothed, with no obvious sign of sexual assault, no car keys, no purse. Her driver's license has her address as Hubbard, Ohio." He scratched his head, looked back at the body. "It looks like she probably bled to death – there are deep cuts along the inside of her forearms – but she didn't do it here. We'll know more when the ME gets done."

"Can I take a look?" asked DeLuca.

Will nodded. "Just try not to disturb the ground around the body too much – the lab is still going over it."

DeLuca nodded and headed off across the grass, following a path already trampled through the dew. Jordan, although he hadn't explicitly been invited, followed. As they approached, DeLuca murmured a few words to the ME, a good-looking bespectacled woman of about forty, and she pulled back the cover about halfway. Poppy Jankovic, a young, somewhat heavy woman, was lying on her back with her head slightly to the side, her hands at her sides, her face unnaturally white. Jordan realized some of the paleness was due to makeup; the victim wore black, piercings, and black fingernail polish – typical Goth apparel. Typical Goth makeup, too, light foundation and dark black eyeliner, lots of it, and her hair appeared to be dyed black. The ME gently lifted an arm and turned it over against the slight stiffness that was already beginning to set in, and they could see long, deep cuts that traversed most of the length between the elbow and wrist, made by something thin, possibly a razor blade, or a sharp knife. There were marks around her wrists and elbows. The ME said, "She appears to have bled to death, somewhere, not here, because there's not enough blood. It looks as though someone tied her down – there are ligature marks around her ankles and elbows, and there was possibly duct tape around her wrists. I would say she struggled based on the rawness of the marks, so she was possibly conscious as she bled out."

"Estimated time of death?"

"I'll know more when I get her to the lab, but no more than eight hours, probably less," said the ME. She glanced at Jordan.

"Sorry, Angie, this is my partner, Jordan Bell," said DeLuca. "He just joined the PDI." He looked at Jordan sharply as he said it; Jordan wondered if he'd overstepped his bounds by following DeLuca over to the body. "Jordan, this is Dr. Angela Washington."

Jordan nodded. "Nice to meet you, Doctor." He couldn't help but stare at the body; he'd only seen one other in his first two years of police work. Neither DeLuca nor Dr. Washington seemed perturbed, and Jordan tried to act as if it didn't bother him.

Angela smiled kindly. "Call me 'Angie.'"

DeLuca said, "It sounds like we may be picking this one up, so we'll need a copy of your report when you've had a chance to get a look." He stumped off, and as Jordan turned to follow him, Angie gave him a grin and a wink. Jordan smiled back, wondering at the reason for the wink. He trailed behind DeLuca again as they walked back toward Detective Lacke. He was trying not to disturb the area, although he was beginning to feel just a bit ridiculous, following DeLuca around like a puppy.

"Who found her?" asked DeLuca as he came up to Lacke.

Lacke nodded to a man standing several yards away on the edge of the lot. "Jogger, his name's Jim Wicks. He's not happy to still be here, but we asked him to stay, and he's cooperating. I think we're done with him, and we've got his contact info – when you're finished, you can tell him to go."

DeLuca nodded and jerked his head at Jordan to follow as he headed toward the man. "Okay, Bell," he said, as they made their way across the corner of the parking lot. "You take this one."

Jordan shot him a glance, but DeLuca didn't elaborate. Jordan had never handled an interrogation before, but he was certainly willing to try. He pulled off the sunglasses and tucked them in his jacket pocket. "Okay."

Jordan took the lead as they approached the jogger, a lean man of about fifty or so. "I'm sorry to keep you waiting. I'm Agent Bell, and this is Agent DeLuca – we're from the PDI. We're going to ask you a few more questions, and then you'll be free to go, although we may contact you again later." The man looked frustrated but brightened at the promise of imminent freedom.

"That's great," he said. "I'm pretty late for work."

Jordan nodded. "We appreciate your patience. Your name is James Wicks?"

"Yes, I go by Jim."

"Okay, Jim, about what time did you find the body?"

Jim sighed a little impatiently, indicating that he'd already answered that question. "It was a little before five. I try to get a run in before I go to work in the morning. I parked and walked over to the trail, and that's when I saw her."

"It was dark then, and she was near the tracks, not on the trail. How did you even see her?"

Jim fished a contraption out of his pocket, a small rectangular light attached to an elastic headband. "I wear a headlight. I was heading for the trail when my headlight picked up something dark lying there on the tracks – I didn't even know what it was at first, but I run this trail every other day – I knew it wasn't something that was usually there. I crossed the trail and walked over to it, and when I got close enough to see it was a person, I kind of freaked, to be honest. I ran back to my car, got my phone, and called 911. They asked me if she was still alive, and I wasn't sure, so I went back, checked her neck, and couldn't find a pulse. They said they were sending an ambulance and the police." He shuddered. "She felt cool. A few minutes later, the police showed up, and they took over."

"Did you see anyone else around?"

"No, there aren't usually many people here at that time of day. Once in a while, there's another jogger, but not this morning. There was no one, no cars or people coming or going except me. There were a couple of cars parked in the lot, but that's not too unusual. I think some of the workers at the place across the street park here, and they must start early or work shifts." He pointed to a small group of cars at the far end of the lot, closer to the street.

"Have you ever seen the victim before?"

"No. Not at all. I feel bad; she looks young. Was it drugs?"

"We're still investigating. Mike, anything you want to ask?"

DeLuca shook his head. "Not right now. You gave the first officer your contact information?"

Jim nodded. "Yes."

DeLuca gave him his card. "Okay, we'll be in touch, and we'd like to have you come down to the headquarters building to give a documented statement. One of us will contact you to set it up. In the meantime, if you think of anything else, give me a call. Thanks for your help, Mr. Wicks – you're free to go."

Wicks nodded gratefully and jogged off. DeLuca watched him go, watched which car he got into and where it was parked.

"Okay?" asked Jordan.

"Okay, what?"

The man's obtuseness flustered Jordan. DeLuca's eyes were on him, waiting for a response, a faint grin lurking on his lips. Jordan realized that he had made a mistake with that question; he had admitted to his lack of experience. He had committed himself, though, so he forged ahead, trying to sound professional. "Any feedback on how I handled that?"

DeLuca stared at him with a cold glint of amusement in his eye, obviously enjoying his discomfort. "I'll give you feedback when you need it. Let's get going. We need to get back and start running down her DMV info, and we have a team meeting this morning – Morrissey will want a report on this."

DeLuca turned toward the parking lot, and Jordan fell into step beside him, face flaming. He'd fumbled somehow; made himself look green and awkward. And DeLuca had taken full advantage.

They got into the vehicle, and Jordan felt DeLuca shoot a glance at him as they wound down 376 toward the office. Jordan put his sunglasses back on and kept his eyes on the street, looking as unruffled as if it had never happened. Professional, in control. He wasn't going to give the man the satisfaction.

Back at the office, the rest of the team headed for a small conference room down the hall, and Jordan followed them. They took their places around the table, and Morrissey started with the murder case. "It looks as if this one is ours," he began. "There is a possible kidnapping here, along with a potential murder. The Feds ordinarily might pick up this case since she was from another state, but there is nothing to indicate for certain that any of the crimes happened in Ohio. They're willing to hand it off to us, at least initially, and so is the PBP." He looked at DeLuca. "We'll start with you and Jordan since you were at the scene."

DeLuca nodded and read through his notes. "Victim is Poppy Jankovic, aged 26; female, from Hubbard, Ohio. The ME's preliminary assessment is that she was restrained – there are ligature marks around her elbows, ankles, and wrists. No obvious signs of sexual assault. The cause of death appears to be exsanguination due to long cuts made to the inside of her forearms."

"Indicating that maybe she was alive when she was killed?" said Jen, frowning.

"That's pretty sick," observed Devon.

Deluca continued. "Dr. Washington thinks that the time of death was within eight hours of when she was discovered but hopes to get a better estimate for us. The doctor believes that the victim bled out at another location because of the lack of blood in the body's vicinity. The victim had her driver's license on her, but no car keys and no purse or wallet, or cell phone. A jogger by the name of James Wicks found her." He looked at Jordan. "Bell interviewed the jogger."

Morrissey asked, "He found her at five in the morning – it was still dark. How did he see her?"

Jordan said, "I asked him the same thing. He wears a headlamp; it sounds as though he's on the trail regularly. Wicks picked her up with his light; said it was still too dark to see what it was until he got closer, and when he did, he dialed 911. He seemed pretty credible, but we'll go back and check out his background, look for any possible associations."

DeLuca added, "The victim was dressed all in black, with white makeup and dark nail polish – it may be noteworthy. She might be part of a group that identifies with death and cutting, like Emo."

Jordan said, "Goth."

The correction earned him an irritated look from DeLuca, but Milt asked, "What's the difference?"

"Goths are into the all-black dress. A typical Emo doesn't usually dress all in black. I knew kids in school in both groups. Both of them have their roots in the punk music scene, but if you were to ask either group, they'd say there was a big difference."

Jordan paused and glanced at DeLuca. "I had a Goth friend who always denied that there was any real connection between Goth culture and cutting, or self-mutilation, but that opinion is out there, at least in public perception. Mike is right; there could be a connection between the Goth culture and the way she was murdered."

It felt good to retaliate; not only had Jordan corrected him, but he'd tossed DeLuca a bone at the end of his little lecture, putting himself squarely in control. The rest of the group was regarding him with newfound respect, although Jordan wasn't sure if it was from the knowledge he had provided or the brazen little political move he had just pulled off – politely making his team leader look like an ass.

Morrissey shot DeLuca a look that said he was enjoying the exchange and said blandly, "Devon was working the DMV angle while you guys were at the scene."

Devon nodded. "Yeah, the PBP found the car right after you guys left – it was right there in the lot, with the keys and her purse inside. PBP forensics guys are still going over it. There were a couple of blood spots in the trunk; they think she was transported there in her vehicle. No cellphone. We've also got a next of kin - her mother, who also lives in Hubbard, Ohio."

"Okay," said Morrissey. He looked at DeLuca. "Next move?"

"Bell and I will ride out to Hubbard this afternoon," said DeLuca, "and do the notification. We'll try to find out if and where she worked, whether she went to school, known associates, the usual, and see if we can pick up any connections." He looked at Jen and Devon. "Jen and Devon, do some background on the jogger – he seems clean, but make sure there's nothing there. I'll try to scare up her cellphone number, and then I'd like you to check to see where it is or where the cell tower last pinged it. Check the area for security cameras - that manufacturing place across the street might have some. Apart from that, we'll be looking for reports to come in from the ME and forensics."

"Okay," Morrissey turned to Marty and Milt. "Anything new on the drug investigations?"

Marty Beran shook his head. "No, sir. We're still watching Carter." He glanced at Jordan as he explained. "We've got a line on a pretty active drug dealer, name of Drayvon Carter. We've been trying to do surveillance on him along with PBP Narcotics, hoping to see who his contacts are. We're trying to work our way up the distribution chain. Carter's careful. He either knows he's being watched, or he's naturally cautious. We haven't seen him make contact with anyone other than with sellers that work for him. We still don't know where he's getting his stuff."

Morrissey sighed. "Okay, keep at it." He looked at DeLuca. "We may need to come up with a different approach here. The drug overdoses are on the news almost every night, and not just here in Pittsburgh. The governor's looking for some progress."

Jordan thought DeLuca would be irked by Morrissey's lecture, which Jordan thought was pointless. DeLuca didn't look happy, but all he said was, "Yeah, we'll take a look, see if we can come up with something."

Much of the ride to Hubbard passed in silence. Jordan suspected he'd irritated his partner by correcting him in the meeting and was expecting a reprimand when they got into the car, but DeLuca was quiet, his expression unreadable as they headed north on I-279. The steep hills rose around them, covered with the green of summer, a blanket that hid the solid rocky core underneath. Those hills were as hard and unforgiving as the steel that had sustained much of the city for so long. Few steel mills remained, but Pittsburgh had transitioned in recent years, buoyed by the healthcare and financial industries, among others. The blue-collar base was still present, although losing ground financially, as the once all-powerful steel unions had dwindled. Small dingy clapboard houses hung stubbornly along the edge of the hills along the highway, punctuated by occasional sleek modern big box store shopping meccas, catering to the wealthier citizens in the northern suburbs.

They transferred onto I-79 and then onto the turnpike at Cranberry and started to head northwest when DeLuca said, "So what did you do for the NYPD?"

His voice was even; conversational, and both the unexpected lightness of his tone and the subject made Jordan tense. He forced himself to relax and offered, "The usual rookie stuff. Patrol. I trained for a while, worked the streets with a senior partner, did foot patrol in the boroughs and subways."

That provoked a sharp glance, and then DeLuca looked back at the highway. "Morrissey said you did undercover work. Said the word was you were pretty good at it."

Jordan's throat felt unexpectedly tight. "Yeah, I did it for part of my second year there." Silence. He added, "I, uh, didn't care for it.

I would rather get into computer investigations."

As soon as the words left his mouth, he knew he'd made his second mistake of the day. He sounded needy, entitled; the expectation was that rookies followed orders, not pick and choose their assignments. DeLuca nodded as if he'd just confirmed a suspicion, a knowing glint in his eye. Jordan looked away at the hills undulating along the highway, and silence descended again.

Eventually, the hills and the lump in his throat receded as they crossed the Ohio border and took the first Ohio exit, Interstate 680. I-680 wound northward from the more affluent south side of Youngstown, up past the city itself. Youngstown had been a steel town once, too, anchored by the mills that now sat ugly and rusting along the Mahoning River. There was still an operating mill, but unlike Pittsburgh, Youngstown hadn't yet recovered from the loss of industry. The steel and auto industries had moved much of their operations to Mexico and overseas. The shortage of jobs was compounded by the fact that the metropolitan area was sprawling, an assortment of smaller towns that had attached themselves to the city's core and had clustered around Youngstown and the smaller neighboring municipality of Warren like a collection of burrs. The number of discrete towns, multiple governments, and the area's size made it challenging to condense projects to focus recovery on the city itself as the jobs collapsed. In its wake, the job exodus had left limited employment opportunities and an environment ripe for drugs and discontent. The Youngstown area was a crucial link in the opioid distribution chain that stretched from Detroit, through Toledo and Cleveland in Ohio, and New Castle and Pittsburgh in Pennsylvania and on southward, along the Ohio River, down into West Virginia. The smaller and more impoverished the town, the more profound the effects of the drug epidemic.

They took US 62 on the south side of downtown, winding through gritty neighborhoods, northward up to Hubbard. Hubbard was a small town that sat on the eastern edge of the Youngstown-Warren area – close enough to be considered part of it, but far enough out that it still had a rural, small-town feel. They found the home of Poppy Jankovic's mother, Ellen Simpson, with little problem, and there was a Hubbard Township police officer waiting for them there.

He got out of his car, nodded, and stuck out a hand as they

approached, a solid man with graying hair. "Sam Miller," he said. "Pittsburgh Police called, and I came and gave Ellen the news already. I know the family. I told her you would be coming to ask questions. She's taking it pretty hard – she lost her first husband and is divorced from her second, lives alone, and Poppy was her only child."

DeLuca nodded and said, "We'll try to go easy. We just want to get a feel for any acquaintances, that kind of thing."

Sam scratched his head. "From the description the PBP gave, it sounded like suicide."

DeLuca said, "I guess we can't entirely rule it out – there's a small chance it could have been an assisted suicide, but there were ligature marks on her ankles and arms – it looks as though she was tied down."

Sam's face twisted. "Shit. I knew her since she was a toddler. I was friends with her dad, Bill Jankovic – he was killed in a car accident when she was ten. Poppy never was any trouble – got kind of weird there with the Goth thing and was just an average student, but she was a good kid growing up. Ellen never had the money to send her to college, and Poppy bounced around in a bunch of minimum wage jobs after high school, but she was out of the house and supporting herself. I know she was working down at Star Beauty Nail Salon recently."

Jordan had a notepad out and jotted down the salon's name, and DeLuca nodded, and they headed toward the house, leaving Sam Miller at his patrol car. It was a small white one-story box of a home, with a sad bedraggled yew hedge for landscaping and graying aluminum siding. Ellen Simpson opened the door as they stepped up on the stoop and motioned them inside, crumpled tissue in her hand. The living room was small, with worn furniture, but tidy. There was a picture of Poppy in her high school graduation cap and gown on a side table. She was smiling and looked much younger, much more innocent, without the heavy dark makeup. Ellen was a short, plump lady with a boyish haircut flecked with gray, and her eyes were red and swollen. She said, "Sam said you were coming. You're from Pittsburgh?"

DeLuca said, "Yes, ma'am. I'm Agent Mike DeLuca, and this is my partner, Jordan Bell, from the Pennsylvania Department of Investigation. We're sorry to intrude, but we need to ask a few questions so we can find out who did this." His tone was kind and respectful with none of his normal brusqueness, and he followed Ellen over to a dark brown sofa and sat next to her. Jordan sat down across from them in a chair with his notebook, waiting for DeLuca to tell him to pick up the questioning, but DeLuca had decided to take the lead. He gently probed Ellen, and in a few moments, they had Poppy's address and the names of her roommates, and the name of her supervisor at the nail salon. Ellen herself had an alibi for the earlier part of the evening; she had been at a concert in nearby Warren with two of her friends. They had dropped her off between ten-thirty and eleven. She had been on her computer until midnight. Not that she appeared suspicious, Jordan thought. She was genuinely grief-stricken.

Jordan took notes as DeLuca said, "No boyfriend?"

A shake of the head.

"Any other friends or acquaintances?"

Ellen shook her head and sniffled. "None that I know. She had a good friend that she hung out with here in town, Leigh, but Leigh moved away a year and a half ago – went with her boyfriend to Tennessee. There were Poppy's roommates, of course, but I'm not sure they all got along that well. She knew some kids in Pittsburgh. There was a bar down there that she liked to go to – Henry's, or Harry's or something. It was a Goth hangout. She was into that Goth stuff, but she was a good kid. Drank a little but never got into the drugs. I'm guessing she ran down to the bar; that's the only reason she would have to go to Pittsburgh, at least that I know of."

"Did she have a cell phone?"

Ellen blinked and gave a short, humorless laugh. "You know any young people her age that don't? Yes, she always had it on her."

"Could you give me the number?" DeLuca jotted it down and handed her his card, and said kindly, "Okay, thank you for the information. If you think of anything else, or anyone else that she knew, call me. We'll do some checking, and we'll keep you informed."

Ellen had been holding up relatively well, dabbing at tears during the interview. Still, she let down at the end of it, crushing the crumpled Kleenex to her eyes and allowing a sob to escape, and DeLuca reached over and gave her shoulder a quick, comforting pat before he rose and nodded at Jordan. Jordan shut his mouth, which had been hanging open slightly in surprise at the display of humanity, and stood, murmuring his thanks, and they left Ellen sobbing quietly on the sofa. In the car, DeLuca called Devon and gave him Poppy's cell phone number.

The trip to the nail salon yielded nothing further, but they did get the bar's correct name from one of Poppy's roommates, a place called Harry's, in Pittsburgh's Southside neighborhood. Both roommates had alibis for the evening before; they were together and out with friends in Youngstown. They couldn't think of any enemies or unusual incidents concerning Poppy. It was by then six in the evening, and DeLuca and Jordan grabbed a burger at the truck stop on the north side of town. They ate in the vehicle, with Jordan reviewing his notes aloud, as DeLuca sat and listened. When he finished, Jordan waited for a response, but none was coming.

DeLuca pulled out of the lot, and they wound out of town toward Pittsburgh, this time heading east on Interstate 80, back over the PA border, and then south on I-376, as the hills began to rise around them again. Jordan looked up the bar on his cell phone. "Harry's is in Southside, but it's not on Carson Street; it's off the main drag down one of the little side streets toward the river."

DeLuca nodded. He got on his phone and instructed Jen and Devon to go down to Southside and investigate the bar; it was Friday night, and the place would likely be full of patrons – an opportune time to look for people who knew Poppy. Devon informed them that they were already on their way. According to the cell phone tower data, the bar was the last place where Poppy's phone had sent a signal. DeLuca disconnected the call, his face closed; the rigid set to his jaw was back. He said, "You have any self-defense training? Martial arts, boxing, anything?"

"No. Just some basic stuff from NYPD training."

"I'd like you to get some. I asked Jen to set up a sparring session with you - she can give you some pointers and steer you toward an instructor. She'll get in touch with you. Make sure you get your notes into a report."

They spent the rest of the ride in uncomfortable silence.

CHAPTER THREE

Jordan called Jen Friday evening as soon as he got back into the office, and she had set up their sparring session for early the next morning. A little before eight on Saturday, he headed downtown to meet her there. The gym was big, with no frills. A raised boxing ring sat in the center, surrounded by several large areas for classroom instruction. On one wall were postings for classes for multiple exercise disciplines, and there was an impressive and somewhat daunting weight room outfitted with machines, free weights, and punching bags. He saw Jen across the room standing next to a recessed area equipped with mats. She nodded to him, and as he crossed the floor toward her, one man yelled out, "Better watch her, boy! She'll kick your ass!"

Several of the other people working out in the gym turned and looked, smirking, interested. They were all men, save for one woman doing free weights in the corner.

Jordan was grateful for the room Jen had reserved. Although one side of it was open to the gym, at least he wasn't in the ring on a raised platform, on display from all angles. He had no idea of what the sparring would consist of, but on the other hand, Jen was slighter than he was and at least an inch or two shorter. He would have a reach advantage and greater strength on his side. The whole thing seemed odd, awkward. He wondered at DeLuca's motives for setting up a session with her. It had to be a test.

Jen nodded as he approached, eyeing his loose gym shorts and tee-shirt. Her blond hair was in a ponytail, and she was wearing a form-fitting T-shirt and knee-length leggings, revealing a fit, solid, muscular frame, without an ounce of fat anywhere except in the places it was supposed to be. "Okay, what you're wearing is fine, but take off your shoes. Do you have any martial arts training?"

Jordan shook his head as he kicked off his shoes. "No."

She pursed her lips. "Nothing?"

"No. Just some basic stuff; crowd control and how to take down a suspect. No real martial arts."

"That's okay. What I'd recommend for you is some boxing training and also some BJJ."

"BJJ?"

"Brazilian jiu-jitsu. You're not a big guy – and neither am I, which is why I started training in BJJ. It's a wrestling discipline that negates an opponent's superior size or uses it to your advantage. It levels the playing field. If you need to take a suspect down without hurting them, it's pretty effective. Some boxing is good too, if for nothing else than for learning how to keep out the way of punches. I'm going to give you a few pointers today and show how both of those can work for you. If you decide you're interested, I'll give you the names of a couple of good teachers."

"Fair enough," said Jordan.

She led the way onto the mat and turned to face him. "Okay, I want you to come at me as if you're going to grab me and try to overpower me. If you want anything to stop, all you need to do is tap out; tap the mat with a free hand, or say 'stop.'"

Jordan hesitated briefly, trying to decide how to proceed – he didn't want to hurt her – and then imitated her stance, feet wide apart, bent slightly at the waist, arms out. They circled briefly, and he lunged and promptly found himself flat on his back. Just before contact, she had ducked under his lunge, grabbed his arm and straightened it, forcing his torso up, and got a leg behind his and used his momentum to upend him, all of it in one seamless move. Once he was on his back, in another series of motions just as fast, she straddled him, grabbed his arm again and forced it straight, swiveled back off of him, twisting it at the same time, and pinned his twisted outstretched arm against her body. He was helpless; he couldn't move his arm without every nerve ending in it firing in pain, and he gasped as she tightened her grip.

"Go ahead and tap out," said Jen, who appeared barely affected by the effort. "You aren't gonna get out of that."

He tapped the mat, and she released his arm and rose. He could hear low laughter and comments from the outer room, and he scrambled to his feet, flexing his arm, his face red.

She grinned. "Don't worry about them. That's called an armbar from mount position. Pretty effective, huh? Now I'm going to teach you how to do that."

She walked him through the steps and had him try them on her a few times, and then they went on to other moves. She pinned him quickly in various embarrassing positions, including one where she had him red-faced and choking between her thighs. That earned him outright laughter and some lewd comments from the rest of the gym patrons, and he realized at that moment that DeLuca had humiliation in mind when he had lined him up to spar with Jen.

Sore and sweating, he put sparring gloves on at her direction, and they moved on to boxing, where he didn't fare much better. He was agile and quick on his feet, but she was faster, especially with the punches. At one point, he moved right into one, and she inadvertently nailed him on his cheekbone. She gave him a few more tips, and they finally broke for the day.

"You're in good shape, aerobically," Jen said with a nod. "And you're pretty flexible. Did you do sports in school?"

Jordan thought back to his high school years. She was trying to salve his ego, and he wasn't about to admit to theater and gymnastics and his failure to make the football team. He settled for, "A little tennis. Now I cycle mostly. Road bike."

Jen pursed her lips, looking impressed. "You cycle on these hills? No wonder I didn't wear you out. Most new sparring partners don't make it this far."

He smiled ruefully. "You don't need to try to make me feel better."

"No, seriously, you have a lot going for you. You're quick and flexible, and you're in good shape. You could use some upper-body weight training, maybe, but as far as BJJ goes, you'll pick it up quick." She studied him for a minute. "DeLuca put you with me for this because I train hard, and pound for pound, I'm the best on the team. I've kicked all of their asses at least once, including his and Bear's. Don't feel bad."

She sat down on the mat and reached for her shoes, and Jordan sat next to her. "I'm not sure I got off on the right foot with him," he admitted, as he laced up.

"With Mike, you mean? You're doing fine," Jen assured him. "It was good that you spoke up so decisively in the meeting yesterday. Most newbies wouldn't do that." She glanced at him sideways. "Although you did correct him in front of the group. I'd think twice about that, at least for a while."

Jordan didn't respond. The fact was, he'd enjoyed putting DeLuca in his place after the man had embarrassed him earlier that morning when he'd asked for his opinion. He had allowed DeLuca to get under his skin, and he'd felt the need to retaliate. She was right; he would need to do better. Not because he was afraid of Mike DeLuca, but because he'd violated his own standards. He didn't let anyone push his buttons. Emotion equaled weakness.

Jen was studying him. Her eyes were remarkable, an intense blue. She said, "Mike's tough, but he's fair. And his bark is worse than his bite. Don't take him personally." She punched him in the arm. "Good session. Get some lessons, and let me know if you want another sparring session down the road." She leaped lightly to her feet and strode through the room, ignoring the admiring glances the men sent after her.

Jordan checked his phone as he let himself into his apartment. It was Saturday morning, but he was half-expecting a call from DeLuca. Mike had told him that if Dr. Washington finished her autopsy over the weekend, they would go in for the report. There was no call, and so Jordan hit the shower, letting the hot water cascade on his already-sore body. He had used some muscles today that he didn't know he had. He shaved, noting the red welt on his cheekbone from the punch he had danced into while sparring with Jen, thinking about her fair skin and blond hair and blue eyes.

It was idle speculation. Jordan had only minimal experience with women – two short-lived relationships in college and nothing since. He wasn't about to start an affair with a co-worker, especially one at least seven years older than he was. Still, she was nice to think about.

He pondered that as he dressed, wondering how many of his coworkers were married. He imagined that DeLuca had been with lots of women – he gave off that kind of vibe. He hadn't noticed a ring, and DeLuca didn't seem like the marrying type. The guy wasn't exactly Mr. Personality when it came to the office. The man seemed unapproachable. He'd effectively put any hopes that Jordan had for a solid partner relationship to rest. Jordan rubbed his face, glanced at his computer with longing, and sighed. He had passed his tests, and it looked as though the job was his. He was in Pittsburgh to stay; he had no more excuses. He should visit his parents.

His parents lived in Fox Chapel, an affluent neighborhood northeast of downtown filled with doctors, lawyers, and CEOs. It was a fourteen-mile drive and a world away from his shabby apartment in Oakland. It took Jordan twenty minutes to get there, and after hitting the code to open the wrought iron gate, he pulled into the driveway of the gray limestone manor where he had grown up, with its leaded casement windows and massive oak door. He parked on the side in front of one of the four garage bays and sat, wondering which entrance to try. He decided on the front door and went up and rang the bell. He had been away for too long; he couldn't simply walk in.

Claudia, the housekeeper, answered the door, gasping in surprise and pleasure, her plump face wreathed in a smile. "Jordan! My goodness!" She opened her arms and gathered him in for a hug, her voice tinted with an accent. She had been a member of their household for years, brought from Bolivia by his mother. "Ah, your mother will be so happy! She is out in the back, come!"

"Thanks, Claudia," murmured Jordan as he followed her inside. They wound through the house and out into a shaded sitting area that looked out on the pool.

His mother was seated at a patio table, reading. "Hi Mom," he said, and she turned and took in a breath, and then tossed the book aside and was on her feet.

"Jordan!" she exclaimed as she hurried toward him and swept him into a hug.

He hugged her back, kissed her cheek. "Hi, Mom. You look as beautiful as ever."

She did. There were some faint wrinkles in the otherwise flawless skin, but her eyes and hair were dark and vibrant, and she was still a beauty who could turn heads. Maria Santos Bell was now wealthy but had once been a clerk at a bank, an immigrant from Bolivia, working to put Jordan's father through medical school. Both of them had earned every penny they had. She was a set of contradictions, carrying herself regally and dressing in designer clothes, but funny, engaging, and approachable. Pittsburgh society loved her, and so did Jordan.

His father was another matter. "Is Dad here?"

"No, oh, he'll be sorry he missed you. He had emergency surgery today. Your brother is gone, too, at the hospital for his internship. What are you doing in Pittsburgh? Why didn't you tell me you were coming?" Her English was much better than Claudia's, nearly perfect, with just the hint of an accent. Jordan felt a sudden urge to lapse into Spanish, like they used to do, only the two of them because his brother Marcus hadn't bothered to learn it, but he answered in English.

"I live here now."

She stared, and an incredulous smile came to her face. "What? How?"

"I transferred back from New York. I'm – doing computer work for the state of Pennsylvania in downtown Pittsburgh now. I'm going back to school on the side in the fall, to take classes in computer science from Pitt."

Her brow furrowed. "Computers? Does that mean no more police work on the street?"

He smiled and lied to her face. "No, Mom, no more work on the street. I'm doing some financial analysis on the computer; it's an office job." That statement would be true soon enough, he told himself. He had told Morrissey that he was taking computer classes and had asked about the possibility of cybercrime work. Morrissey had hinted that he might eventually end up in the computer lab. Once Jordan got through training and got himself assigned to cybercrime full time, he would have an office job. And much of that work was financial analysis, following the money.

"Oh, thank goodness!" she said, "And I'm happy you are home; your father will be, too." She winked at him. "Although I think he would be more thrilled if you finished law school. Me, of course, I always saw you on Broadway. Or in the movies." She fanned a hand at her face. "It's getting hot out here. Let's go inside."

She bustled in ahead of him and waved him into the sitting room while she went into the kitchen to ask Claudia for iced tea and to start lunch. Jordan wandered into the room, his eyes falling on old photos; one of him in costume on a stage at about age thirteen, his arms outstretched, his mouth open in song. It sat next to a shot of his older brother, Marcus, imposing even at age fifteen in a football uniform. They couldn't possibly have been more different, Jordan thought. Marcus took after their father, tall and blond, athletic, analytical and efficient, smart, outgoing, popular. Jordan favored their mother, slight and dark, artsy, bookish, introverted. In high school, he had tried to follow in his brother's footsteps, and although he'd eclipsed him academically, he was definitely in a lower stratosphere, socially. Jordan had been two grades ahead of his peers and by far the youngest in his high school classes. He and Marcus had graduated the same year even though Jordan was two years younger, Jordan first in their class and Marcus second, and he was sure that Marcus hated him for it.

Jordan had spent those years trying to fit in, too small for most sports, too young for the girls, too intelligent to be cool. He had survived by studying the behavior of his peers intently, trying to figure out what made the popular kids popular – mannerisms, dress, speech – attempting to adopt each detail, and had inadvertently discovered a talent for acting. He had finally found his niche in the theater group and had managed to become just hip enough to blend in and avoid harassment. Anonymous, in plain sight. He stared at his picture, blushing. Theater had been fun at the time but seemed embarrassing, frivolous, now. He had already seen more ugliness than he'd ever expected, and those innocent times were long gone.

His mother bustled in with iced tea and questions, and they sat. "So, how long have you been here? Where will you live? You can stay here, if you like, in your old bedroom. How did you get here?"

He smiled. "I've been here just a few days, and I'm living in an apartment in Oakland, close to campus."

She was staring at him, and she cocked her head, and the next question threw him. "Is everything okay? You seem – so serious."

He brushed it off. "Yes, Mom, I'm fine. Moving and starting a new job are both a little stressful; I'm just tired."

"You have a mark on your face."

" A moving accident," he grinned. Lying was effortless, even with his mother. It was a good thing. There was a lot she shouldn't know. "I caught a falling box with my head."

"Ai," Maria said under her breath, shaking her head. "You should have called. Your father and Marcus would have helped you."

"No, they wouldn't," said Jordan, agreeably. "Dad would have called a mover."

She sighed and smiled. "You're probably right." Claudia came in with a tray of sandwiches cut into neat triangles, and they both helped themselves to one. Maria gestured at him with hers. "There is a party at the Martins' house next Saturday – you should come. All of our friends will be there – they will want to see you. You remember their son, Peter – you and Marcus graduated with him. He lives at home. He will probably be there, as well, and there may be others your age."

"I'll see," said Jordan. He honestly couldn't think of anything he would like less than going to a stuffy party, especially if his father would be there. He remembered Peter, a hulking acned disagreeable sloth of a boy. Nothing about that invitation sounded good.

They chatted and ate sandwiches, and Jordan left well before his father was due home.

Max Weinberg glanced at the time on his burner phone as he stepped out of the little hotel room. The place was one of his favorites - a decrepit isolated one-story motel off the highway on the Maryland-Pennsylvania border, with a few individual rooms. A private business that took cash and asked no questions; cottages that ensured privacy, the distance between them swallowing the occasional scream. Max had thoroughly enjoyed the services of the young man he had brought with him and had paid extra for a late checkout.

It was almost two in the afternoon; his boss, Derek Mason, would be walking to the back of his sixty-acre property on the edge of the Poconos. Derek had guests at his estate this week, so he'd had to set a time for communication and make a plan to get away from the house. Max slung himself into his blue Porsche 911, checked his face and hair in the rearview mirror, and adjusted his sunglasses. He started the car, pulled out of the lot, and dialed. Derek answered. "Max. How are things?"

"Good. Nothing serious to report. Things have been quiet, and sales are up. The cops got nothing out of that raid."

"Anything on our young friend?"

"No. I couldn't find anything - nothing to indicate that Carlos Moreno was not who he seemed to be. No indication that he was a cop. We still think Lucaya was the snitch."

"They were close, the two of them."

"I know, but not that close. Did you see Moreno's face? He looked shocked."

"The issue is that he has seen *my* face. I need to know for certain that he's not the police or another informant."

"I know, he's seen me, too, but he probably didn't get a good look, and he doesn't know our names. We've looked all over the city. The word on the street is, he's gone back to South America or possibly Mexico. Or maybe South America via Mexico. He can't bother us from there."

"True. If that's the case, okay, but I want you to verify that. Keep looking until you do."

"That's the plan."

The call disconnected, and Max frowned. He had to agree - the incident at the warehouse had been disconcerting, much too close for comfort. It was unfortunate; things had been going well up until the unexpected appearance of the police. Max had dispatched the informant, that traitor, Lucaya, in a most spectacularly gruesome way, over the top even for him. It had sent an unforgettable message to the others. He privately thought that Derek was too paranoid about Moreno, but on the other hand, they had accounted for everyone who had been there except for him. Most likely, Lucaya's murder and the close call with the police had scared him away.

Max shrugged and punched the accelerator. Although he and Derek worked as partners, there was no question as to who called the shots. If Derek wanted him to keep looking, he would.

CHAPTER FOUR

Monday morning, Jordan put one leg out of his car into the office parking lot and grimaced. He was still somewhat sore from his sparring session on Saturday, and on Sunday, he had decided to add insult to injury and had hopped on his bike. He had cycled across the Birmingham Bridge to Southside, over to Harry's Bar. The bar was closed, but Jordan rode around the block, checking out the street and its surroundings. Neither the neighborhood nor the bar looked like much; it was run-down, shabby. The one-story brick building was truly a dive, not the spiffed-up dive wannabes a few blocks up on Carson Street. He stood straddling his bicycle, considering the parking lot where Poppy must have parked her car. Crumbling asphalt, sporting the occasional cigarette butt. Had she been abducted there? Or had she gone on to somewhere else after Harry's? There were no cameras in the lot and no witnesses to her disappearance. He'd thought about that for a moment. Then he'd made the unfortunate decision to ride the five miles or so over to Beechview and try a run up Canton Avenue.

Canton Avenue was the steepest residential street in the country, with a thirty-seven percent grade. It was featured in an automobile commercial and was part of an annual bicycle race that included Pittsburgh's steepest hills. Jordan had ridden it more than once in high school for no particular reason other than to challenge himself to see if he could make it up without stopping.

At the bottom, he paused, looked up at the expanse of quiet road that rose above him, and second-guessed himself. It was more daunting than he remembered, a nearly vertical conglomeration of differently paved sections of cracked concrete slabs, asphalt, and cobblestones. He decided to backtrack to get some momentum and then started fast, changing gears several times to get into the lowest one. He charged the hill at the bottom, standing up in the saddle to begin the torturous climb, step after step. He was winded at a quarter of the way up, his legs trembling and screaming for oxygen at one third, and he had to stop short of halfway, nearly falling as he tried to disengage his clip shoes from his pedals on the steep grade. His bike shoes, stiff and slippery, scrabbled for purchase on the pavement, and he barely stopped himself from rolling backward.

He muttered to himself, breathing heavily and wiping his brow. It had never been easy to get up the hill, but he'd never had to stop before. He was out of shape. He'd ridden his bike almost daily in New York City, but it was stop-and-go traffic and flat terrain. It hadn't been enough to keep him in proper form to ride the hills of Pittsburgh. The thought irked him enough to try it once more with a similar result, reaching a point just short of the first try.

Now on Monday, he was feeling his aching, stiff muscles, a reminder of his failures over the weekend – the embarrassing sparring session and his foiled attempt at the hill. He was starting his week sore, tired, and irritated with himself.

His mood didn't improve as the week progressed. Although Monday and Tuesday were slow, case-wise, and he was able to get a fair amount of time working with one of the PBP guys in the computer lab, a vague sense of irritation still nipped at his heels. DeLuca had given him no assignments concerning the drug investigations, even though he had volunteered to try to track Drayvon Carter's movements on the computer by monitoring his cell phone if they could get a warrant to obtain his number. DeLuca had dismissed that, saying that getting that warrant wouldn't do much good because Carter was undoubtedly using unregistered burner phones for his drug transactions.

The coroner's and forensics reports hadn't come in yet on the murder case. Jen and Devon were going back to the bar Tuesday night to spend more time interviewing the regulars, and Jordan had even volunteered for that but had DeLuca had ordered him to stay put. Jordan had the feeling that he was being marginalized, shoved aside. It gave him what he wanted – plenty of time in the computer lab – but with nothing to work on, Jordan felt like a neglected step-child. He had considered going over DeLuca's head to Morrissey to ask for a project, but it was way too early for a step that drastic. So, he cooled his heels in front of the monitor, tucked back away in the computer lab, and when Jerry, the PBP technician, wasn't around, used the opportunity to do some searching of his own, looking up crimes in the New York area.

He was coming back from the lab Tuesday morning and had turned the corner to go down the hallway to the PDI offices when he heard Jen say, "…and he seems to be trying hard."

Jen and DeLuca were standing in the hallway along the wall, Jen leaning against it and close to DeLuca, maybe a little closer than was necessary.

DeLuca grunted something noncommittal and then said, "Okay, thanks."

Jen pushed away from the wall with a smile and a sideways glance at DeLuca that made Jordan think, "Huh." And then they both saw him, and their faces went blank. They'd been talking about him. 'Trying hard?' Ouch. Had Jen told DeLuca about their sparring session? Jordan followed them into the bullpen, and as DeLuca turned to go into his office, Jen shot Jordan a smile and a wink. So maybe she hadn't thrown him under the bus.

DeLuca was in the process of sitting at his desk, and as Jordan passed, he looked at him, judging the response. There was none; DeLuca simply looked back, blandly.

Tuesday night, Jordan went to the University of Pittsburgh to pay for his fall computer class and stopped to see Professor William Latimore. Latimore seemed never to change in all of the years that Jordan had known him – he was portly with a full head of white hair and bushy white eyebrows and always dressed in a formal three-piece suit. His blue eyes were as sharp as ever.

"Jordan – great to see you! Come in, sit down. How are things? Getting settled in your new job? You started with the PDI, you told me."

Jordan nodded and changed the subject. "Yeah, I started last week. Hey, professor, I've got a question for you. Do you know anything about the Dark Web?"

Latimore peered at him, his smile dimming. "The Dark Web!

Some. Why do you want to know?"

"It has to do with work. I'm going to be doing computer work going forward."

"I would assume your work computers have a secure method of accessing the Deep Web – and the Dark Web."

Jordan nodded. "They do. It's just that I may want to do some work from my home computer."

Latimore frowned. "I would advise against that, but if you must, you need to make sure you have a secure, untraceable connection."

"I realize that – that's exactly what I need."

Latimore studied him for a moment, then reached for a piece of paper and began jotting down notes. "The first thing you need to do is get yourself a good VPN. I would do that and use it all the time, whether you are on the Deep Web or not. If you are compromised or hacked – which is a distinct possibility if you are out browsing on those sites, they won't trace your computer. I am listing a few sites where you can get one."

"The second thing you need to do is to download TOR," he said, continuing to write. "TOR is a browser that accesses the Dark Web, which is a subset of the Deep Web. Make sure you download it from this site," he underlined a portion of the scribble. "Once you do that, you'll be able to access the Darknet menus. Also, make sure you set up a new email account that has nothing to do with any of your current email accounts on the regular internet." He handed Jordan the paper.

Jordan glanced over it. "Okay, thanks. One more question – is there a way to trace someone who is looking for something specific? In other words, to find someone who is making queries about something or someone?"

Latimore nodded. "There are programs and algorithms that can do that. I can give you the titles of some reading material on the subject." He reached for the paper and made a few more notes.

"Can the people see that someone is searching for them?"

"Possibly, if they know what they are doing. They could try to track you back – but if your VPN is good, they won't be able to tell where you are." His brow furrowed as he handed the paper back again. "What exactly are you trying to do here?"

Jordan smiled. "Nothing criminal, don't worry. Hopefully, tracking down some bad guys."

Latimore shook his head. "I strongly advise against doing anything like that on your personal computer, VPN or not. However, if you are intent on it, at least let me help you with the programs." His voice dropped. "You should probably use a computer at another site for more anonymity – although you should never use a public Wi-Fi – it's a hacker's heaven. Find somewhere more secure. It would be safest to use your work computer." He stopped short of suggesting the campus computers, but Jordan knew what he meant.

"Understood," said Jordan. "Maybe I'll take a stab at the program and have you check it if you would."

"Certainly."

Jordan nodded, waving the paper at him as he turned for the door. "Thanks for the help."

"No problem. I saw your schedule – you'll like Professor Anderson."

"Thanks, Professor."

"Don't mention it."

Jordan could feel Latimore's eyes boring a hole in his back as he shut the door.

Wednesday morning, Jordan was working with Jerry in the computer lab when DeLuca stuck his head in the door. "Come on, Bell," he snapped. "Staff meeting. Or did you forget?"

He stalked away, and Jerry raised his eyebrows and looked at Jordan, who shrugged. The others were already in the conference room, and Jordan eased into a chair, eyeing DeLuca. The man seemed more brusque than usual. Jordan had the impression that he had made him angry, somehow.

DeLuca plopped some papers on the table and said, "Forensics reports are in. Dr. Washington thinks the victim died between three and four in the morning. There was evidence of alcohol and Rohypnol in her system."

Bear's eyebrows rose. "She'd been roofied."

DeLuca nodded. "Probably in one of her drinks, and possibly, maybe even probable that it happened at Harry's. There wasn't a lot of alcohol in her system. Dr. Washington estimated two drinks worth or so, which matched what the bartender thought she'd had. That would indicate that maybe she hadn't stopped anywhere else after Harry's, or if she did, she ordered a drink without alcohol. That is a possibility – she had a long drive back to Ohio, so maybe she stopped somewhere for a coffee or a soda, but it's also possible that Harry's was her only stop. Her last cell phone ping was at Harry's – the murderer could have turned it off. Of course, she could have done that herself if her charge was low."

Devon said, "When Jen and I were there on Friday night, we hit the closest bars up on Carson Street to see if she had stopped in any of them. No one recognized her picture."

DeLuca pursed his lips. "That helps, a little – although there are more bars than just those, in Southside, not to mention the rest of Pittsburgh. Still, it's starting to look like Harry's was her only stop." He looked at Jen and Devon. "Did anything else come out of your interviews?"

Jen pushed a sheet of paper forward. "We compiled a list of names of the people who were there that night. We haven't talked to all of them yet, but we did cover some key people. There have been some turf wars going on at the bar lately. Nothing too bad, just arguing over space and music selection. According to the bartender and owner, Harry Jessup, that bar has been a Goth hangout for a long time. He said back in the day, that's all it was, but the Goth crowd's size has decreased over the years. The Goth group that still goes there are die-hards and are pretty territorial. He said another crowd has started hanging out there – a bunch of college kids, and there's another group of mostly working men in their twenties or thirties."

She continued, "The bartender says the working group doesn't cause much trouble, but they create some additional underlying tension because they take up some space. And everybody fights over the music on the jukebox. Each group has very different tastes. However, he said the real friction is between the college kids and the Goths. He thinks part of that reason is that one of the college kids used to go out with one of the Goth girls. The kid used to be Goth but isn't anymore. The bartender wasn't sure who dumped who, but then the guy started showing up with his new crowd of friends and being kind of pushy. The bartender thinks he's doing it to get back at the Goth crowd, and the Goth kids are rallying around the girl and their turf."

"Doesn't sound like enough of a motive for murder," said

DeLuca. "Now, if one of the two ex-lovebirds had been the victim, the breakup could be the motive. But I don't see a bunch of frat boys killing a girl from Ohio just because her girlfriend broke up with their friend."

Devon nodded. "That's what we thought. And it turns out that the two girls weren't even great friends – just acquaintances. Some of those Goth kids are there all the time, and I think they're pretty tight, but it sounds like the victim was only there once in a while. Someone said she wasn't 'real Goth,' whatever that means."

"Some kids dress Goth because they like the look," said Jordan. "For people who truly identify as Goth, though, it's more than just clothes. It's music, it's books, poetry, art, among other things. According to the Goths that I knew at school, it's a mindset. Maybe Poppy wasn't into all of that."

Milt picked up the list of names, examined it, and then passed it to Mike, who did likewise and gave it to Morrissey. Mike asked, "Which one of these names are the girl and the guy who broke up? Is there any chance that the girl was the target, and the victim was picked up by mistake?"

"I've got double asterisks next to their names," said Jen. "The Goth girl is Suzanne Weir. I talked to her. She doesn't look much like the victim, so I don't think it's likely that Poppy was mistaken for her. Suzanne comes from a middle-class family in the South Hills; she's got an associate degree in business and works at one of the local libraries."

"I talked to the ex-boyfriend," said Devon. "His name is Will McCann. At the bar until one that night, he got a ride home with one of his buddies. He lives over in Oakland in student housing, got home around one-twenty. The victim left the bar an hour before he did. We can't rule him out – he still had time to meet her somewhere else later in the evening, before the projected time of death."

Morrissey finished reading the notes and handed the page to Jordan, who glanced down the list. Jen had organized it under various headings corresponding to the groups in the bar. Under the first heading, Goth, Jen had written several names, and one, in particular, jumped out at him. Peter Martin. Granted, both the first name and surname were common, but there was a chance that maybe this Peter Martin was the same one his mother had mentioned – her friends' son. The ones who were having a party on Saturday. He thought back, trying to remember if Peter had been Goth in high school, and then he realized that DeLuca had said something to him.

"Sorry, what?" he said.

DeLuca frowned. "I said, you're the right age for this crowd – maybe you could stop at the bar for a few nights and blend in, and see if you hear anything. You have all that undercover experience – you could put it to use." Inexplicably, Jordan's tongue seized up, and he just stared back at him.

"I don't think that's such a good idea," Morrissey was saying quietly, at almost the same time.

When Jordan found his voice, what came out was, "I don't think so, either."

DeLuca tried to keep his tone reasonable, but Jordan could tell that he was angry. He turned to Morrissey. "I don't understand what the big deal is. According to NYPD, he's supposed to be good at undercover work. Or was that just some story?" He glared at Jordan. "No one else on this team would argue if asked to do something, especially something that simple."

Morrissey's jaw tightened. "Let's discuss this outside of here."

Jordan felt the others' eyes on him, curiously, and he fought to keep his composure. He couldn't speak; he couldn't even reason against the rising tide of panic. He slid the paper onto the table and tried to even out his breath. Damn it, where was this coming from? The sensation of panic was so intense he felt sure that it was splashed across his face, but the others ignored him and moved on to the forensics results. Those reports had provided little else, other than some unspecified dust from a concrete floor on the victim's clothes and adhesive residue on the victim's face and wrists. The killer had transported Poppy from the murder site in her own vehicle and had wiped down the car to remove any fingerprints.

Jordan tried hard to focus on all of that and eventually calmed down as the meeting moved on to the drug investigations. He still felt rattled, though, when he walked out at the end of the discussion. The rest of the group filtered off down the hallway into the main office, except for his two bosses. Jordan felt his shoulders tense as the door shut behind him and Morrissey and DeLuca started to argue, and he slipped away down the hall, back to the computer lab.

CHAPTER FIVE

Jordan let himself into his apartment after work, plopped his backpack on the kitchen table, sank into a chair, and sat for a while, deliberating the incident in the conference room. DeLuca had proposed simple, basic undercover work, and even the thought of it had been enough to produce unreasonable fear. The reaction was frightening in itself, the irrationality of his response unsettling. He'd done that work before, he knew he was good at it, and as undercover tasks went, this one was simple; there was no good reason not to take it. And he'd panicked. Refusing the assignment had made him look weak and uncertain, and that was intolerable. He stood, agitated, and began to pace.

He had the impression that DeLuca was trying to set him up to fail; maybe he had even made the proposal knowing that Jordan would push back, that his reluctance to take the assignment would make him look bad. Jordan had the feeling that he was at a divide, a crossroad. The computer lab assignment was a safe, controlled environment, and Jordan sensed that the job was what he needed, at least until he felt mentally settled. If he pushed for it, however, DeLuca might not give him another chance. It was probable that parking him in the computer lab was just what DeLuca wanted; he would get the rookie off his back, and he wouldn't be in any hurry to put him in a more challenging assignment when Jordan felt ready for it. Jordan would become *that guy*, the one who they had to hide in a backroom because he couldn't hack it on the street. He could almost hear the talk around the PBP water cooler.

He thought it through logically, trying to weed out the emotion, and eventually regained some perspective. There was only one way to make DeLuca eat his words, and the idea made Jordan feel both apprehensive and oddly, powerful, in control again.

He went and changed and got his bike, clipped in, and headed out in the rush hour traffic over the Monongahela to Canton Hill. He was crawling with adrenaline; he had to burn it off somehow. He tried the hill four times before he was too spent to try again, getting just over halfway on his best attempt. Then he went home, showered and called his mother, and told her he would be attending the Martins' party on Saturday.

He was glad he hadn't told her that he was still doing police work. She didn't need to know that; it would just worry her. But more importantly, she was friends with the Martins. If the Martins' son Peter was the same Peter Martin on Jen's list, Jordan couldn't have him knowing that he was a cop.

He showered and grabbed a sandwich and ran out to do some shopping before the stores closed.

Jordan stalked through the hallways past the PBP offices the next morning, ignoring the looks, although they made him want to grin. He turned and went down the hall toward the PDI offices; it was empty. Jordan was coming in a little late, purposely. His chair was the first one upon entering the bullpen, and he slid into it without anyone noticing and leaned back lazily. DeLuca was in Morrissey's office; they had the door closed.

Marty Beran, in the desk closest to his, took a sip of his coffee and then did a double-take, and Jordan knew what he was seeing: a stranger, a punk, dressed in tight black jeans and boots and a short black leather jacket adorned with chains, with a pierced ear and dark hair standing on end in unruly spikes.

"Hey, you," said Bear roughly. "Get out of that chair. Are you here to see someone?"

"Yeah," said Jordan. He didn't bother to sit up or turn to face him. "Mike DeLuca."

"I said, get out of the chair." The others – Milt, Jen, and Devon – were turning to look now. "Do you have an appointment with him?"

"Naw." Jordan kept his eyes on Morrissey's office, waiting for DeLuca to come out.

Jordan saw DeLuca turn and stare through the window, and Morrissey rose to his feet behind his desk. Bear came out of his chair, bristling; time to move. Jordan stood, and as DeLuca opened the door, he began to walk toward his bosses with a cocky swagger, keeping Bear in his peripheral vision.

Bear moved forward, but Milt said, "Bear, hold up."

Recognition finally flashed into Bear's face. Jordan moved right up to DeLuca and said, "You wanted someone undercover in the bar? You got him." He knew his demonstration was over the top and that his coworkers were staring at him, but instead of relaxing his stance, he dialed it up. He swiveled to face them with a smile, but it wasn't his usual polite grin. It was a scornful smirk, and he slouched, laying it on thick. He shrugged and turned back to DeLuca and Morrissey. "So, how's this?"

Morrissey said, "Both of you, in the conference room, now."

Once in the room, Jordan dropped the swagger and the sneer but coolly returned DeLuca's gaze. DeLuca, to Jordan's satisfaction, couldn't stop staring at him. He might just have gotten himself fired, but it was almost worth it to see that look on DeLuca's face.

Morrissey gestured at Jordan as he sat. "So, what is this?"

Jordan shrugged. "Mike said he wanted me to go into the bar and get some information. I figured I'd get more from the Goth crowd if I showed up as a Goth."

Morrissey frowned. "I thought you weren't too keen on that idea. And when you came here, you came with instructions from NYPD that maybe you should stay off the street for a while, keep a low profile. I told Mike about it yesterday. Does NYPD have a reason for that?"

That broke the façade. Jordan blinked at him. "They told you that?"

"Yes. But NYPD didn't tell me why. Does it have to do with your undercover assignment in New York?"

Jordan sat back, trying to regather his composure. "Maybe," he said. "But the person I was in New York was nothing like this. There's nothing to link me to him." He saw DeLuca frown. He knew that sounded a little, well, nuts. As if he had a multiple personality disorder.

"And who are you now, exactly?"

Jordan lifted a shoulder. "Jordan Bell. Office worker and clean-cut by day, Goth in my free time. A lot of Goths adopt that routine to conform to workplace dress codes. No one at the bar would need to know my daytime office job is with the PDI."

Morrissey pressed. "You told me you wanted computer work. I got the impression you weren't interested in anything else."

Jordan looked directly at DeLuca as he answered. "I'm interested in whatever it takes to do my job. I don't shy away from assignments when asked, despite what some people think. And yes, I worked undercover in New York, and for the record, I was pretty damned good at it."

DeLuca shot back, "No one is trying to pressure you into something you're not comfortable with."

Bullshit. Jordan shrugged and leaned back in his chair, and turned on the punk again, bored and insolent. He smiled humorlessly. "Do I look uncomfortable?"

Morrissey and DeLuca looked at each other, and Morrissey said, "Okay, we'll think about it. The idea isn't bad if the incident began at the bar, but we don't even know that yet. The victim could have left Harry's, and someone drugged her elsewhere. Go home and change and come back to work. If we decide we want you to do this, we'll let you know."

Jordan inclined his head, coolly, rose, and left the room. He'd stood up to DeLuca and made his point, for better or for worse. Whether or not they would take him up on his proposal was up to them.

Two hours later, they had their answer.

Victim number two was found floating in a shallow area along the banks of the Monongahela, caught up in some shrubs that hung out over the water near Sandcastle waterpark. A kayaker out for an afternoon paddle had spotted him.

When the call came in, Pittsburgh police notified the PDI immediately, and Mike DeLuca, Jordan, Jen, and Devon made it to the scene just as the forensics team pulled into the lot. The riverbank was rocky but degenerated into mire near the water's edge. There were no footprints in the mud, which meant the body had probably floated there from elsewhere. The forensics team came in snapping pictures, and then some of them waded in to retrieve the body, which was lying partially on its side, rocking back and forth as the water lapped at it.

The man was young, in his twenties, somewhat stocky. He was wearing a short jacket with a double row of brass buttons, heavy boots, and what looked like an old leather helmet with a chinstrap with brass goggles perched on top. His body was somewhat bloated, as was his face, especially the submerged side of him, but it didn't appear that he had been in the water too long. There were long cuts along the inside of his forearms and ligature marks on his wrists, similar to those on Poppy Jankovic.

"What in the hell is he wearing?" asked DeLuca, looking at the odd helmet and the goggles.

"It's a helmet of some kind, like a World War I pilot's helmet," said Devon. "I saw this guy hanging out at Harry's with the Goth crowd when we went to the bar Friday night."

Jen nodded. "I interviewed him. His name is Jon Hurly. He wasn't at the bar the night Poppy was there."

"What he's wearing is called 'steampunk,'" said Jordan. "Steampunk is a romanticized version of dress tied to the Victorian era. It's not truly Goth, but some people who identify as Goth can dress this way."

Jen nodded. "He was hanging with the Goth crowd."

DeLuca frowned. "So, another Goth victim, but maybe not considered 'true Goth.' Someone at the bar described Poppy Jankovic that way, too."

Jordan said, "Yeah, that's right. The murderer could be a Goth person with a beef against Goth poseurs. Or on the other hand, he could be a non-Goth person who doesn't discriminate – to him, all Goths are the same. It might be someone who might not pick up on subtle variations."

Devon looked at the helmet. "I'd fall into that second group, myself. Weird is weird."

"One thing's for sure," said Jen. "We're probably talking about a guy, or someone pretty strong. This victim wouldn't be easy to move around. I'll bet he's over two hundred pounds."

The ME arrived, and they backed away to give her access. DeLuca looked at Jordan. "Well, I guess this seals it – two Goth victims who frequented the same Goth bar is a connection to the bar, no matter whether they were kidnapped there or not. You still interested in that undercover assignment?"

Jordan returned his gaze levelly. "Sure."

Jordan and DeLuca ended up in Morrissey's office that afternoon, and DeLuca told him about what they'd found. By that time, the lab techs had found the victim's wallet with his ID, which confirmed Jen's identification – one Jon Hurly, from the nearby suburb of McKees Rocks. As with Poppy, there was no cell phone; it had last pinged from Hurly's home in McKees Rocks, the night before.

"So," said DeLuca, "we've got a definite connection to Harry's Bar, and Bell has offered to go in. We wanted to make sure you were okay with that."

"I'm more interested in knowing if Jordan is okay with it," said Morrissey, looking at Jordan over tented fingers.

"Yes," said Jordan. "I think I made that clear this morning." His voice was calm, but he realized that he was gripping his pen and notebook tightly. He forced his hands to relax.

"Okay," sighed Morrissey. He un-tented his fingers and looked at DeLuca. "I'll talk to you about particulars after this." He turned his gaze on Jordan. "When can you go into the bar? Tomorrow night is Friday – maybe a good night to start?"

Jordan hedged. "I'm going to need some time to get ready. I need to do some research. I need to know details on Goth music and maybe things like literature, at least enough to get by. Otherwise, they'll realize I'm a fake – or at best a poseur.

"Here's what I'm thinking. I'm going to a party Saturday night – some friends of my parents, the Martins. They have a son named Peter – there was a Peter Martin on Jen's list of Goth patrons. I think it could be the same guy. I'm going to try to make a connection with him, maybe even see if he invites me to Harry's to hang out. It would help me get access to the group. If Peter brings up the bar, I'll suggest that we leave the party and head over there Saturday night. If it turns out that he's not the same Peter Martin, or if he doesn't want to go, I'll go anyway."

"Okay," said Morrissey. "Take the time to do your research; we don't want to go in unprepared. But keep in mind, there's some urgency here. As soon as this second Goth victim hits the news, all hell will break out. I'll handle the press, but we need to move on this."

There was a knock on the door, and Devon poked his head in through the doorway. "They found Hurly's car. It was parked upriver between Homestead and Whitaker. There's a short piece of road that sticks off East Waterfront Drive and dead-ends at the Great Allegheny Passage. The car was pulled all the way down to the end of that road by the trail. They've got forensics down there now – but the first thing they saw were drag marks, down to the river. They think the body floated down from there."

"So, a similar manner of disposing of the body," said Jordan. "Use the victim's car to transport it, and park it near a deserted piece of the trail near the river. Only this time, it was the other side of the Monongahela."

"And he didn't just leave the body near the river; he dumped it in the river," said DeLuca.

"It sounds a little haphazard," Morrissey observed. "If he wanted to get rid of a body and not have it found, he'd drive out in the sticks below town, weigh the body down, and throw it in the Ohio. It sounds like someone either not too bright or inexperienced. Either way, I want him reeled in." He looked at Jordan. "Okay, I want a word with Mike, here, for a minute."

Jordan nodded and rose, and as soon as the door closed, he could hear Morrissey say to DeLuca, "You need to be all over this," and then Mike said something about someone named Kinney, but he lost the rest of it as he walked away, over to his desk. He could see them talking, and they didn't look particularly happy.

Later that afternoon, he crossed paths with Bear in the hallway, and he pulled him aside. "Hey, I've got a question for you," he said. "Who is Kinney?"

"Kinney!" repeated Bear, surprised.

Jordan stretched the truth. "Yeah, Mike said something about him."

"Huh," said Bear. He hesitated. "Well, I guess if Mike brought it up… Kinney was Mike's old partner. They got caught in a shootout one night, and Kinney took a bullet in the spine. He's in a wheelchair, on disability, for the rest of his life." Jordan frowned, and Bear went on, "There was an investigation, and no one accused either of them of any breach of protocol; it was nighttime, and they were outgunned. Kinney always said that Mike saved his life. But I think Mike took it kinda hard." He stopped short, perhaps realizing that he had said too much, and changed the subject. "You put on quite a show yesterday. You had me going."

Jordan shrugged and grinned. "Well, Mike said he wanted someone undercover."

Bear peered at him. "Did you pierce your ear, just for that?"

"No, I did some undercover work in New York. I - uh - did it then." Jordan stopped; he felt that he'd revealed something he shouldn't, even though DeLuca and Morrissey already seemed to know something about his assignment in New York. His slip didn't matter; Bear looked skeptical. Jordan added, "There were a bunch of us doing a little street work. No big deal."

"Well, you've sure got a knack for it," said Bear. "Let me know next time you're gonna do that, so I don't shoot you." He gave Jordan a grin and a wink and walked off.

CHAPTER SIX

Jordan had the lousy luck Saturday evening to pull up in front of the Martins' house at the same time as his family. He grimaced, but he got out of his car and met them in the Martins' expansive curving driveway just as the sun was setting.

His mother was beaming. She looked radiant in an expensive teal silk blouse, and she gave Jordan a warm hug. As they parted, Jordan nodded. "Dad."

Everett Rowland Bell smiled tightly and eyed him with the same judgmental expression that Jordan had come to both loathe and expect. Same cold blue eyes, situated over a nose that made him look like a hawk. No attempt at a hug or even a handshake. "Jordan. I heard you were in town. It would have been nice to know you were coming back." Jordan smiled back, just as tightly, and began to walk toward the door, and they fell in beside him.

His brother Marcus smirked. "What happened – did you get booted from the NYPD?"

Jordan eyed him. Marcus had put on some weight in the last couple of years. "No. I got a chance to do some computer work there, and I liked it. I saw an opportunity listed for the State of Pennsylvania, and I applied for it. It happened to be here in Pittsburgh, which is fine with me. I enrolled in some computer classes at Pitt."

"All of this jumping around from career to career – aren't you getting a little old for this?" said his father. His lean face was sour with disapproval. "You graduated early from high school, and now you're going back to school at twenty-three. You should have stuck with law school. You would have passed the bar by now and be working your way up in a law firm. This job-hopping; it's immature."

"Everett," said Maria, warningly.

Jordan shrugged. "It's okay, Mom. I'm out on my own; I don't owe anyone any explanations." He looked directly at his father. "I'm paying my own way. It's my life."

"Nice," sniped Marcus. He was still living at home while he finished medical school and had taken Jordan's comment as a jab at him. Which it was. "We haven't seen you in two years, and this is how you act."

"He's a punk," said Everett coldly. "He's always been an argumentative little punk." They had reached the door, and he punched the doorbell with a forefinger, viciously.

"That went well," Jordan thought, and he shook his head; nothing had changed. "Nice to see both of you, too," he said pleasantly and offered his arm with mock gallantry to his mother as the door opened. "Mother, shall we?" The gesture wiped the distress off of her face.

She took his arm, and they stepped inside. She immediately caught sight of some friends, and they saw Jordan, and he was the center of a group of females for a moment. "My, look at you! So handsome! I would never have recognized him!" He smiled at them and was charming, and he could see his mother beaming with pride. He circulated and made small talk for a while, looking around for Peter, and then he spotted Peter's older sister, Meg, in the kitchen, leaning against the gleaming quartz counter of a built-in wine bar, talking with a friend. Meg was five years older than he was; he wasn't sure if she would remember him, but he wanted to find out where Peter was.

"Meg, how are you?"

She looked at him and smiled uncertainly. "I'm sorry; do I know you?"

"Jordan Bell."

"Oh, my gosh!" she exclaimed. "No! Little Jordan?"

He smiled. "That's me."

Her brow furrowed. "You went away for a while somewhere, Mom said. New York?"

"I was. I'm back in Pittsburgh as of this month, doing financial analysis for the state. Hey, is Peter around?"

She rolled her eyes. "Yes, Peter's up in his room. He's not a big fan of the parties. Go up and see him; I'm sure he'll want to see you. It's the first room on the right after you go upstairs. Good to see you."

He nodded at her and her girlfriend, a curvy blonde. "Nice to see you." He could hear the girlfriend ask about him as he walked away.

"Who is he?" And then, at Meg's murmured explanation, "My Gawd, is he hot!"

He grinned to himself on the way up the stairs; he reckoned he did look pretty sharp. He'd dressed in gray slacks and black Italian dress boots, and a black button-down shirt. Although he'd gone with dark colors, it was not Goth apparel by a long shot; he'd have a sales job on his hands with Peter.

He paused at the door, gathering his wits, then knocked.

"Yeah."

"Peter?"

There was a moment of silence, some shuffling around, and then the door opened. Peter was pulling on a long-sleeved button shirt. He left it open in the front, over a black T-shirt featuring an album cover from The Cure, covering a hefty mid-section. He peered at Jordan, scowling, then recognition came into his eyes. "Waterboy? Is that you? Holy crap."

Jordan let the old nickname slide. He had never been a water boy, but after his failed attempt at football in high school, someone started calling him that, and it had stuck, at least among the football players. Jordan was sure his brother had something to do with that. He smiled. "What's up?"

"Not much," said Peter, eyeing him dubiously. He hadn't changed much; the acne was less pronounced, and the weight had been augmented by at least twenty pounds, but he was the same old Peter, big and ugly. Peter had played offensive line on the football team, Jordan remembered. And he'd walked around school with that same scowl. It seemed to be permanently affixed.

"Your sister said you'd be up here," said Jordan. "I thought I'd come up and hang out for a while if that's okay. My mom talked me into coming, but I'm not too big on the social scene."

Peter's expression softened infinitesimally. "Yeah, I hear that.

Come in." He shuffled backward and pushed a dirty paper plate sitting on his desk into a trashcan. Peter had helped himself to the party food and had come upstairs to eat it in his bedroom, like a bear in his den. Sociable.

"I was just gonna put on some tunes, maybe do some video games." Peter pointed to his computer screen, which displayed a playlist, much of it Goth and punk music.

"Sweet," said Jordan, as he studied the list. "How about Sisters of Mercy?"

Peter gave him an appraising look. "You like that stuff?"

"You're the one who has the album. Don't you?"

"Yeah, I do. You just never struck me as the Goth type."

"Yeah, well, likewise. I always thought you were a basic jock. I was into the music in school, but I never got the whole scene until I moved to New York. There were a couple of really intense clubs there. Besides, you know my dad, plus I was just a kid, a little young for high school. He would never have let me get away with the clothes." He looked at Peter curiously. "I don't remember you being Goth in school."

"Well, I was," said Peter, as he cued up the music and turned on the speakers, louder than they needed to be. "We had a dress code at school, so it's not like anyone at school would know if you didn't tell them. And my hair is already dark, so I didn't need to dye it." He eyed Jordan. "Kind of like you, I guess."

He had some old vinyl albums on a shelf above his head, and Jordan pointed, "Shit, is that Joy Division?"

Peter turned his bulk, a grin coming to his face. He reached a big paw toward the shelf, and as he did so, his sleeve fell. Peter turned his arm deftly, but not before Jordan saw the telltale marks and a few small healing cuts on his arms. He had suspected that Peter was either a cutter or a drug user when he pulled on the long-sleeved shirt. Cutter, then. Interesting. Peter pulled down the album and dusted it off, and Jordan pretended to admire it.

Peter studied him. "So, are you visiting from New York?" He sat and pointed to a chair, and Jordan sat, too.

Jordan shook his head. "I moved back. New job. I'm doing computer work for the state, some financial stuff, and I'm going back for my degree in computer science on the side. I start in the fall at Pitt."

"My mom said you were a cop in New York."

"Yeah," sighed Jordan. "I was. I did some computer work for them and decided I liked that better. I was just a beat cop, patrolling subways, and that kind of stuff. It wasn't as exciting as TV makes it out to be. I started looking for computer jobs, and this one came up."

"You wanted to come back?"

"Not really, but it's okay. I did like New York City, but the cost of living there is a killer. I miss those clubs, though."

"We've got a club here," said Peter, defensively. "I mean, it's not really a club, it's a dive bar, but it's a Goth hangout. There are some pretty cool people there. We have some intense discussions on Goth stuff – poetry, literature. It's not for poseurs."

"I'm down with that," said Jordan. "What's this place called?"

"Harry's. It's in Southside. I was thinking of running over there later. Wanna go?"

"Yeah, sure, sounds good."

"Well, let's eat first," said Peter as if he hadn't already. "My mom catered the food for the party from Wellington's."

They got plates, talked for an hour, and listened to Goth punk, with Jordan watching while Peter played a war video game with some online players. He had some impressive computer equipment, courtesy of his parents, no doubt, because Peter admitted he was still plodding through business school, apparently on the eight-year plan. Then Peter glanced at the time on his monitor and said, "It's early, but I'm sick of this place. Let's go."

"Okay," said Jordan. "I'm gonna stop at home and change; I'll meet you there."

"You staying at your Mom and Dad's?"

"Naw – I got an apartment in Oakland to be close to Pitt."

Peter nodded. "That's on the way, then. Okay, I'll see you there."

He followed Jordan downstairs, detouring to the kitchen again, and Jordan gave his mother a wave and was out the door. She looked disappointed at his quick exit, but he needed the time.

At his apartment, he changed quickly into the Goth outfit he had worn into work, wincing as he put in his earring. It wasn't a new piercing; he'd gotten it in New York for his undercover assignment, but he'd let the hole close most of the way, and getting the post back in again had been tough. Then he went online, looking up New York

Goth clubs.

He'd spent the entire day before the party and most of the last evening cramming on Goth subjects – music, literature, poetry, art – and some subset cultures, like Vampirism and steampunk. He had never thought of looking up the New York Goth scene until he'd mentioned it to Peter, which had turned out to be a risky move; if Peter had asked for details, he would have had none. He now needed to back up his lies with some facts. Jordan quickly found an article on the top five Goth clubs in New York and clicked on the linked websites of each, memorizing details such as the décor and the local band scene, as much as he could determine from the pictures. He closed his eyes, his head spinning from the intense study of the past two days, and could feel a hint of anxiety starting to spiral. Jordan took one more look at the article, and finally satisfied, he pulled out his cell phone and called Mike DeLuca. It was just after ten.

The call went to voice mail, and Jordan said, "Mike, this is Jordan. I got an invite to Harry's from Peter Martin. I'm going in."

The bar was less than two miles from his apartment, and, traveling via the Birmingham Bridge, took precisely seven minutes to get there. Jordan scanned Harry's parking lot as he pulled in, wondering if Peter had gotten there yet. He had no idea what car Peter drove – but that four-year-old Lincoln might fit the bill; it was easily the most expensive car in the lot. It was likely that the Martins were bankrolling Peter's vehicle, along with his tuition. Sure enough, when he strolled inside, Peter waved at him from some tables along the far wall.

That section was readily identifiable as Goth territory, with several Goths clustered around one of the back tables. A few of the working crowd were seated at the bar itself; no college kids as of yet. The bar was limited to one room and boasted scarred paneled walls adorned with dusty random artifacts and pictures, an ancient scuffed wooden bar, and a worn tiled floor. The tables were no-frills, fake wood tops with dark painted metal legs, and the chairs had cheap vinyl seats. A jukebox sat against the wall nearest the Goth group. Jordan took a breath and inhaled something musty and the scent of stale beer. Curious eyes were on him as he moved forward, and as he came up to the table, he nodded at the group.

"This is the friend from high school that I was telling you about," said Peter. "Jordan."

'Friend,' thought Jordan; the word was a promotion of sorts. Maybe. Not all of the expressions were welcoming. They weren't necessarily hostile either, just watchful.

Peter went around the table, introducing the group, who all appeared to be in their twenties. George Lilt was tall and lean with chin-length dark greasy hair, Sammy Farineau was small and skinny, with a pointed nose and a weak chin. There were two girls: Victoria Jensen, who had a curvy figure tucked into a corset and was wearing a long black skirt with ruffles, and Suzanne Weir. There was an air about the place, around the group: toughness, a touch of hostility. Every one of them had a chip on their shoulder.

Jordan took another look at the girls. Suzanne was the ex-girlfriend, Jordan remembered. Victoria was pretty, even with the dyed hair and the nose piercing and the black lipstick, but Suzanne was stunning. She had dressed more simply, in black leather pants and a sleeveless black leather vest over a form-fitting long-sleeved black T-shirt. Both girls wore dark lipstick and eyeliner, and both had long black hair; Victoria's curly, and Suzanne's straight and silky. Victoria pulled out a chair next to her and said, "Have a seat, Jordan."

He sat, and she glanced at him coquettishly and said, "We were just talking about a book that George read."

Jordan glanced at George to see if he would expand on her comment, but he was watching a man at the jukebox with a look of annoyance. The man selected a southern rock tune, and Sammy said in a nasal voice, "Oh Gawd, I hate that song."

Suzanne said, "Jordan, you're closest. Would you mind putting something decent in the queue after that song?"

Jordan nodded, "Sure." They were testing him already.

He went over to the jukebox, slipped in a credit card, and perused the offerings, taking a bit of time to think. The group wasn't a think tank, by any means, but they were discussing books. Intellectual wannabes, maybe. He needed to align himself with their mannerisms, their choice of words, although he already had a sense of who Jordan the Goth might be. A working man, but something of a rebel, not entirely satisfied with his lot in life.

Unsurprisingly, there was a large selection of Goth music. Jordan put in some early work from The Cure, something from Corpus

Delicti, and followed that up with two songs by Souxie and the Banshees. The Cure had gone more mainstream later in their career, so when the southern rock tune ended and that song came on, Jordan could still see some skepticism in the faces of the group; approval, but grudging. Not yet quite sure.

Sammy asked, "You into poetry, Jordan?"

Jordan said, "Yeah, I like poetry."

Victoria batted her eyelashes at him. "I like Lord Byron. Who's your favorite?"

Jordan smiled at her. "I like the classics too. But I guess my favorite is The Dance of Death, by von Goethe."

He plopped that one out there, and a moment later, Corpus Delicti came on, and his answer and the second song seemed satisfactory. The entire group seemed to sit back and relax. Peter said, "Jordan said he hit some Goth clubs in New York City when he was there."

"Awesome, dude," said George Lilt, who was smiling at him now. "They had to be incredible."

Jordan nodded. "They were. My favorite was Apocalypse at Night Shades." He went on to describe the place, and the last of the suspicious looks faded. Jordan was under no delusions that he was permanently accepted, however. Early in life, he had found out that acceptance was a misconception or at least a fleeting state of being. He had a foot in the door, that was all. The talk grew more animated and less focused solely on him, and he started to work on Victoria.

She was flirting with him, there was no doubt, and he listened to her prattle on about the latest movie by one of her favorite directors. After a few minutes of that, Jordan got up and went to get drinks, following her lead and ordering a diet soda for both of them. Most of the Goth crowd opted for soft drinks. It probably didn't break the bartender's heart that the Goth group was dwindling; the other patrons were ordering the pricier hard beverages. Jordan's music selections had chased away a few people – either that or they were working stiffs who had called it a night – but some of the college crowd was filtering in, mostly young men, with a few girls. He wondered if the ex-boyfriend, Will McCann, was among them. Each of the college kids seemed to be getting equally hostile stares from the Goth group, but one young man, in particular, seemed to be drawing furtive looks from Suzanne Weir and Peter Martin.

Jordan had been watching Peter all evening, and he hadn't left Suzanne's side. Then again, neither had George Lilt. Both of them seemed to be very attentive to her – maybe hoping to fill in the empty spot left by Will McCann. As Jordan returned with the drinks, he got a dark look from Sammy Farineau, who seemed interested in Victoria. Jordan ignored him and retook his seat.

"Thanks," said Victoria, and hit him again with the eyelashes. They were false and so thick that Jordan swore she generated a small breeze every time she blinked. Across the table, Sammy scowled. Victoria leaned in conspiratorially, revealing ample cleavage. "So, have you heard about all of the crazy shit that's been happening here?"

Jordan widened his eyes in feigned surprise. "No. What shit?"

"Two of our friends were murdered," said Victoria. "Two Goth kids who hung out at this bar. One of them was on the news – that girl from Ohio."

"Oh, yeah, I think I did hear about that."

"They didn't say exactly, on the news, but the rumor is going around that her wrists had been slit."

Jordan frowned. "That sounds like suicide."

"I know, right?" said Victoria. "But on the news, they said it was a murder investigation. So, someone must have cut her." She took a drink and continued. "Then the cops came back here asking about Jon Hurly. The girl, Poppy, wasn't here too much, but Jon was. He lived right over in McKees Rocks. We knew him pretty well. Anyway, that one hasn't been on the news, but Peter talked to Harry, and Harry told him."

"Harry?"

She gestured with her head. "The bartender and owner. The cops came in and told Harry, and Harry told us, but he said the cops wouldn't say how he died."

"Wow, that is some freaky shit," agreed Jordan. He glanced around the bar and then back at her. "Doesn't that make you paranoid? Two Goth kids dead, and they both hung out here?"

"A little," she admitted. Her eyes tracked around the room nervously, unconsciously following the path of Jordan's gaze. "We try to go out in groups to our cars now when we leave. That's why I'm telling you this because you should be careful. But we don't know what happened. Everyone remembers Poppy being here the night she died, but she left at around midnight. It wasn't that late yet. She could have gone somewhere else, or someone could have just randomly jacked her car at a stoplight, y'know? And we still don't know what happened to Jon. Maybe he wasn't even murdered. He drank – he could have wrecked his car, and the cops were trying to find out from Harry how much he'd had that night. It could be anything with him. George is going to call his mom tomorrow and see if there are any arrangements." She sighed and shook her head. Then she glanced at him, her eyes bright with interest. "Peter said you were a cop in New York. He said you were scary smart in high school."

"Yeah, I did okay in school. The cop thing wasn't for me, though." He grinned at her, with a gesture at his clothes. "I'm not exactly a conformist."

She smiled, her eyes meeting his, holding his gaze. "Me neither."

Their conversation was interrupted by Sammy pulling up a chair, trying to fit it into a rather tight spot between Victoria and George, and Victoria made a face and shifted to let him in. She gave Jordan an apologetic look as she turned to Sammy; he was asking her something. Jordan took the opportunity to get up and walk around, and he saw the look of satisfaction on Sammy's face as he left.

He went over to the bar ostensibly to get another soda, and he made sure to plant himself next to the college kid who had drawn Suzanne Weir's attention while he waited for it. The young man was staring, and Jordan called him on it. "Need something?"

"No." The kid was unflustered, his blue eyes hard and cold. "Who are you?"

"Jordan Bell. Who are you?" Jordan tossed back, a challenge in his voice.

"Will McCann. You're new here."

Jordan shrugged. "From what I hear, this place is a long-time Goth hangout. I came to check it out." He looked McCann up and down. McCann was six feet, maybe 190 pounds, almost all of it muscle. His breath smelled strongly of beer, and his eyes were glazed; he had probably been drinking before he got there. "You're looking pretty mainstream, dude. Maybe you didn't get that memo." Someone had come up behind him, and Jordan turned just enough to see him in the mirror behind the bar. Peter.

"It's a public place," said McCann. "Goth assholes don't own it."

Jordan smiled. "Goth assholes? Really? That's intelligent. Go crawl back in your dorm, frat boy."

McCann bristled. "Who the hell are you, you little punk? Step outside, and we'll see who ends up crawling." A cloud of beer breath accompanied the threat.

Harry, the bartender, listened in now as he hustled drinks, with one ear and one wary eye on the conversation. Jordan winced and averted his face from McCann. "Geez, buddy. You smell like shit. *You* step outside. That's where you belong."

Harry set the soda down, and Jordan reached for it, and as he did so, McCann gave him a hard shove in the shoulder. Peter said, "Back off, McCann!" and Harry barked, "Back away, Will, and pipe down, or you're out of here!"

Will made a face, but he took a step back, both hands up. "Okay, okay." He sneered at Jordan, who had picked up his drink and was regarding him coolly. "Later, freak."

Jordan tossed a few bills on the counter and shook his head and smirked, which wiped the sneer off McCann's face. Anger was returning to it as Jordan turned to go back to his table, and out of the corner of his eye, he saw one of McCann's buddies speaking quietly into his ear, trying to calm him down. Peter fell in alongside, putting his bulk between Jordan and the college boys. He was grinning. "You okay?"

"Me? I'm fine. It'll take more than a little shove to hurt me."

"McCann's an asshole," said Peter, unnecessarily. He stopped a few feet short of their table, speaking in a confidential tone. "Will used to be Goth and used to go out with Suzanne. Then he went mainstream, and she dumped him. I mean, I think the dump was coming anyway, but he fell in with these college kids – they're freakin' obnoxious. McCann was always a jerk, but he started being more of one, and she couldn't take him anymore. We didn't see him for a while, and then all of a sudden, he started showing up here with his friends. I think he's doing it to get back at her and us. They come in and take over the bar, do stupid stuff like commandeer the jukebox. And Harry lets it happen because he wants the extra business. Hard to blame him, I guess, but college kids have a ton of bars that they own already. They could go anywhere, but they have to come here. It's hard to take sometimes."

Jordan nodded sympathetically. "I get that. I was happy to find out we had a place in Pittsburgh."

"You handled him pretty good," said Peter. "I'm not scared of him, and neither is George, but the rest of them are. Jon wasn't scared of him either, but he's gone now."

"Jon Hurly."

Peter nodded. "You heard about him and Poppy?"

"Victoria told me."

"Yeah, well, I'm not sure what's going on there, or how Jon died even. But we're all watching our backs." He looked apologetic. "I guess I should have told you about all this stuff before you came down here. My bad."

Jordan shrugged. "It wouldn't have changed my mind. I wanted to check it out." He grinned at Peter. "I'm not scared of the pretty frat boys either. And I'll be coming back. Tonight just made it interesting."

Harry pushed up the last call to forty-five minutes before legal closing time to minimize the chances of fights in the parking lot, even though it cost him a few drink orders. That effectively cleared out the college crowd – they went on up to Carson Street, just a couple of blocks away, to try to get in one or two more drinks. Jordan ended up closing the place down with the Goth group, and they all left together, the girls peering around nervously as they got into their cars. Jordan got into the Impala and glanced at his phone. There was a message from DeLuca, asking him to check in when he got out, but it was late, after 2:00 a.m. Way too late to call. He pulled out of the lot and headed toward home.

CHAPTER SEVEN

Jordan's phone buzzed at six a.m., and he groaned, fumbled for it, and hit answer. DeLuca's voice came on the line, with a hint of nasty in it. "Hope you had a good night's sleep, buttercup. Where was my phone call?"

"Sorry." Jordan sat up. "I didn't get out of there until after two. I didn't want to wake you up."

"Okay," said DeLuca. "Let's get one thing straight. When I say call, I mean, call. Here's another thing. I'll be at your place in about ten or fifteen. Be outside. We're going for a ride. Don't bother with coffee. I got it."

Jordan was waiting when he got there, and DeLuca almost drove past him. Jordan suspected that DeLuca didn't recognize him; he was wearing jeans and a T-shirt, and his hair was sticking up in random tufts from the gel he'd used to spike it the night before. Jordan imagined that he probably looked like a college kid from a distance. As Jordan opened the passenger door, DeLuca thrust a bag at him and jerked his head at the console, where two cups of coffee sat. He mumbled something.

"What?" asked Jordan.

"You're like a freakin' chameleon," grumbled DeLuca.

Jordan got in and took the bag, eying him warily, and said, "Thanks," quietly, as he went for the coffee. He took a sip and closed his eyes briefly in appreciation. Black, strong, and hot. "Where are we going?"

"I was going to have you meet me for breakfast over on the Strip, but I'm not sure that's such a good idea. If we stumbled on anyone from the bar, it wouldn't be good for us to be seen together. If I end up at the bar during this investigation, I wouldn't want anybody to place me with you." DeLuca glanced sharply at him. "Unless you've blown your cover already."

Jordan ignored the comment and tamped down a scowl. "Of course, I haven't. If anything, I cemented it last night. I'm in, at least with the Goth crowd. And conversely, I'm not in with the college crowd. Jen was right; they don't like each other much."

DeLuca drove over to the Point and parked. They watched the morning light steal over the water and ate egg-and-sausage biscuits and drank coffee, and Jordan told him about the party at the Martins' house, and hitting it off with Peter, and getting invited to go out to the bar.

"There was a small group at Harry's when I got there at around ten. Two girls, Suzanne and Victoria, and the rest were guys. George Lilt, Sammy Farineau, and Peter. I think they're the regulars; well, Jon Hurly sounded like a regular, too. A couple more Goth types came in later, but they kept to themselves. I don't think they're part of the usual group, but if they show up again, I'll find out. And I met Will McCann."

"The college kid that broke up with Suzanne."

"Yeah. McCann's a belligerent type; came in already plastered, looking to pick a fight. So, I picked one with him."

"What?"

"Relax, it was just a little argument." Jordan took a swig of coffee. "The Goth group was testing me, right off the bat. It was a good thing that I studied. I think I passed those tests, but I figured it wouldn't hurt to draw a line between the college kids and me. I also was trying to stir things up – not a lot, just a little – so I could watch what happened."

"And?"

"There's a lot of tension in that little bar, and McCann is causing most of it. He came in with a group of guys and girls at eleven. They're noisy, and they take over the bar and start hogging the jukebox. The Goth group pretty much kept to their corner, but they weren't happy. McCann goes in there just looking to make trouble. He's still apparently pretty bitter over the breakup."

"So, she broke up with him."

DeLuca was engaged now, not judging, just listening. Jordan took a bite of his sandwich and chewed. "That's what Peter told me. The thing is, I think both Peter and George are interested in Suzanne now. They sat on either side of her all night. I can't blame them – she's attractive."

"What's she like?"

"That'll have to wait for my next visit. I didn't get much of a chance to talk to her. I sat near Victoria, who was pretty chatty. She told me about Poppy and Jon – although no one at the bar knows what happened to him."

"It'll be in this morning's Pittsburgh Post-Gazette," said DeLuca. "Morrissey got permission from the family and met with the editor on this one last night. Morrissey let them know we think it's linked to Poppy's murder. It'll be all over the news by the end of the day. So, what happened with McCann?"

"Nothing. It was like poking a bear; it didn't take much to rile him. I went up to the bar to get a drink and made sure I was next to him. McCann had noticed me, alright – he was watching the Goth crowd all night. I was purposely mouthy. I wanted to see how he'd react. I knew he was trying to cause trouble, but sometimes that kind of thing can be light-hearted, mischievous. That wasn't. McCann was downright hostile. He's a very angry guy."

"Is McCann big?"

"You mean, big enough to cart bodies around? Yeah. He's probably just over six feet and a little under two-hundred, mostly muscle. Of course, Peter and George Lilt are big guys too. And so are several of McCann's buddies."

"You said you went for a drink. You were drinking?"

Jordan shook his head. "Just soda. A few of the Goth crowd had a beer, but a lot of them didn't drink at all."

"Okay. Keep it that way."

Jordan ignored that and drained the last of his coffee. "Anyway, Peter came over to the bar and heard most of my little altercation with McCann. I think that episode just strengthened my relationship with the Goth group."

DeLuca shook his head. "Watch your back. You might come out to find McCann and his buddies in the parking lot some night."

"I know. I'm careful. So is Harry, the bartender. He closes his bar down forty-five minutes before the others do – it clears out the crowd pretty quick. The college kids all run up to Carson Street for last call, and they're long gone before the Goth crowd hits the parking lot." He paused, remembering. "The whole Goth crowd came out together last night when the bar closed. I think they're all pretty spooked."

"Yeah," said DeLuca. "So am I – spooked about our heads rolling if we don't get this guy soon. That said, now that you tried this for a night, I need you to tell me honestly what you think about it. I don't want you in there if your head's not in the game."

This time Jordan didn't try to hide the scowl. "Who said my head's not in the game?"

"You didn't seem too excited about this when I brought it up the first time."

DeLuca was asking him what he thought about the assignment. Concern, or some other motive? Jordan gave him the benefit of the doubt and answered, more or less honestly. "I wasn't. But the more I thought about it, the more I thought I could handle it. I think it's going pretty well. I'll let you know if it seems like it's going sour."

DeLuca nodded. "Okay, fair enough. I'll drop you back off – make sure you put what you saw into a report. And be ready to report out at the team meeting tomorrow morning."

Jordan was in early Monday morning and was reading over his report as DeLuca came in. He wasn't sure, but he thought he caught a look of approval on the man's face as he passed by. The morning meeting the day before had gone better, too. Granted, DeLuca had dragged him out of bed to interrogate him, but for once, the man seemed on the level. He'd seemed honestly interested in the answers instead of trying to belittle Jordan's efforts. Unless he wanted to count the 'your head's not in the game' comment.

The fact was that the first visit to the bar had made him feel a lot better about the whole thing. Picking up the Goth punk role had been easier than expected. It wasn't a full-time act, and he was still Jordan Bell. He could go into work every day and be himself. This assignment might be just what he needed. He grinned cheerfully at Marty Beran as he trudged into the office. "Morning, Bear."

Bear peered at him as he passed, with a nod. "Mornin'. You're looking – uh – normal – today."

Jordan's grin widened, and he said, "Normal is relative."

Bear chuckled. "You got that right. And I'm living proof. You want a coffee, kid?"

He bought Jordan a coffee, and as they stood at the coffee pot, Jordan said, "Let me ask you something. Mike calls everyone here by their first name, except me. Is that supposed to be a hint?"

Bear grinned. "No, no hint. He did that with all of us when we came in, at least to start. It took most of us two years before he'd start calling us by our first name. Milt was quicker, but in his case, that was because he's a year older than Mike, and they came in at the same time, so he'd earned a little more respect. Rookies get last name status until he decides otherwise – nothing personal."

Jordan turned that over in his head, with a glance at Milt as he came through the door. Was Milt only a year older than DeLuca? He looked at least ten years his senior. The others filed in, and the office filled with the sounds of drawers clunking, coffee cups plunking down on the counter in the corner, the click of keyboards. Jordan headed back to his desk as Milt and Bear started discussing the Steelers game from the day before and their prospects for the season, and fueled by his second cup of coffee that morning, kept typing. He had his report done in time for the team meeting and made copies.

As they all filed into the conference room, Morrissey was right in front of Jordan, and he turned and murmured, "Mike said it went pretty well for you Saturday night."

"Yeah, I think so," said Jordan. He glanced at DeLuca. Had the man paid him a compliment? More likely, Morrissey had put his personal spin on DeLuca's report.

Morrissey kicked off the meeting. "The news was out yesterday, in the paper and on the local news stations, and I confirmed that we think the two deaths are homicides and that they are related. I did not mention why, and I did not elaborate on the connection with the bar. Those are things we want to keep confidential while we investigate. With it being Sunday and with the game on TV, the stories got less attention than they might have. Today it'll be worse. The reporters will be out in full force, looking for the latest for their nightly broadcast. I'm going to try to run interference and hold a press conference but be advised that they may try to approach you when you leave the building. We've been through this before – you know the drill – do not comment on the case.

"We also do not want to lead them to the bar inadvertently. Some of the local press know the members of our team, except for Jordan. For that reason, Jen and Devon, you need to try to stay away from the bar if you can help it. They could follow you there. Jordan will be our eyes and ears as far as the bar is concerned. All of the rest of you, during this investigation, if you have any questions for anyone at the bar, you will do it by phone or meet them elsewhere, or if it makes sense, and Jordan can ask the questions without blowing his cover, have him do it."

He looked at Jordan. "That brings us to you. Until some of the attention dies down, you should not try to come into the office; you should work from home. If the camera crews catch you coming out of this building, even in the background, and anyone from the bar sees it on TV, you'll blow your cover. Mike will talk to you about it after the meeting."

Jordan felt an uncomfortable clutch in his gut but nodded and kept his face neutral. He hadn't counted on this. The part-time undercover job had just gone full-time, with DeLuca, in essence, as his handler.

Morrissey looked around the table. "That's it, then, concerning the press, except for the fact that if there is another victim before we solve this thing, you can bet the national news will get involved, and the press situation and the pressure from the mayor and the governor will get exponentially worse. I cannot stress enough that we need to make some progress here. Jen and Devon are still the leads on this, and Marty and Milt, you are still the leads on the drug case, but I need your eyes and ears on the murder case, along with Jordan's. We need all hands on deck with this one. And with that, I'll turn the meeting over to Mike."

DeLuca passed out copies of Jordan's report. "As you might have assumed, based on John's comments, Bell was successful at getting accepted by the Goth group at Harry's this weekend. You can read the details in his report. He'll be frequenting the bar in the evenings and turning in reports afterward. Bell, any comments?"

Jordan said, "The bottom line is that there are several key people who frequent the bar and are big enough, physically, to be able to subdue a suspect and cart around a body. Two men in the Goth group, and several of the college kids. As far as motive goes, we still don't have a strong one, but Will McCann's hatred toward his ex-girlfriend also seems to be directed at the Goth group in general."

DeLuca said, "Jen and Devon, I need you to focus on McCann and his alibis for the night in question. Look at the places he went in the later hours of those nights and see if we can scare up any surveillance camera footage in the body dump areas. Find out if we can place his car there or anywhere in the neighborhood. Check with the cell phone company to track where his phone was those nights. Also, look back at his record and see if there is any other indication of violence. You two have anything to add?"

Devon nodded. "We have a few more forensics results, and the ME worked overtime this weekend, so we have some more information on the second body. The ME concurs with our suspicion that Victim Two was dead before the killer put him in the river. There was little aspiration of river water and some air left in the lungs; that's why the body floated instead of sinking. It made it several yards down the river before it caught on bushes near the bank because it was placed in shallow water, too close to shore for the current to pick it up and pull it out into deeper water."

DeLuca said, "So this time we had more of an attempt to hide the body, but a poor attempt."

Devon nodded. "The ME determined the cause of death to be the same as Victim One – he bled to death from long deep cuts along the inside of his forearms, and there are similar ligature marks on the arms and ankles. The ME is checking for sedatives."

Jen added, "We did get a couple of footprints near where the body went into the river. They're not clear; the mud was too soft to hold any details, but the crime techs think someone sizable made the tracks, wearing at least a size eleven shoe and fairly heavy. They didn't see any other prints right down on the water's edge, so it appears that whoever dumped the body was working alone. The body was dragged from a vehicle to the river bank on a tarp - they found a fragment of it, a small piece of blue plastic reinforced with fiber, caught on a rock, and evidence of drag marks in the dirt and grass."

"Okay," said DeLuca. "Anybody have anything else on the murder case? No? Where are we with the drug distribution ring?"

Bear rubbed his face. "We're not too far, I'm afraid. We've tracked Drayvon Carter all around Pittsburgh, and he's a pretty boring guy. He gets up and goes down to the Mon near the

Glenwood Bridge and goes fishing nearly every weekday morning. He occasionally visits his buddies, and a couple of them we think are part of his distribution ring, but they're not his suppliers. He visits his mom a couple of times a week. He volunteers at his church; he heads up a food bank on Saturdays and attends services on Sundays. Sometimes he goes around town, driving through territories where he has his guys set up, selling. We've tracked him to all of those places, and we keep seeing signs of the selling, but not the buying. We've been watching him for weeks, now, along with the PBP, and nothing yet."

He plopped some copies of reports on the table and pointed at them. "Those are the locations where we've spotted Carter recently, with photos. For the last four of those weeks, we had someone on him twenty-four seven. If anyone has any ideas, we're open to them."

The meeting ended without much more discussion, and Morrissey's lips were in a tight line when he left the room. No one looked happy. DeLuca remained sitting and crooked a finger at Jordan, and Jordan moved opposite him as the others filed out. DeLuca said, "I have the IT guys working on your remote access. They'll give you instructions on how to hook up to the office website securely from home using your work laptop. Your work cell phone came in; you can use it to contact us and call into meetings. I will be your main contact for developments; report them through me. If you have any issues or questions, get hold of me. When you leave here today, I suggest you do it around noon and avoid the parking lot. We'll get someone to give you a ride to your apartment. Leave your car keys, and someone will drop them off there at the end of the day. There's a side entrance to this building. Your ride will come around to that side and pick you up there."

He paused, waiting, and Jordan shrugged and said, "Okay." What else could he say?

"I want you to call me at least once a day. If you go into the bar and the visit was uneventful, send me a text to let me know you got back okay. For anything big, call me anytime, day or night. Otherwise, let's shoot for a phone meeting at 7:30 a.m. every morning. You can catch me up on anything that happened the day or night before." He paused again. "I don't expect you to go to the bar every night if you think it will look odd."

Jordan nodded. "I know. I'll try tomorrow night again; see who's there. If it looks like most of the Goth crowd shows up every night, then fine, I will too. If not, I'll try to match what they do."

DeLuca nodded. "I'll trust your judgment. You may want to touch base with Jerry in the IT lab and see if there's anything you can work on at home if you get a slow day. This case takes priority, though, over anything he gives you." He paused. "You did a good job this weekend, getting in there so fast. I liked that assertiveness, but don't take any undue risks. If you feel that anything doesn't seem right, don't take time to analyze – just get out of there."

Jordan thought to himself that those were fine words from the guy who had pushed for him to be in the assignment to begin with, but he kept his mouth shut and nodded. Their talk over, he went back to work for a while at his desk and then went down to the IT lab to square things up with Jerry. Someone from PBP Narcotics named Joe called him, and Jordan arranged for a ride home. He left his car keys with DeLuca, gathered up his laptop, his new phone, some notes, and the latest copies of the case reports for both the Goth murders and the drug case, and shortly after noon, he was back at his apartment. He put his things on the small kitchen table and sighed.

He'd felt good that morning, as though he was contributing and was part of the team. Now, even though his primary assignment hadn't changed, he felt exiled. That was one of the worst things about being undercover - the sense of isolation, of being tethered to the real world by only a handler. His job was looking more and more like the one he had had in New York. He rubbed his forehead and thought back over the last week. Part of this was his fault, and he had to make the best of it. Besides, he had nailed it last weekend. Waltzed right in, sweet-talked Peter Martin, and became a part of the group. And he had to admit, playing the bad boy was growing on him. He had thought he didn't want to do this anymore, but maybe it did beat sitting in a dark room in front of a computer.

He looked in his refrigerator and grimaced; it was nearly empty. He rummaged through the cabinets, found some ramen noodles for lunch, sat down to think, and made some notes while he ate, trying to get down what they knew.

Both victims were Goth, at least as far as most others were concerned. However, both might have been considered poseurs –

Devon had said that there had been a comment by someone that Poppy wasn't a real Goth. Who had made that comment? And what had they meant by it, exactly? It could be significant. He made a note and underlined it. Then there was Jon Hurly, not the usual all-in-black version of Goth, but a steampunk, a Victorian dresser with a penchant for leather helmets and brass goggles. Still Goth, but not the archetype. To an outsider, those deviations wouldn't matter, but to a Goth, they might.

What else? Poppy had been barely an acquaintance, traveling in rarely from Ohio, and Jon had been a regular, from Pittsburgh. Female and male. No similarities there. Both around the same age, but all of the Goths there were in their twenties. The group seemed a little - he searched for a word - *intense,* compared to the Goth kids he remembered from school. His classmates had been more laid back, mainly into music and dress. This group took the culture seriously.

What about the cutting, the murder method? Jordan fired up his work laptop, got out on the internet, and looked up Goths and cutting. As he expected, most of the Goth-friendly sites denounced cutting and maintained that it was a myth that Goths cut themselves more than others, but here and there, he found hints of other websites that espoused cutting. There was one study that found that adolescents predisposed to cutting were also inclined to admire Goth culture and join Goth groups. There were a few webpages on the regular internet about cutting, but he knew where he would probably find other sites – on the Dark Web. He thought for a moment and then tied his computer into the link that Jerry used to surf the Dark Web to look for cybercrime evidence. That link was secure with its own VPN, and through it, he could access TOR.

He searched for a while, and it didn't take long before he turned up all sorts of dark sites, many of them professing to be Goth. These were not the tame Goth sites on the regular internet, not even close. Some websites espoused death and dying, torture, witchcraft, vampirism, blood, and some of them, cutting. He examined two of the cutting sites. They had links to another webpage called True Goth, and the name caught his eye. The site's moderator went by the pseudonym of Darkness and proposed rigid rules for the true Goth, which didn't necessarily agree with the other Goth sites on the internet. Apparently, it was Darkness's personal creed. The presentation of the information was unsophisticated, except for the art. The links to topics and forums were simple, but the artwork on each page was elaborate. Type font in a Victorian script, page edging in swirls of black and dashes of red and purple, with figures lurking in the borders; anything from knives dripping blood to goblins.

Topics ranged from Goth poetry to treatises on what happened to the human body after death, to what constituted 'true' Goth dress, among others. And cutting. There were instructions on how to cut (shallow and crosswise was safe) and how to hide the fact, and the entire section began with a bold statement: 'True Goths cut. If you are not a cutter, you cannot be a true Goth'. A description of the dark joys of self-mutilation followed that directive, a treatise on the rush of endorphins, the high. The topic had hundreds of followers. He felt a chill down the back of his neck. Something about the site felt more than just dark; he could feel evil oozing out of it, curling around him like tendrils of smoke.

He sat back in his chair. Could someone possibly take the Goth culture so seriously that they would follow a site like this to the letter? And if they were obsessed enough, would they kill others that they deemed to be poseurs? It seemed unlikely but reading this, maybe not impossible. That might explain the method chosen for killing the victims. Sacrifice them, turn them into True Goths at their moment of death.

Or, the motive for the killings could be something more commonplace, as old as the dawn of man; jealousy, scorned love. That would point to Will McCann, but why take out his anger on two other people related to the object of his desire only by Goth culture? Was he blaming that culture as the cause of their breakup? The fact that he was no longer Goth meant he had cast the behavior aside for one reason or another. And Suzanne's desire to continue to pursue the Goth culture could have led to the breakup and possibly have made him blame the lifestyle and anyone who followed it. Or, McCann could be using the Goth murders as scare tactics to drive her away from Goth and toward the mainstream and, by extension, dissolve their differences.

He shook his head. It seemed convoluted, and convoluted was unlikely. McCann was all angry emotion, not a rational thinker. Jordan could see McCann attacking Suzanne herself, or maybe another man who had claimed her affection, but not thinking through the killings of two other people simply to play with her head – with one exception. It could be that he was mentally ill. Then it might be possible that he would take out his anger on a target that he saw as related, merely because that target was Goth.

That brought him to the killings, which were contradictory themselves. The set-up was meticulously planned – the kidnapping and killing itself. The site of the actual murders was still a mystery; there was little to describe where it might be, other than some concrete dust on Poppy's clothes. But the body dumps were sloppy. Effective, because they didn't leave much in the way of clues, but amateurish. He sat up as a thought occurred to him. The killer meant for them to find the bodies. The first was left poorly hidden on the train tracks; the second was a badly-executed disposal, an unweighted corpse in the river. The killer was sending a message. What that message was, and who the murderer intended it for, was anyone's guess.

He could get no further without more information, but he needed to clear his head of the darkness, and so he sat and thought about the drug case for a while, trying to ignore the irony in that. He read the reports from Marty and Milt and looked at the details; Drayvon Carter lived in Larimer, only five miles away. He thought about that for a moment. Jordan didn't have a car at the moment - it was still at the office - but he did have a bicycle. Wheeling it over from its home against the wall, he changed out the pedals. He wouldn't be wearing fancy cycling clip shoes for this ride.

A few moments later, he was on the road. Jordan's route took him past Schenley Park, past the Carnegie complex, including the Carnegie Library and museums, and through the hip neighborhood of Shadyside. It was mostly uphill, but thanks to his stints on Canton Avenue, his legs were slowly getting into Pittsburgh shape. Larimer was northeast of where he lived and was considered one of Pittsburgh's roughest areas, along with its neighbor to the east, Homewood North, and its neighbor to the west, East Liberty. It was not an area that Jordan would have visited at night on his own – not on a bicycle, but he figured he'd be safe enough in the daytime, especially if he looked as if he belonged there.

He had donned torn jeans and a sleeveless hooded shirt that had seen better days and tousled his hair. No bike helmet, oversized aviator sunglasses, hip hop sneakers. No wallet, just keys and phone.

Ellsworth Avenue turned into Broad Street. Jordan rode past a trendy grocery store, and the hipness of Shadyside abruptly ended as Jordan entered Larimer. Roughly paved streets, sprinkled with older clapboard and brick houses and the occasional vacant lot, took over. The area was slowly rebuilding due to an urban renewal grant, and construction crews were razing some of the old buildings and replacing them with newer housing. Jordan meandered through the neighborhood and found Drayvon Carter's house, one of the bigger brick homes on the block. Overgrown shrubbery, vines, and trees surrounded the house. The street was empty. Too quiet. No one out mowing a lawn, no children were playing.

A newer but dusty black SUV sat in front of Carter's house. An alley ran down the left side of the residence, and Jordan swung down it. It led to a second alley that ran behind Carter's house and four others on that block. There was a high fence around the back yard, with a gate that let out onto the back alley. Convenient for deliveries, thought Jordan. A car could turn down that alley, swing behind the house, and pick up or drop off a package to someone waiting at that back gate, and be gone in seconds - all of it out of sight of the main street.

He turned right and passed by the back of the house and continued down the back alley, which ended at a side street. Jordan turned to the right and went past the house on the corner, and then turned right on the main road again, pedaling slowly past the front of Carter's house, making a full loop. There was no sign of life. He rode on up the street for a block, turned around, and came back down again, stopping at a building just across the side alley from Carter's house. It was a two-story brick building connected to a small Baptist church. The church and the building next to it had seen better days, although the church had a new coat of white paint over the brick. Jordan wheeled his bike over and propped it against the side building wall and knelt, pretending to tie his shoe to give himself more observation time, and then straightened again. As he did so, he froze. A man was striding across the alley toward him. At the same moment, he heard the crunch of a footstep behind him, coming from around the corner, and a voice said, "Don't move." He didn't. He heard footsteps as the person advanced, and Jordan felt something hard press into his back.

He stood still, his mind running wildly over his options, as the other man came up in front of him. He looked angry, suspicious. "What do you want here, kid?"

Jordan forced his body to relax, let it slouch, and lapsed into street vernacular laced with a Latino accent. "I don't want nuthin."

"Don't tell me that," said the man. "We saw you ride around the block, go up the street, and then come back."

Jordan shrugged and shot a glance at the man behind him. "Are you a cop?" he asked him suspiciously.

The man behind him looked at him, and then at the man in front of him, and then back at Jordan, and said scornfully, "No, we ain't cops! Do we look like cops to you?" The men were imposing, one five-eleven, and the other perhaps an inch taller. Both wore designer sports shirts and gold chains, and they were heavily muscled. And both of them looked as tough as nails.

Jordan eyed him for a moment and then looked back around and sized up the other man, the one in front of him. "I heard I could get some — stuff — around this neighborhood. Good stuff."

The men exchanged glances, and the man in front of him said, "Who told you that?"

"I ain't sayin'. I don't know you. You could be cops."

The man in front of him rolled his eyes. "Jesus, kid. We told you, we ain't cops." He motioned at the man behind Jordan. "Put that thing away, Dee Dee."

Jordan felt the hard object drop away from his back and suppressed a shudder as Dee Dee holstered his gun. The man in front of him said, "We may know someone who can help you, but I gotta make a call. What you lookin' for, in particular?"

"White China," said Jordan, giving the man the street name for heroin mixed with fentanyl.

The man narrowed his eyes, scanning Jordan's arms, looking for needle tracks. "You don't look like a user."

"I don't *use* the stuff. I ain't stupid. I sell it. I got a bunch of clients, and my bizness is growin.' I need some more sources."

The man looked at Dee Dee, then back at Jordan, and then said, "Wait here," and he stepped around the corner of the building, pulling out his phone as he went.

He came back after two minutes and looked Jordan up and down. "How old are you, kid?"

"Eighteen."

He weighed that information. "Okay, here's the deal. We can introduce you to someone, but you better not be lyin' about nothing, here, you understand? If he decides to do bizness, you're in - but bein' in with him ain't nothin' to take lightly. We find out you're lyin' about anything; you're a dead kid. You got it? This ain't small-time shit. Now, if you think that's too heavy for you, you can walk away, and we'll all be done with this, as long as you never come back here. Or, if you're the big bizness man you say you are and you want in, then you should follow us."

Jordan fought down a sudden urge to run. Instead, he said, "I'm in."

The man cocked his head, then nodded. "Grab your bike and walk with us."

They headed across the alley. "Leave your bike on the lawn," the man said. "Won't nobody mess with it there."

Jordan laid his bike down on the grass and followed the man up concrete steps, stained and crumbling at the edges. The man opened the front door and motioned, and Jordan stepped inside the home of Drayvon Carter.

CHAPTER EIGHT

Like many older homes, the rooms were small by modern standards. The house had a small slate floor entryway with a coat closet and a low arched doorway leading into the living room. It was cluttered, crammed with furniture, and a big-screen television far too large for the room hung on one wall, with cords running down to a TV stand littered with a DVD, stereo components, and scores of videos and CDs, the latter primarily by rap artists. The curtains were drawn, and the room was dim. Drayvon Carter sat in an overstuffed armchair with its back to the opening for the next area, which was probably supposed to be a dining room. It did hold a table, but the surface was laden with clutter and random junk – boxes, papers, plastic cups, a fake plant.

Carter was a big man. His face was somewhat in shadow from the glow of a ceiling fixture in the dining room behind him, his forearms resting on the arms of the chair. A chunky gold ring on his index finger caught the light, gleaming. He nodded, and Jordan stepped in front of him, aware that he was now inside and out of sight. No one knew he was here. If he said anything that Drayvon Carter didn't like, he would earn himself a spot on the missing persons list. He had to become someone else. The accent and the attitude came naturally; Jordan had practiced them as Carlos Moreno for a year in New York. He could never be Carlos again, however.

"What your name, kid?" Carter's voice was deep and husky and deceptively soft. His delivery was lazy, steeped in the street.

"Juan Gonzalez."

"Where you live?"

"South Hills."

"Where in the South Hills?"

Juan/Jordan's brain was working furiously. He'd had a friend, Jake, in his theater group in high school, who had lived in the South Hills. He stuck to the only place in the South Hills he was familiar with – Jake's borough. "Dormont."

"You go to high school?"

"Not anymore."

"Graduate?"

"Yeah. This year."

"You kind of a punk. You got –" Drayvon waved a hand, "*attitude*. You in any gangs?"

"No. I don't mess with that. My ma's from Ecuador; I got younger brothers and sisters. My dad left us. I'm trying to help 'em meet the rent and pay my tuition. I got some kids from school and my old neighborhood who buy from me. The guy I was getting my stuff off of is small-time. He can't keep up."

"That area's pretty white."

Juan shrugged. "White kids got money. And white kids use drugs."

Carter waved a hand at Dee Dee. "Search him."

The sleeveless hoodie was thin and fitted to Jordan's torso; it was evident that there was nothing under that, but Dee Dee patted him down anyway. He took more time with the jeans, pulling out pockets, going through them thoroughly. Dee Dee appeared to be looking for more than a weapon; he was checking for something smaller, like a wire or a transmitter. He pulled out Jordan's cell phone and apartment keys, looked at them, and put them back in the pockets. At length, he straightened. "He's clean."

Carter said, "If you got stuff from me today, where you gonna put it? You ride in here on a bike – makes me think you're not serious. And you didn't bring no money."

"I got a car. Some kid I sell to said he heard you can get stuff up on this street. I just came up here on the bike to check it out, see if it was true, you know."

"You think it's true?"

"Yeah, man, I do."

Carter sat and observed him for a minute. "You look a little nervous to me."

"Hell, yeah, man, I'm nervous. I'm in a room with three big guys I don't know, and at least one of 'em has a gun. But I wanna do bizness, so I came."

Carter frowned at him. "You rode all the way up here from Dormont on a goddamn bike?"

Juan allowed himself the shadow of a grin. "No, man. My ma lives in Dormont – I live in Oakland. I'm taking computer classes from Pitt in the fall. I got me an apartment there." He puffed out his chest. "I'm gonna make somethin' of myself."

Carter looked at his men. "Dee Dee, James, what do you think?"

They both shrugged.

Carter cocked his head, considering, and nodded. "Okay. I'm gonna start you out small. Maybe twenty grams, at sixty-five per. Thirteen hundred bucks – you think you can swing that?"

Juan frowned, and Carter held up a hand. "I know that's a lot per gram. But you can charge more to your buyers 'cause this is some serious stuff. You can charge ten bucks a stamp bag, easy. And if you work this right, you'll sell more and more, and even with the higher price, you'll be makin' more in the long run. You got it?"

Juan looked skeptical. "Yeah, I got it."

"Let me be straight here – you don't get a choice, you understand? You sign up with me; you do what I say. Period." He jabbed a finger at Juan, the finger with the gold ring. "Now I'm asking you again, boy, you got it?"

Juan, meekly: "I got it."

"Good. You ride your little bike home, and you come back here with your car. Come after dark, and call me before you come. You got a phone?"

Juan slowly pulled his cell phone out of his pocket.

"No, no, your burner phone, man."

"This *is* my burner," Juan lied. "I bought it used on the Internet – loaded it with a prepaid plan. It ain't tied to nuthin. I'm not stupid."

"Okay, put this number in it." Carter recited the number. "That's my burner. You want to talk; you gotta give the code first." He grabbed a CD from the side table, held up a rap album. "This is the code. *Makin' Change*, by Big Jimmy P. Remember that. I don't hear the code; I hang up. You call before you come; don't just show up here again. I'll tell you if it's okay to come or not. I'll tell you exactly how much I have and how much it will cost you when you call. You need to cover the cost of the dope upfront. And remember this – do not cross me. If you do, I will hunt down your skinny little ass and kill you. Now get outta here, punk."

Juan nodded and loped between Dee Dee and James, and on out the door, devoutly thankful that Carter hadn't asked to look at his phone. He hopped on his bike, not too fast, taking his time even though his knees were shaking.

Inside, James looked at Drayvon and said, "You think he'll call?"

"Hell, I don' know," said Carter. "If he gets scared and he don't, it won't bother me none. You gotta admit, he has guts to come up here like that. But if he does call, he might be useful. We don't sell much in the South Hills – it could be a way to break in. Plus, you know, the cops just pinched a couple of our people. We could use some replacements." He cocked his head again, thinking. "But just in case, follow him. See if he goes to Oakland like he say. And make sure there ain't no one else following him – that he really came alone."

It took Juan several minutes of pedaling, and he got most of the way through Shadyside before he thought it might be safe to be Jordan again. He was stopped at a light and was just about to relax when he spotted Dee Dee and James. When he glanced to the side, the shop windows on the street caught the reflection of their car. He saw James clearly, behind the wheel. They were just two vehicles behind him.

He let his chin come up, tried to look cool, tried to project attitude. The rest of the way home, he took his time, casing the shop windows, ogling the occasional pretty girl, like Juan might. He still made good time because it was downhill, and after what seemed like an eternity, he pulled onto his street and got off his bike.

He wheeled it to the front entrance of the building next to his. There were three identical apartment buildings on the street, all owned by the same agency, and the key for the entrance fit all three of the outside doors. He went into the middle building, wheeling his bike, and let the outer door fall closed. The top panes of that door were windows, and he could see that the car went on past. He waited a minute and then carefully peeked out through the door. There was no sign of the car, but he waited another two full minutes before he ducked back out and jogged his bike over to his unit. They might know where he lived, but they wouldn't have the right building, much less the actual apartment.

Once inside, he didn't stop; he put his bike on his shoulder and hustled up the three flights of stairs to his apartment. He unlocked the door and carefully wheeled his bike against the wall, locked the door again, and then he went over to the table, pulled off his sunglasses, sat down hard in a chair, and ran a hand down his face. He took two deep breaths and then shot to his feet as a knock came at his door. The interior doors were old, with no viewing holes. There was no way to see who it was. He ran into the bedroom, got his Glock, and ran back to the door as another knock sounded.

"Who is it?"

"It's Mike. I've got your car keys."

Jordan unlocked the door, and DeLuca paused in mid-step as he came through it and then kept coming. He shut the door, glanced around the small shabby apartment, and said dryly, "Nice place. Why don't you go put that gun away?"

Jordan blinked and looked down at the gun and realized that he was pointing it at DeLuca. He dropped his arm, then turned without a word and went into the bedroom and came back out without it. He paused two steps into the room and said, with a mix of wonderment and apprehension, "I think I just got in with Drayvon Carter."

DeLuca stared at him and said, "What?!"

Jordan shrugged with one shoulder. "What I said."

He walked past DeLuca toward the tiny kitchen and said, "I need some water. Do you want some?"

DeLuca watched him go and said, "Yeah, I'll take one. And then you'll tell me what in the hell you meant by that."

Jordan nodded and got them two tall glasses of water with ice. He pulled out a chair at the kitchen table, and DeLuca took a chair too, setting Jordan's car keys on top of Marty and Milt's latest report on Drayvon Carter.

Jordan took a big swallow of water and a deep breath and said, "I was working on both cases this afternoon. I was thinking the murder cases over and thinking about how the victims died – by cutting, basically – but pretty much getting nowhere with that line of thought. So, I switched over to the drug case, and I read the latest report. It had Drayvon Carter's address in it, and I had some time, so I decided to take a ride up there on my bike and check it out."

"You did what?" DeLuca stared at him, mouth open.

"I was careful," Jordan assured him, and he pulled at the sleeveless hoodie. "Look at me. I dressed the part. Who would pay attention to some neighborhood kid on his bike?" DeLuca shook his head, and Jordan continued, "Well, anyway, that's what I thought. I didn't have any particular plan; I was only going to check out his place and the neighborhood. I rode up there, found the house, and made a loop around it by going down the back alley. If I'd kept going, I would have been fine, but I rode up the street and then turned around and came back. There's a church building across the alley from his house. I stopped there and pretended to tie my shoe to get a better look. His house has a back gate that opens onto the alley. He probably takes deliveries and makes some of his own deliveries to his customers – they could drive up -,"

DeLuca interrupted him. "We know. There are four guys from PBP Narcotics that take turns surveilling the back gate from a house on the other side of the alley. That's been going on for a while. Carter makes deliveries there, sure, but he's only getting stuff out to his sellers. They haven't seen one drop or delivery to him at that gate."

That was disappointing. Jordan moved on. "Well, anyway, as I stood up, I saw a guy coming out of Carter's house, headed straight for me. And at about the same time, I heard a voice behind me and felt a gun in my back."

"God damn it, Bell."

"I know," said Jordan, nodding. "Scared the hell out of me. They wanted to know what I was doing there, so I told them that I'd heard I could buy stuff in that neighborhood – I asked for White China."

"And they believed you?"

Jordan shrugged, and then he slouched, lazily, and gave DeLuca his best insolent expression. He spoke, his voice tinged with a Latino street accent. "I needed another source, man. My bizness is growing. I got my ma and my brothers and sisters to take care of, you know, man?"

DeLuca was staring at him. He shook his head.

Jordan said, in his normal voice, "At that point, one of the men made a phone call, and then they walked me over to Carter's house.

They told me to leave my bike on the lawn and to go inside. I have to admit: I wasn't sure which way it would go at that point. It was a little freaky. But I went in, and Carter asked me a bunch of questions. I told him my name was Juan Gonzalez, that I was eighteen, just graduated from high school and taking computer courses at Pitt, and I was selling to make ends meet. I told him my current source couldn't get me enough to keep up with the demand, and some kid I sold to told me to come up to Larimar. Carter had them search me. At the end of the conversation, Carter told me to go home and come back later with a car and gave me his burner number and a code word. He said to call when I was ready, and he would tell me how much stuff he could give me and how much it would be. He's asking for sixty-five bucks for a gram and suggested twenty grams would be good for starters -,"

DeLuca couldn't contain himself any longer. "That was just plain asinine! What in the hell were you thinking? You could have been killed!" He stared at Jordan's attire – the hoodie was thin and clung to his torso – no room to hide a piece. "You probably didn't even have your gun with you."

"Look, there's no harm done," said Jordan. "The two guys with Carter – one called Dee Dee and one he called James – followed me home. I had told them that I was living in Oakland, near Pitt, so that jived with my story. They have no reason to be suspicious. I'm in if we want me to be. If we don't, no harm done; all I have to do is not call them. I think Carter was ambivalent about it. There's a risk in taking on a new dealer, but there's also an upside if the dealer can sell enough. If we could get some money from Morrissey to fund this, I could make some buys from him. Once he sees me funneling money to him, he'll relax. Maybe I'd be able to get in a little deeper."

DeLuca was silent. Finally, he said, "I don't know. This stuff is a lot heavier than the Goth assignment. But I'll run it past Morrissey; see what he thinks." He watched Jordan's face as he said it.

Jordan nodded, careful to keep his expression neutral. "Let me know."

"Okay. I need a ride back – you can drop me a couple of blocks from the office."

The phone rang a few minutes after five. Jordan listened without comment as DeLuca told him that Morrissey had liked the proposal and had approved the assignment. Oddly, DeLuca didn't sound very happy about it. "Good," was all that Jordan said, "I'll get ready."

He disconnected the call, then sat down and put his face in his hands for a long minute. Then he got up, showered, and changed. He took the car and went first to the mall to get three more black T-shirts, one of them with long sleeves, and another pair of black jeans for his Goth assignment. He had plenty of appropriate clothes in his wardrobe for the Carter mission – Juan Gonzalez was very much like Carlos Moreno. Jordan still had the clothing he'd bought for his New York assignment: essential street punk couture. Then he went and picked up some groceries.

Jordan made dinner and spent the rest of the evening going over the drug case files and doing some background research on Dormont, where Juan Gonzalez was supposedly from, and area high schools, where Juan Gonzalez was allegedly dealing. He submitted an expense report for the Goth clothing he had gotten so far. Routine, matter-of-fact, calm. Brush your teeth, get ready for bed, look at the face in the mirror and see Jordan Bell the Cop, Carlos Moreno, Jordan Bell the Goth, and Juan Gonzalez. Take your pick.

He woke in the middle of the night sweating and sitting straight up in bed, with the image of the New York warehouse and Lucaya's screams reverberating in his head.

CHAPTER NINE

The next night, Tuesday, Jordan was back in the bar. Being a work night at the beginning of the week, it was a slow night, but the Goth crowd was there. The after-work crowd was sparse, and there was no sign of the college crowd. Victoria looked happy to see him, and Sammy Farineau looked irritated. Victoria was sitting next to Suzanne, and Jordan pulled up a seat between them. That earned him an uncertain smile from Victoria, unsure if she should be happy with the arrangement or not. Jordan didn't care. Tonight, he was determined to talk to Suzanne Weir.

He figured that action would generate some hard feelings. If Peter and George were interested in Suzanne, he would make them jealous, and paying attention to Suzanne would probably irk Victoria. He wouldn't be making any friends that night, but he wasn't there to make friends. He was there to stir the pot and see what rose to the surface.

He let the conversation flow on and just sat there at first, observing. They talked about a book that George had read; he was the self-proclaimed intellectual in the group. Lilt was tall and sallow, with dark, wavy, greasy hair that he wore long, cascading in soft waves to his jawline. He was on the thin side, but he looked wiry; strong muscles lined his arms under the long-sleeved T-shirt that he wore.

That shirt made Jordan wonder about cutting, and he glanced around the table. Sammy, George, Suzanne, and Peter all wore long-sleeved shirts, even though it was August. He already knew that

Peter cut, but what about the rest of them? Were the long sleeves merely a nod to Goth style, or did they hide telltale scars? Victoria was the only one with bare forearms, and they were free of marks. Every time one of the others gestured, Jordan watched the edge of their sleeve, seeing if it would ride up enough to reveal something, but he could see nothing of interest, even on Peter's arms, where Jordan knew the scars were present.

He thought about that. To bleed to death from slitting one's wrists, a cutter would need to make long deep cuts along the length of their inner forearm, like the cuts on the victims. Most cutters didn't intend to kill themselves or inflict severe damage; they were after the endorphin rush. Safe, shallow, crosswise cuts. The mechanics and the intent behind what Peter did to himself were utterly different from those behind the murders. Still, it seemed there was at least something symbolic about the method that the murderer had chosen to kill the victims. Or maybe, the murderer wanted them to think that.

It was too quiet, Jordan decided. He wanted to talk to Suzanne without everyone listening in, so he went over to the jukebox and picked out several Goth punk selections. George, who was in the middle of expounding upon the book he was reading, sent him a scowl, but Victoria beamed. Music blared, and Jordan returned to his seat and spoke into Suzanne's ear over the din.

"So, what do you think of George's book?"

She smiled and had the presence of mind not to look George's way, and leaned over and said in his ear. "It's okay. That one, in particular, is not my thing."

She sat back, smiling at him, and Jordan was struck again by her looks. Her skin was flawless. High cheekbones, a delicate nose, and a clean-lined jaw, brown eyes flecked with gold. Her hair was silky, natural soft black, not the jarring jet black that Victoria sported. She was slender, and he thought what an easy target she would make - unless the murderer was after poseurs and had decided that she wasn't one.

He smiled and turned on the charm. "What *is* your thing?"

Her smile was coy, mysterious, and she held his gaze, then blushed prettily. "Gothic romances," she admitted. "I work in a library, so I read a lot. How about you?"

"I'm more along the lines of Poe." He smiled. "Typical

guy."

She smiled back. "You're not typical. And I mean that as a compliment."

"Neither are you." He gave her his best smile; held her eyes.

They talked loudly enough to be heard over the music, at least sitting next to each other, but no one else could hear them. Already though, their conversation was having an impact; Victoria was pouting, and Sammy was smirking. George and Peter were involved in a sober discussion, although George looked distracted and glowered each time he looked their way. Peter seemed less threatened, but he did look perturbed. And then there was Will McCann.

McCann had walked in with a couple of friends while Jordan was talking to Suzanne, and the look he was giving the two of them was dark and angry enough to be disturbing. Jordan jerked his head toward McCann and said to Suzanne, "What's with him?"

A pained expression crossed her face, a look of distaste. "We used to date," she said. "Will used to be Goth, and then he decided to go mainstream. But that wasn't the reason we broke up. We just argued too much. And looking back on it, he probably wasn't the best choice I've ever made in a boyfriend. He's very – controlling."

"Controlling?"

She glanced sideways at McCann, and Jordan could read just a hint of fear in her face. "He had to call all of the shots and didn't want me out of his sight. You can see how he is still. He comes here every night that I'm here."

Jordan frowned. "That could be construed as stalking. Did you ever think of getting a protective order against him?"

"I've thought about it, but I'm not sure they would give it to me. Will only shows up here – nowhere else that I go – and he was coming to this bar before we were dating. He doesn't try to talk – he just watches me. But it is kind of creepy."

"Maybe," said Jordan, with a meaningful look in his eyes, "if you made it clear you were with someone else – I mean from a romantic standpoint – he'd give up and go away."

She stared at him, and then she smiled, blushed, and dipped her head. Her eyes held his. "I, uh, think I see what you mean."

He felt guilty – but not guilty enough to stop flirting. He played it up, laughing and talking, leaning in a little too close; it wasn't difficult to pretend to be attracted to Suzanne, he admitted. She was captivating. Quiet, a bit shy, but he could feel the sexual attraction when she turned her gaze on him. Eventually, he could tell that his playlist was coming to an end, so he asked Suzanne what she wanted to drink and headed for the jukebox.

He got there just before one of the college kids did, and Jordan put in ten more songs and then sauntered toward the bar. In the mirror behind the bar, he saw the college kid make a face when he saw the number of selections ahead of his, saw him turn, and throw up his hands toward his buddies. Jordan grinned and leaned over the bar and ordered two colas. He sensed movement beside him and picked up Will McCann, moving into view in the mirror.

"What in the hell do you think you're doing, asshole?" growled McCann.

Jordan looked innocent. "Me? I'm just ordering a couple of drinks. It *is* a bar if you haven't noticed."

"Yeah, and it's my bar and has been for years."

Jordan raised an eyebrow. "I think Harry might contest that."

"It's my bar," repeated McCann. He was slurring his words. "Quit hogging the jukebox. And if I were you, I'd stay away from Suzanne."

Jordan picked up the drinks and slipped cash across to Harry, way more than was necessary for two sodas, and Harry nodded his thanks. Jordan turned to McCann. "This bar is a public place. It doesn't belong to anyone except Harry. And I'll talk to whoever I want. If you get pissed off when you come here, why do you keep showing up?"

And with that, Jordan turned and walked back to the table, half expecting a big hand to come down on him from behind. However, nothing happened, and he slipped back into his seat and offered a soda to Suzanne. Victoria sent him a look black enough to put her eyeliner to shame, and at the bar, McCann was fuming. Apart from Suzanne, Sammy Farineau was the only person in the place who looked happy. He was doodling something on a piece of paper; it looked intricate and somehow familiar.

"Hey, that's pretty cool, Sammy. Are you an artist?" said Jordan, looking at the paper. He had to yell across the table for Sammy to hear him over the music.

He got what he wanted; Sammy, eager to show it off, pushed it toward him and yelled back. "Yeah, man, I do a little art now and then. This is nothing, though, just a doodle."

Jordan examined the paper and immediately realized what had looked familiar; it looked exactly like the elaborate scrollwork on the dark website called True Goth. "Wow, this is something, man. Did you get this design from somewhere?"

Sammy grinned, looking pleased. Even Victoria looked mollified at Jordan's praise. "No, it's original. I do some artwork for web pages for Goth sites."

Suzanne spoke in Jordan's ear. "I want to go out and get some air. Do you mind coming with me? I don't like to go out alone with Will around."

Jordan nodded, his mind on the artwork. He hated to leave the conversation, but Suzanne had risen, so he followed, with her leading the way not to the front door but the rear of the bar. They were watched all the way out. There was a rear exit by the restrooms, and as they went out, Suzanne wedged a small rock in the door to prop it open. "It locks when it's closed," she said. "Harry usually keeps it locked unless one of us is out here. Sammy comes out here to smoke sometimes. Harry trusts us. We lock it again if we're leaving or when we go back inside."

Jordan gave her his best smile. "Good to know." He glanced around them. The parking lot was more sizable than it looked; it extended around to the back of the bar. The entire property was hemmed off from the next building over by a tall weathered wooden fence. Its wide slats loomed like sentinels in the harsh glow of a streetlight. A few cars sat in the lot casting black shadows, blobs of varying shades of gray, their color washed away by the darkness.

"We've all been parking on the side of the bar by the road, lately, instead of back here," she said. "We go out through the front door at closing now, unless the lot is so crowded that we have to park in the rear. It's safer out front."

"I heard about the two people who died."

She looked troubled. "The news said their deaths were connected. We didn't know the girl that well, but Jon, he was one of us." She shivered and leaned into Jordan, and they both leaned against the brick wall, still warm from the summer sun. "It's scary."

He put an arm around her, even though it was probably not the best idea. "Yeah," he said softly, "it's not good. I'm glad that you're careful."

She looked up at him, her face right next to his, and for a moment, they just gazed at each other. She reached up with one hand and stroked his face. "I think you may be the most beautiful man I've ever seen," she breathed.

Her lips were open slightly, her eyes searching his, pulling him in closer. He leaned down and kissed her, watching her striking eyes drift shut, feeling a thrill at the soft pressure of her lips. She returned the kiss, deepening it, making a small sound in the back of her throat that sent a jolt through him. His mind told him he needed to stop, needed to back off, but his body wouldn't move. Finally, she broke the kiss, smiled up at him, and then blushed. "I usually don't kiss on the first date," she teased.

He tried to catch his breath and smiled at her. "Is this a date?"

She smiled back. "It is now."

She leaned back against the building and took a deep breath, and he did the same – more than one. She was pure seduction; she tasted as sweet as she looked. Her eyes drifted upward, toward the moon, a pearl-white half sphere. "When did you know you were Goth?" she asked.

Jordan thought back to his conversation with Peter; he had to be consistent. "I'm not sure I thought it through, but I knew I liked the music in high school. I did do some reading, but it was just that, reading and music until I got to New York. I was on my own, and when I wasn't working, I could dress the way I wanted – and then I started hitting the Goth clubs. Those were some intense scenes. I had some good conversations with other Goths there about literature and art and music. And some other stuff – witchcraft, vampirism, although some of that was little too out there for me."

She made a face. "Me too. I'm straight Goth – I never went for that Wiccan stuff. The dark side of things can be beautiful – it doesn't need to be scary or evil. Even death – death as an abstract concept can be beautiful – dark and mysterious and sometimes sad – but beautiful," she smiled, "as long as it's not happening to you."

She traced a finger down his forearm. She seemed to think, hesitating, then blurted, "Did you ever – you know – cut?"

Jordan kept his face expressionless. Just the topic he wanted to know more about, and she had brought it up herself.

"Uh, no. I've thought about it sometimes but wasn't sure

how, or at least how much was safe." He looked at her. "Did you?"

She flushed and looked away and then back at him. "Promise you won't judge me?"

He shook his head. "Of course not. I think it's kind of – cool."

Relief flooded into her face. "Many people don't understand. There are a few of us here who do. I'm one of them." She turned to him, earnestly. "You should try it sometime. It's so, such a – it's hard to explain. Tension builds up, and when you cut, it's such a release." She smiled teasingly. "A little like sex, when you think about it." Her voice lowered. "Maybe you can come over some night, and we'll try it."

He wasn't sure if she meant sex or cutting or both, but he gave her a seductive smile. "Maybe I will."

They talked a bit longer, Jordan gently probing, trying to find out who the other cutters were, but to no avail. After a little more conversation, she turned toward him again, and they kissed, long and slow, Jordan fighting to keep his distance, mentally, even while his body was telling him that she was just what he needed. Finally, they broke apart.

"You," Jordan said, "are amazing."

She smiled at him and blushed again. "Likewise, Mr. Bell." She laughed self-consciously. "Your last name sounds like it should be in a Gothic romance." She gestured grandly. "The dashing Mr. Bell." Her color deepened. "I'm sorry. I read too many books."

He put an arm around her as they turned to go inside. "No one can read too many books."

She turned to him and smiled as they walked back in, kicking the rock away and letting the door lock behind them, and he smiled back, and he knew that not one person in the bar had missed the exchange. He was feeling cocky, euphoric, and when he went up to the bar for two more sodas, he grinned at Will McCann. "So, whose bar is it now, McCann?"

McCann took a step toward him, fury flooding his face, but two of his buddies held him back, one of them talking earnestly into his ear. Jordan waited, a challenging look in his eye, but McCann's friends kept their grips, so he finally shrugged and went back to his table. He was looking for an opportunity to talk to Sammy about the artwork, and he got it just then; Sammy got up and headed for the restroom. Jordan put their drinks on the table, then gave

Suzanne a grin and said, "I'll be back," and followed Sammy toward the back of the bar.

Sammy was just hitting the urinal when Jordan came through the door, and Jordan stood next to him, doing his own thing, and said, "You know, I think I've seen your artwork on the web."

Sammy smiled and snorted and said, "I doubt it," as he zipped his pants.

"No, really," said Jordan as he zipped up. "True Goth, am I right?"

Sammy was at the sink, and Jordan could see his jaw drop in the mirror. "You surf the Dark Web?"

Jordan shrugged. "Sure. Why wouldn't I? Some of the best Goth sites are out there – including True Goth. Was that your artwork on it?"

Sammy looked pleased. "Well, yeah."

"That's pretty impressive," said Jordan as he stepped to the sink. "How'd you get that gig? Do you know the people who run it?"

Sammy shrugged. "I just got it by someone recommending me. I gave them the artwork, and they liked it. They paid me – not much, but they paid me. And that's all there was to it. I've sold some mainstream artwork for regular web pages, too." He headed for the door, and Jordan turned on the water. Sammy hadn't answered his question – did he know who ran True Goth or not?

Harry made his usual early last call, and McCann's friends talked him into going with them up to the bars on Carson Street. Even though McCann was gone, Jordan walked Suzanne out to her car at closing time and, lingering, told her good night. She wanted to exchange cell phone numbers, and so they did, as the rest of the crowd got into their vehicles.

The Monongahela looked like black oil under the Birmingham Bridge. As he drove, Jordan took stock of the night. He'd talked to Suzanne as he'd intended – and then some – but still wasn't much further than when he'd started. He was convinced that cutting played a part somehow; it had to, considering the method the killer had used. Maybe a motive in itself, or at least a symbolic way of delivering death.

The only other intriguing item was Sammy Farineau's artwork on True Goth. Jordan had been hoping Sammy could tell him who ran the site, but it sounded like a simple business transaction; Sammy hadn't created the site itself. That seemed to be another dead end.

Jordan had the sense that the answers were there, just out of reach. Everything he'd tried so far had made that conviction stronger; he was closing in, slowly, but on what? There was a wall there, blocking his way, and all of those answers were on the other side.

There was one other thing that was nagging at him. He shouldn't have kissed Suzanne.

CHAPTER TEN

Jordan called DeLuca promptly at 7:30 a.m. the next morning and told him about finding the site called True Goth and researching the cutting angle at the bar. "Peter cuts – I saw the marks on his arms at his house," Jordan said. "And Suzanne asked me outright if I cut and told me that she did, and so did some of the others. Victoria probably doesn't unless she picks an area of her body other than her arms. And Sammy and George possibly do; they wear long-sleeved shirts."

"I thought you said that cutting among Goths is a misconception."

"It is – among most of them. The True Goth site promotes it, however. It seems there is a subset of people in the group at the bar who cut, and one of them did the artwork for that site."

"And the significance of this is?"

"I don't know," admitted Jordan. "Just a hunch that this is all connected. The True Goth site is a little far out – fanatical. What if someone follows it who is even more of a fanatic and has decided to knock off Goth pretenders? And what if that someone is part of this group? Neither Poppy nor Jon Hurly was a cutter, so maybe they were considered by the murderer to be poseurs. I know it's pretty weak as a motive, but so is the idea that Will McCann did it. If he was mad at Suzanne for breaking up with him, why didn't he take it out on her? The only alternative is there is some other motive out there, and we are just missing it."

He paused. "On the flip side, McCann continues to be one very angry dude, and I think he has a drinking problem. I spent a lot of time talking to Suzanne last night, and we were both openly flirting with each other. I encouraged it because I was looking for reactions. At one point, we stepped out in the back to have a quiet conversation. When I came back in, McCann was pissed. He was drunk, as usual. He told me that the bar was his and to stay away from Suzanne. Of course, I don't think either Peter or George was too happy about me spending time with her, either. Especially George."

"You'd better watch yourself," said DeLuca. "You're sitting on a land mine. If you push too hard, it could go off in your face."

"Yeah, I do think I need to cool it a little," Jordan admitted. "When Suzanne and I went outside, well, I got a vibe. She was interested in me."

He could hear the disapproval in DeLuca's voice. "I don't think I need to tell you that you're getting in too deep there. Every regular in that bar is a person of interest. You can't go starting personal relationships, at least not until this case is over."

"I know, I know. I already came to the same conclusion. I'll back off. I want to find out who runs that True Goth site. It turns out that Sammy Farineau did the artwork for the web pages, but it sounded like a contract job – I didn't get a clear answer from him when I asked if he knew who set it up. I'm going to try him again tonight."

"Better make that tomorrow night. Morrissey got the money approved for your drug deal with Carter. We have cash – Bear will run it over to you today. You can call Carter and set something up, preferably for tonight. Let us know what time – we'll have the PBP narc guys on the watch from their house across the alley – they can help out if something goes south."

Jordan stood at his apartment window later that morning and waited for Marty Beran. After he'd given his report to DeLuca, he had phoned into the Wednesday morning team meeting and listened in, mostly. DeLuca gave updates based on Jordan's statements, and Jordan filled in a detail or two but otherwise just sat, neither heard nor seen, feeling somewhat disconnected. Jen and Devon reported that they had gotten warrants to trace Will McCann's cell phone for the nights of the murders, but the trace showed that once he got home those nights, his cell phone, at least, had never left his apartment. Maybe McCann was smart enough to leave it at home before he went to meet his victims, but Jordan was beginning to wonder if the guy ever stopped drinking long enough to think straight - unless the drinking was an act. Maybe he had kept sober those nights, knowing what he had planned.

Jen and Devon reported that McCann had finished high school and drifted for a while, living at his parents' house. Last spring, he had enrolled in college at Robert Morris but only took two classes that semester. McCann had taken one five-week class in the summer session, but that had ended in early June, and he didn't seem to be doing much with his free time in the past few weeks other than working part-time as a busser at a diner, with his usual shift being lunch, and then going to Harry's. His parents had some money, and he was living in Oakland, renting an apartment not too far from Jordan's.

Regarding McCann's history, he'd gotten in trouble once in high school – a fight with another boy, and someone had made accusations of bullying against him. Other than that, nothing. The bullying fit with his character but was a far cry from making him a murderer. He seemed too impulsive to have carried out the two murders without leaving a clue as to their locations – unless he'd been lucky – or was a consummate actor. That was a possibility that Jordan never ruled out – he knew how easy it was to fool someone.

In addition, Jen and Devon had searched for security cameras, looking for them in any areas between the bar and the body drop locations. They had found a few cameras aimed at the parking lots of nearby businesses, but none picked up the main road, and there were none at the body drop locations. All in all, their efforts had been a bust, as far as McCann was concerned.

Morrissey had reported that some of the uproar from the press had died down. It had been almost a week since the second victim, Jon Hurly, had been found, and a shooting in a mall parking lot had taken over the news. With nothing new, the press had relegated the Goth murders to a brief mention on the nightly news and the fourth page of the Pittsburgh Post-Gazette.

Bear showed up shortly after the meeting, and Jordan met him at the outside door, and they stumped upstairs to his apartment. He opened the apartment door, and Bear stepped in and said politely,

"Nice place."

DeLuca had said the same thing when he came in on Monday. Jordan scratched his head. Was the place that bad? He'd cleaned it up. Compared to his tiny dark efficiency in New York, it wasn't terrible. On the other hand, compared to the house he'd grown up in, maybe it was pretty bad.

Bear set a backpack on the table. "There's two grand in here. Morrissey got approval for more – we'll get it to you as you need it. It's more than enough for the twenty grams that Carter suggested. Twenty grams would do about two hundred stamp bags. There's an extra seven hundred for slop, but try to stay close to what he quoted you. If he tries to sell you more, you've got a little to play with."

"Since I'm not actually selling the stuff, what do you want me to do with it?"

"We'll have someone from the labs come here and pick it up. They'll take a sample and test it, and we'll put the rest in evidence. It's always good to look at another batch, see if we can learn anything, like if Carter has changed sources – sometimes the chemical makeup will show a difference. I'd tell Carter that you need a few days before you come back to him for more. If you were an active small-time dealer, you'd probably need at least four days to unload two hundred bags. Anything less than that, and he'll get suspicious. Oh, and there's a burner phone in the bag – use it to contact Carter – and we got a fake driver's license made up for you. We used your DMV photo: Juan Gonzalez, age eighteen."

"Okay."

"One more thing – a little information on James and Dee Dee. Dee Dee is Deondre Dawson. James is Marcellus James, sometimes goes by Big M. They are both convicted felons for armed robbery and are long-time associates of Carter. After they did their time, they joined him in the drug business. They started as dealers, worked their way up to lieutenants. You shouldn't take either of them lightly." Bear paused. "You okay with this? It's some pretty heavy stuff."

Jordan shrugged. "I've done it before, in New York."

Bear gave him a nod. "Somehow, that doesn't surprise me. It would have a week or so ago – but…" he trailed off and headed toward the door, his movements more graceful than his muscular bulk would suggest. "Anyway – good luck. I emailed you some back information on Carter, some stuff that we picked up during surveillance. The info should help, but if you have any questions, Milt and I would be happy to answer them." He paused at the door and looked back. "Be careful, man. Carter isn't anyone to mess around with. If you don't like what you see, get out. And don't forget to call Mike when you find out what time you're going in, so he can have the narc guys on standby."

After Bear left, Jordan looked up Carter's number on his cell phone and dialed Carter on the burner phone. Carter came on, and Jordan said, in Juan's voice, "Makin' Change, by Big Jimmy P."

Carter said, suspiciously, "Who this?"

Jordan knew he didn't recognize the number. "It's Juan."

He could hear Carter's voice lighten. "I wasn't sure you were going to call. I got some of what you want."

"Good, I want twenty."

"Ok, the price is still what I gave you. Pick up in the back at 9:30 p.m., sharp. Just drive up."

The transaction was mostly uneventful. Jordan called DeLuca on the way there, who notified the narc guys across the alley. DeLuca had described the narc house, so Jordan would know which one it was. As he turned into the alleyway, he glanced at it. The upper window was dark, but Jordan knew there was a man there, watching. It made him feel a bit better as he pulled up next to Carter's back gate.

Vines shrouded the gate itself, and Jordan rolled down his passenger side window as it creaked open and slumped in his seat, turning on Juan Gonzalez. James came through the gate wearing a hoodie and glancing up and down the alley, and Juan picked up the envelope of money and slid it to him through the window, keeping it low. James said, "All here?"

"Thirteen hundred, just like he said."

"Better be, or we'll come and find you. We know where you live." He delivered the words without hostility, like a standard warning, a ritual. They were beginning to trust him. "Pop your trunk." James stuffed the envelope in the deep pockets of his hoodie and pulled out a bag, keeping it close to him, eyes moving, checking out the surroundings.

He went behind the car, put the bag in the trunk, closed it, and stepped back to the window. "Mr. Carter is interested in getting set up on the computer, anonymously. You said you were taking computer classes. You know how to do that?"

"Yeah, I do."

"How long you think you'll take to sell the shit?"

Juan cocked his head. "Give me through the weekend."

James nodded approvingly. "That's pretty quick."

"I told you, I got demand."

"Okay, Monday night, be here at nine with the money for your next buy. When you come that night, park the car in the alley and come inside. Mr. Carter is gonna want you to work on his computer, set him up with an untraceable email."

Juan nodded. James stepped away and walked back through the gate, and Juan pulled away.

Jordan waited until he was back at home and had the stash safely upstairs, and he looked at it before he called DeLuca. It was all there – a baggie of white powder and two hundred empty stamp bags to package it in.

DeLuca answered on the second ring, and Jordan said, "Got it. It went smoothly."

"Good," came DeLuca's voice. "I got a call from the narc guys – they saw you make the drop. They said it looked pretty standard, nothing out of the ordinary from what they've seen before."

"I got another request from Carter," said Jordan. "I told him I was taking computer classes at Pitt, and James told me tonight that Carter wants me to set him up with an untraceable email. I'm supposed to go back Monday night, and he will give me more stuff to sell. And he wants me to come in that night and work on his computer."

DeLuca was silent for a moment. "You think that's the real reason he wants you inside?"

Jordan frowned. "I think so. I don't have any reason to think otherwise."

"Maybe you should wear a wire."

"No, not a good idea. Carter had Dee Dee search me the first time I was there, and it was a pretty thorough search. I know they were looking for something like that. Look, Carter put himself out on a limb by giving me the drugs. He would have called me inside tonight to check me out again before they incriminated themselves if he suspected something. And I could hear it in James' voice – they trust me."

"Okay," said DeLuca, but he still sounded unconvinced. "How long will this thing take you – and do you know how to do it?"

"I haven't tried to set one up yet, but I'll try it tonight. I have good instructions from a reputable source. I'll see how long it takes on my computer, and then I'll let you know. The good thing is, I'll know Carter's real IP address. We'll be able to track his online activity."

"Did he say what he wants it for?"

"I'm assuming for selling more drugs. Carter may be trying to expand his business to internet sales on the Dark Web. He already seems to have a fool-proof supply, so I doubt he's looking to buy. But we'll be able to track him and find out once I set this up."

"Okay. What are your plans for tomorrow?"

"I'll head back to the bar tomorrow night. I'm going to try to work on Sammy Farineau; see if he can give me any more information on who runs True Goth."

"Okay. No need to call in tomorrow morning. Get some rest. I'll talk to you on Friday morning unless something comes up. And Bell? Good work."

"Thanks."

Jordan hung up and rubbed his face. He was exhausted, but there was a small grin lifting the corner of his mouth. DeLuca had finally paid him a compliment.

CHAPTER ELEVEN

Jordan spent the day setting up a secure VPN and TOR access on his computer per Professor Latimore's instructions. He took his time, making sure he was doing it correctly. He estimated that it would take about an hour or two at the most when he set up Carter's system, now that he knew what he was doing. Around noon, one of the guys from PBP Narcotics showed up and picked up the package of drugs.

Jordan went to his usual Thursday lesson at the gym, a session with his trainer that went long; he worked on both Brazilian jiu-jitsu and boxing that evening. He went home for a shower, changed into his Goth attire, and didn't pull into Harry's parking lot until around nine. The lot on the bar's side was nearly full, and Jordan thought it might be necessary to park in the back, but there was one empty spot in the middle of the side lot. He pulled in and opened his car door, thinking about how to set up a conversation with Sammy Farineau. Stepping out, he shut the car door and stretched, arching his back against some post-workout stiffness, and as he straightened, he caught movement in his peripheral vision near the car parked in front of his.

He turned toward it; whatever he had seen was gone, and then he heard the scrape of a foot on the pavement behind him, just as a fist slammed into his lower back. The pain was like an electric jolt, and he staggered, but he managed to come around and face his attacker, who charged forward. He grabbed the man's arm, twisted and straightened, precisely as he'd been taught in his jiu-jitsu class, and was honestly surprised when the man yelped and dropped to his knees. Jordan caught a glimpse of his face in the streetlight. McCann. Just then, lights exploded in Jordan's head from a hit from behind. He went down, dazed but not quite out, and then hands were grabbing him from behind, two men holding him up as McCann punched, delivering two breath-stealing jabs to his gut. Jordan's head lolled upward as McCann hissed, "You come back here, and we'll give you some more!" and he saw McCann grin just before the man's fist came crashing into his face.

Jordan barely registered the sharp blip-blip of a siren and completely missed the flashing lights of the cop car that pulled alongside the parking lot. He wasn't even entirely aware that the hands had released him; he didn't hear the running feet through the parking lot and the calls of the cop to halt. He was too busy retching and coughing on his hands and knees.

As his head cleared, he heard a voice beside him and managed to turn his face toward the sound. A PBP cop squatted next to him. "How are you doing, buddy? Why don't you sit back against the car here and let me take a look at you?" He had a thick Pittsburgh accent.

Somehow Jordan managed to get from his hands and knees to his rear, and he leaned back against the car with a grunt. The cop shined a small flashlight in his face, and Jordan winced, and so did the officer. "I was parked a half a block down, and I saw 'em jump you. It looks like they got in a couple of good licks. Do you need me to call an ambulance?"

"No."

"Did you know the guys who did it?"

Jordan started to shake his head, but the resulting pain made him think better of it. "I'm not sure – I didn't get a good look." His head was still swimming; he wasn't thinking clearly, but for some reason, he didn't want to finger McCann.

There were other voices outside the bar now – the flashing lights had drawn the others' attention inside, and the Goth group hurried over, followed by Harry. "Jordan!" exclaimed Suzanne. "What happened?" She looked distressed. Even George and Peter looked taken aback.

The cop let him answer, probably to see what he would say. Jordan lifted a shoulder. "Got jumped – I think it was three guys." He gingerly lifted a hand to touch his cheekbone, which was already swelling. The side of his face hurt like hell, but that was nothing compared to his ribcage, or his head for that matter. He rubbed the back of it; there was a knot forming.

"They take your wallet?" the cop asked.

Jordan reached around to his back pocket. "No." His mind was starting to clear; it occurred to him that he didn't want the cop to ask for his name. If the man recognized the name and blurted out that he was PDI, he would blow his cover. He struggled to get up. "I'm okay."

He managed to get on his feet using the side of his car and leaned against it, fighting a wave of dizziness. The cop looked at him with narrowed eyes. "I'm not so sure about that."

The others clustered nearby, murmuring, and the cop, thankfully, waved them away. "Give us a minute, folks." They moved off with sideways looks, and the officer turned back to Jordan. "If we find these guys, you want me to file charges? I'm going to file a report anyway; the boss has us watching this bar because of the two people who got murdered, and they're probably going to investigate this, either way, or at least turn it over to the PDI. I'm going to need your name for the report, even if you don't want to file."

Jordan shot a look at the group; they were out of earshot. "Jordan Bell."

He waited, but the man didn't react; he just jotted the name down in a notebook and said, "Okay, you said you thought there were three of 'em, and that's what I thought, too; although yunz were kind of down between the cars, here, so I couldn't see, exactly. I caught a glimpse of someone running around the back of the bar as I drove up."

"I'm not sure I want to press charges; I'll think about it." The only thing he could think about at the moment was getting home and lying down.

The cop wrote something on another page and tore it off. "My name's Officer Gilly, and that's my number. You think of anything, please call me. You can also call down to headquarters tomorrow to see if they've assigned the case yet, and you can still file charges later if you want to. You come here often?"

Jordan stuffed the paper in his pocket. "I've started to, in the last couple of weeks."

"Anyone ever give you any trouble in here?"

"No, not really."

"Okay, I'm going to let you go for now, but I recommend you get checked out at an emergency room. You took a couple of good hits."

He moved away and went over to talk to Harry, and Suzanne immediately trotted over to Jordan. "Oh my God," she said, as she got a closer look at his face, reaching out a hand as if to touch it but stopping just short. "Jordan, who did this?"

He shook his head, wincing at the movement. "Not sure. They jumped me – there were three of them – it happened pretty fast."

Her eyes flashed. "It had to be McCann and his guys."

"Maybe." He looked at her apologetically. "I don't think I'm up for hanging out tonight; I'm sorry."

"I should say not," she said firmly. "I can drive you to the emergency room and then drive you home. We can worry about your car later."

"I'm okay; I just need some ice and ibuprofen. It probably looks worse than it is."

Her forehead furrowed in a pretty frown. "I don't know. You were looking and sounding woozy there, at first. Are you sure?"

"Yeah, yeah, I'm fine." He reached out a hand and grasped hers gently. "Thank you. Are you going to be here tomorrow night?"

She nodded, still looking at him anxiously. "Yeah, I'll be here." Damn, she was pretty.

He released her hand and pushed himself away from the side of his car. "Okay, I'll see you then." He managed a lopsided grin.

"Okay, but if you feel bad while you're driving, call me and pull over, and I'll come right away. And text me when you get home."

He gave her a wave, smiling, waiting until she'd turned around before he tried to pick up his car keys, in case he had a hard time getting back up. Jordan had to bite back a groan as he straightened;

his back was quickly becoming the most painful spot on his body, and he fought off a wave of dizziness as he opened the car door. Once in his seat, he let his head clear for a moment before he started his car. Harry and Officer Gilly were still conversing, and they shot a glance over their shoulders as Jordan's headlights came on but kept talking.

He made it home, and it took him a full five minutes to get up the three flights of stairs and down the hallway to his door. He remembered to text Suzanne, got his ice and ibuprofen, and plugged in his phone next to his work phone on the nightstand. A trip to the bathroom was worrisome – he was peeing blood – the shot to his back had apparently hit a kidney, and the side of his face was red and swollen with blue in the center of the red part, just below his cheekbone. His head was spinning again. Maybe he should have gone to the emergency room – but he didn't want to risk having to deal with his father. They would take head X-rays, and his father was head of neurosurgery… He crawled into bed with a groan. He'd rest a minute, then call DeLuca. Somehow, he managed to fall asleep despite the pain.

Jordan got a call from DeLuca early the next morning, telling him to come into the office. According to DeLuca, Morrissey had gotten a disparaging phone call from the governor the night before. As a result, he'd scheduled an all-day workshop to focus on their cases. Morrissey wanted Jordan there; DeLuca told him to call for a ride and come through the side entrance.

Jordan set the cell phone down and slowly, painfully pushed himself up to a sitting position. Getting to the office would be easier said than done.

Somehow, he managed a shower, got dressed, and called for a ride to the office. The trip down the hallway was slow and painful, and he got looks from some of the PBP officers. As he turned the corner, he could see Bear ahead of him, just entering the PDI office. The rest of the group was standing outside of the door to Morrissey's office, listening to Morrissey.

Bear looked at the group in the doorway and beamed, his teeth shining through his beard. "Is this a party?"

They turned. "Yeah," called out Morrissey, from behind his desk, "a work party. We're going to do some brainstorming. Everyone, cancel what you've got on your calendars today. We're going to spend all day in the conference room, working on our top two cases."

There were a couple of good-natured groans, and the group was beginning to head off to the coffee pot or a desk when Jordan shuffled into the room. Jen saw him first and gasped and said, "Oh, my God."

DeLuca turned to look at him, just as Bear blurted, "Holy shit, kid! What happened to you?"

Jordan managed to scowl, even with a severely swollen face. "What does it look like?" he groused. "I got jumped in the parking lot at Harry's."

He made it to his desk and sat, and everyone stood around while he told the story. "Why didn't you tell Gilly that it was McCann, man?" said Devon.

"I don't know," said Jordan wearily. "I wasn't thinking too straight at first, and something was telling me we shouldn't let him know we're watching him; we need him to screw up, lead us to something he shouldn't. It's hard for him to do that if he's in jail for assault."

Morrissey said, "The ER released you?"

Jordan looked sheepish. "I didn't go."

"You're not fit to be in here," said Morrissey. "You need to go get checked out, and you need to go home."

"I'm fine," Jordan said irritably. "If I have to stay off my feet all day, it might as well be here."

DeLuca said, "Are we going to prosecute McCann, or not? Because if we are, I can help."

Morrissey frowned. "What?"

"I was in a bar up on Carson Street last night." DeLuca looked at Jordan. "I went down there for a while. You said that McCann and his buddies went up to the other bars on Carson Street at the end of the night, and I wanted a look at him, but I didn't want to show up at Harry's. I saw McCann and two of his friends come in panting and sweating as if they'd been running. The attack must have just happened, although I didn't know it at the time. I hung out there, keeping an eye on them until eleven. I can identify all three of them if we get them in a lineup. I say we go after him, rattle his cage a little."

"I think it's better if we let him think he got away with it," said Jordan, quietly. "If he's the murderer, he's been getting away with a lot more than throwing a punch or two. Maybe he'll get cocky and slip up somewhere."

Everyone looked at Morrissey, who said, "I'll think about it. Get your coffee and your notes and whatever you need, and let's get to the conference room."

It was one of the longest days Jordan could remember. He had never hurt like that before, and the ache in his back made it difficult to sit in the conference room chairs. They worked solidly up through the morning, writing out what they knew on the sheets of paper blanketing the walls, first working the murder cases and then the drug case. Morrissey ordered lunch in, and they ate and worked through lunch. Well, the rest of them ate. Jordan was still feeling nauseous, and he picked at his sandwich. His lower back kept going into spasm, and he was getting tired of the pain – tired and irritated.

He made a trip to the restroom while the rest were still eating, and DeLuca came in a minute or two later. He stood, blocking the doorway with his arms crossed. "Why didn't you call me last night?"

Jordan shrugged and stepped to the sink. "To be honest, all I could think about was getting home and into bed. I figured we had our morning meeting lined up – I was going to report out then."

DeLuca's scowl deepened. "I told you to call me day or night if something came up, remember? You don't think getting attacked by our number one suspect qualifies?"

Irritation spiked, and Jordan faced him. "Stop treating me like a kid, okay? I know what I'm doing."

Anger flashed into DeLuca's face. "Yeah, you know what you're doing, all right. I warned you about pushing too hard on McCann, and look what happened. And you *are* a kid. You're twenty-three goddamned years old. You've been doing this for two years, and you think you know everything? Wise up." He turned and stalked out.

Jordan stared after him for a moment, an angry retort on his lips, and then his shoulders slumped. He couldn't blame DeLuca. The guy was right; he had warned him. Jordan sighed and shook his head. The truth was, he was annoyed with himself for not being more careful. And above all, he was angry at Will McCann. Despite his request to not press charges against him, he'd like to smash a fist in that guy's face. He'd love even more to put him behind bars for murder.

CHAPTER TWELVE

Jordan went home exhausted and still in pain at the end of the day, almost too tired to stand and wait for his ride. He debated about going back to Harry's that night; both DeLuca and Morrissey had ordered him to go home and stay there. But Jordan had told Suzanne that he would be at the bar, and he didn't want McCann to think he'd scared him off, even for a minute. He tried to force down some food and took a three-hour nap.

He woke feeling like he had more energy, but he was still unbearably stiff. Inertia claimed him for a moment; sleep seemed like just what he needed. But he pushed himself out of bed and got dressed, spiked up his hair, and put his earring in. He looked at himself in the mirror, at his bruised face and red eyes and his Goth getup, and decided he looked positively frightening. He wouldn't have to worry about Suzanne wanting to kiss him tonight.

He pulled into a parking spot by a streetlight and looked around before he stepped out of the car. He made it inside without incident, and almost the first face he saw was McCann's; he was standing about ten feet from the door at the end of the bar, with his usual crowd. Jordan walked right up to him, and McCann turned. The surprise was evident on his face, and Jordan got in close, nose to nose, and said, calmly, "You're going to be sorry for that." Then he turned and walked over to the Goth crowd, McCann sputtering something behind him.

Suzanne was pulling up a chair for him between her and Victoria, and for a minute or two, he enjoyed both girls fawning over him. Everyone wanted to know what happened, and he told them about being hit from behind, then turning around and trying to face his attacker, and being tackled and held by two others.

Peter frowned and shot a glance at the group at the bar. "Are you sure it wasn't one of them?"

"Oh, I'm sure it was," said Jordan. "There's no doubt McCann was behind it. The problem was, it was dark, and it happened so fast, I only got a look at one of them, and that wasn't a good look." He grinned. "Hard to tell them apart. They're all big and ugly."

That earned him roars of laughter. The only person who looked less than delighted was Sammy. He smiled, but he was playing with his phone, preoccupied.

George Lilt said, "My playlist is almost up. I'd better get over to the jukebox before they do."

Jordan said, "I got it."

He got up, trying to move smoothly and as quickly as he could, because one of the McCann crowd had started to move toward the jukebox, as well. Jordan had the jump on him, though. He got there and stuck his credit card in, sucking in a breath and leaning on the box as his back tightened. The other man leaned against the jukebox with his hand in plain view, showing off a set of bruised knuckles. "You are an obnoxious little punk, aren't you?"

He had at least four inches and 50 pounds on Jordan. Judging by the condition of his knuckles, he was the man who had punched him in the back of the head. Jordan just smiled at him and paid for twenty songs.

He picked some of the angriest, darkest Goth punk he could find, and it took him a while to queue them all up, and his back kept getting tighter. By the time he got back to the table, there was a sheen of sweat on his forehead, and he sat down gingerly. The girls fussed, and he tried to muster a smile. He knew he wanted to talk to Sammy, but he couldn't generate the energy to try to figure out how to get him alone to talk.

He stuck it out for another hour and then headed for home.

He slept for ten hours straight, and Sunday morning woke feeling twinges of anxiety again. He'd been dreaming last night about Lucaya and the warehouse in New York. The need for the bathroom drove him to his feet, and he found that he was somewhat less sore and that, thankfully, the bleeding in his kidney had stopped. Some of his facial swelling was starting to recede, but the bruise was starting to turn purple, tinged with red. He looked at all three of his phones, slipped on a pair of gym shorts, started the coffee pot, drifted into the living room, and sunk into the sofa.

He was at a loss. The bar wouldn't be open that night, and he wasn't due to go to Carter's until the next night. He thought about what he would tell Carter about his face because the man would surely comment. That took all of about thirty seconds. He didn't feel well enough to go out for a bike ride. He might have considered a visit home to see his mother, except he'd have to explain his face. So, he was stuck in the apartment again. He would go over the case files some more, he thought, although the idea didn't appeal to him. He was getting burned out, and they didn't have anything more to go on than they'd had yesterday. Maybe it would be good to get a day of rest and heal up and try to get ready for the week.

He got coffee, managed a shower, and was toweling off when his work phone rang. Wrapping the towel around his waist, he picked it up. DeLuca was on the other end.

"Bell," he said. "How are you feeling today?"

"A little better." Jordan tried to keep suspicion out of his voice – DeLuca couldn't simply be calling to see how he was. The call had to be work-related.

"Good – how do you feel about getting out for a field trip?"

"*I knew it*," thought Jordan. He said, "Fine, what's up? Did something happen?"

"No, no, not for work," said DeLuca. "I'm heading over to my mom's for Sunday dinner – she has the whole family over every week. Typical Italian – homemade sauce, pasta. I go right past your place; I could pick you up on the way. I think you could use a break, right?"

"I – uh – yeah, sure," said Jordan. The gesture was unexpected. He thought of the sauce, and his stomach growled. "That sounds great."

"Okay, see you at around noon."

Jordan hung up the phone and scratched his head. His hair was getting long, and he'd been wearing it mussed and spiky lately. He'd better spend some time with the hairdryer and try to tame it into something respectable.

He shaved and found a decent polo and some jeans without holes in them and thought it felt good to look like himself for a change. He got down the stairs and into Mike's vehicle; he was moving a little better, too.

"Hi," he said.

"Hi," said DeLuca. He pulled out of the lot, and without taking his eyes off the road, muttered, "Sorry about yesterday. I meant what I said, but it wasn't the best timing."

If he'd said he was about to drive them off the Liberty Bridge, Jordan couldn't have been more surprised. Was that an apology?

"Yeah, well, you were right," Jordan said. Silence descended, and then he said, with a quick sidelong glance, "So, I went to the bar last night."

DeLuca gave him a look of disapproval. "You could hardly walk yesterday. We told you to stay at home."

Jordan shrugged. "I didn't go for long. I didn't find out anything else, either; I wasn't there long enough. I wanted to talk to Sammy, but I couldn't get him alone, and I just ran out of steam."

"So, why'd you go?"

"Like I said, to talk to Sammy." He paused. "And to let that asshole McCann know he wasn't scaring me away."

DeLuca shook his head and shot him a glance. "You didn't get into it with him again, did you?"

"Nope. I just held my ground and hung out with the Goth crowd. If I wasn't in with them before, I sure am now. They feel persecuted by that college crowd, and they certainly are sympathetic." He paused and said, "Your mom doesn't make meatballs, does she?"

DeLuca grinned. "Just the best ones in the state."

DeLuca's parents lived on a quiet street in Morningside. There were two cars parked at the curb, and DeLuca pulled in behind one of them and said, "There'll be a crowd here today. I've got two brothers and a sister, and they're all married with kids. If it gets to be too much, just say so. We can eat and get out."

He led the way into the house, a decent-sized ranch. Two men were in the living room, one of them slightly older than DeLuca and one much older; Jordan pegged them for Mike's brother and father. They both stood up as they entered, and both of them gave DeLuca the same handshake/arm slap combination as a greeting. "Dad, Bobby," said DeLuca.

"Michael," boomed Bobby. "How ya doin'?" Their eyes went immediately to Jordan. The kitchen door pushed open simultaneously, and three women came out, who DeLuca introduced as his mother, his sister Susan, and Bobby's wife, Carol.

"I'm good," said DeLuca. "Guys, this is my new partner, Jordan Bell. He's in training; he started a couple of weeks ago."

He stepped over and gave his mom and Susan a hug, and Carol a half-hug and buss on the cheek, as Jordan nodded and said hello.

DeLuca's mother, a trim woman with neat salt and pepper curls, immediately went over and gave Jordan a hug, which made him both embarrassed and pleased, and she said, "Welcome, honey." She looked at DeLuca. "Oh, my goodness, you start them young." She studied Jordan, holding his shoulders at arms' length. "What on earth did you do to your face?"

Jordan gave her his best smile, and he could see all three women melt. "Took a tumble on my bike. It's nothing." He glanced at DeLuca, and DeLuca gave him a faint nod, sanctioning the falsehood.

Carol liked to cycle, and she started chatting, and she and Jordan moved toward the kitchen along with his mother and Susan. There was a screech from outside; the kids were out there running around the yard, and Bobby said, "Damn kids. I'm gonna check on 'em; be right back," and was out the door. In the kitchen, Susan offered Jordan a beer, but even the mention of it made him realize that the morning's coffee was working on him. "Would you mind if I used the bathroom?"

Susan directed him back out through the living room, and as Jordan re-entered the room, he heard DeLuca say, "I said he's my *partner*, Dad, my work partner. What did you think he was?"

The senior DeLuca scowled. "Well, I didn't know," he complained. "He looks kind of young to be a cop. And you never seem to come around with a girl anymore."

DeLuca rolled his eyes. "Jesus, Dad."

Jordan cleared his throat. "Sorry," he said, his voice shaking with repressed laughter, "I was going to use your bathroom and wash up."

DeLuca turned and saw him, and one corner of his mouth twisted in a rueful grin as they exchanged a look, and he said, "It's right down that hall."

Jordan had to pass them on the way, and he veered over to DeLuca's father and gave him a robust pump of a handshake and a hearty slap on the arm – the DeLuca handshake on steroids. "How ya doin,' Mr. DeLuca? I didn't get to shake your hand yet!" His voice was deep, a near bellow, heavy with Pittsburgh accent, and reminiscent of Bear. He saw DeLuca turn away to hide his smile.

"Uh, good, good," his dad stammered, giving Jordan a few more hand pumps than necessary. "Nice to have you, kid."

Jordan shot Mike a wicked grin and strode off to the bathroom, as Bobby came in from the yard, sweating. "Damn kids. I need a beer."

They ate outside in the back yard. The DeLuca residence boasted a small concrete patio in the back yard covered by an awning, and there were two folding tables with folding chairs set up there, one for the adults and one for the children. It was a noisy and happy crowd, and it was a beautiful August day – green grass and trees vied for admiration with a deep blue sky dotted with fluffy clouds. Jordan was hungry, and he was sure that it was the best Italian meal he had ever eaten anywhere: Italian sausage and peppers, meatballs, homemade gnocchi, and homemade sauce. And he enjoyed the company. The DeLucas didn't seem to change their normal conversation because he was there, and they included him in their banter. It made him feel like a part of the family instantly.

He couldn't help but compare it to his upbringing – stiff family dinners, permeated by an air of disapproval, judgment hovering over every conversation. In retrospect, he could see how his mother had worked as a mediator, smoothing over the jabs by his father, both veiled and overt, bringing life and positivity to the table. It had been enough to make the atmosphere bearable, but never comfortable, never loving. Not like this. Even when the senior DeLucas asked Mike if he was patching things up with Janine (a name Jordan filed away for future reference), the inquisition, while pointed, was well-meaning at heart. Jordan enjoyed it all immensely and was envious of DeLuca for having it. However, he couldn't help but wonder what he was doing there.

As evening descended, they were both sent home with leftovers, poor bereft bachelors that they were; at least that's how DeLuca's mother seemed to see it, as if they were unfortunate clueless saps who couldn't feed themselves without a woman to cook for them. Jordan liked that, too; it was nice to be fussed over. In the car, he glanced sideways at DeLuca. The man never gave up much about himself, and today had been a revelation, a glimpse into a piece of DeLuca's world. Plus some bonus information: the fact that DeLuca had had a girlfriend named Janine and that they had broken up. They rode in silence for a while as he pondered that, then Jordan said, "Thanks for that. It was great."

DeLuca shook his head. "Don't mention it. I thought you could use a break, get some normal for a while. And Mom always makes enough to feed an army."

"You have a great family."

"Yeah, they're okay," said DeLuca, offhandedly, although he smiled. "They ask too many questions. And they're a little old-school. Be prepared; my mom and my sister and sisters-in-law will be trying to fix you up with a girlfriend. Pairing up unmarried people seems to be their mission in life." They were nearing his apartment, and DeLuca changed the subject. "You good to go for tomorrow night?"

"Yeah, I tried setting up the VPN and TOR access on my own computer, and it went fine. I think it will take an hour, two at the most, to do it on Carter's computer. I'm going to need thirteen hundred more to buy another round."

"Yeah, we've got it for you, and I already set it up with one of the narc guys to drop it off tomorrow. What time are you getting there?"

"They want me at nine. I'm supposed to park alongside the

house, in the side alley."

"Okay, we'll have PBP Narcotics watching out from their post. You still feel comfortable that you don't need a wire or even a GPS tracker?"

"Yeah, it should be fine." Night had descended, and the street lights had come on as DeLuca turned down the road to Jordan's apartment. They were both looking for surveillance and didn't see any. Still, DeLuca pulled into the rear parking lot to drop him off – it was less conspicuous.

It had been a good day, and Jordan felt as though they had gained some ground. Not really partners yet, but perhaps starting to get beyond whatever they had been before. Maybe. He had the impression that DeLuca's invitation was based on an ulterior motive. DeLuca put the vehicle in park, and even in the gloom, his eyes looked icy, piercing. And then he asked again, "You're sure you're okay?" and Jordan knew.

He reached for the door handle and said, as he got out of the vehicle, "Sure, I'm good. Thanks for the invite." He shut the door and strode toward the apartment building, keenly aware of DeLuca's eyes on his back. Jordan heard the vehicle start as the outside door swung shut behind him, and safely inside in the gloom, he watched the SUV pull out of the lot. DeLuca hadn't brought him to his family's house out of the goodness of his heart. He had done it to check his mental status, to assess his behavior in a casual setting, to see if he acted normally. DeLuca knew something that he wasn't telling him, and he still didn't trust him.

CHAPTER THIRTEEN

Monday was a slow day, made slower by the thought of the pending activity in the evening. Jordan spent the time in his apartment, going over the story behind his new undercover role, cementing the details that he thought would apply to Juan Gonzalez. He put together a few notes on the web access project he would be doing for Carter, making sure there wasn't anything incriminating on the pages if Carter demanded to see them. The person from narc showed up and dropped off the money: thirteen hundred for the next round of drugs. Jordan still had seven hundred from the first delivery, and he put it in his wallet as a backup, along with the thirteen hundred, took out his credit cards, and replaced his driver's license with the Juan Gonzalez version.

Physically, he felt much better. His bruised areas were still sore to the touch but didn't hurt when he moved, and the swelling was nearly gone. The welt on his cheek exhibited some yellowish areas among the red and purple spots but was receding in size. He had a lot more energy after all the sleep he had gotten over the weekend, but even so, he forced himself to take an afternoon nap. He would have a late night tonight, and he needed to go back to the bar the next night.

He ate a sandwich for dinner – he had those magnificent leftovers from Mrs. DeLuca, but nerves were starting to intrude, and he didn't have the stomach for all of that food. He'd save it for a victory meal. At least, that's what he told himself. It wasn't because DeLuca's apparent lack of trust in him had tainted the entire outing. And so what? So, DeLuca was all business; that was as it should be. Jordan would prove to him that he was as tough as he needed to be. He spent the next hour getting his things together and going over the game plan for his assignment at Carter's house that night. At around 8:30 p.m., he sent DeLuca a text message that he was heading out, packed up, and took off for Carter's place.

He got there a few minutes early and parked in the side alley, as James had instructed. The bushes on that side blocked his view of the house where they had stationed the narc guys, and he wondered if they knew he was there; they had to have seen his headlights at least, he reasoned. He waited until two minutes before nine, and then Juan Gonzalez grabbed his backpack, got out of the car, and went to the front door. It opened just as he got to it, and he slipped inside.

Dee Dee ushered him in. James stood off to the side, and Carter was sitting in his chair, waiting, and he said, "Check him out."

James grabbed his backpack and went through it as Dee Dee patted him down. Carter said, "What happened to your face?"

"I, uh, got me into an altercation," said Juan. "Some punk was trying to stiff me on the correct amount for a bundle. I called him on it, and he sucker-punched me."

Dee Dee stepped away. "Clean."

Carter's eyes narrowed with interest. "And so, what'd you do, kid?"

Juan shrugged. "I took him down, took the bundle back. He was whinin' and cryin' for his drugs back and finally gave me the money. So, he got his drugs and a lesson."

Carter looked skeptical. "How'd a skinny little punk like you take someone down?"

"I got some MMA training. A little boxing, a little BJJ."

"That so?" said James. He had a disbelieving smirk on his face, his big arms crossed over his chest. "I think you're a lot of talk, punk. I think you got your assed kicked and don' wanna admit it."

Juan hesitated. He hadn't wanted to take it this far; he had figured they'd buy his excuse. He should have used the bike story instead. He had no choice; his credibility was at stake. "Okay," he said to James, cockily, "Come at me. Come on."

A grin spread over James' face, and he crouched, his arms out, and Juan readied himself, his heart thumping. Carter rapped out, "Stop!"

James straightened, reluctantly. "I don't need this foolishness in my house," snapped Carter. "This ain't no high school gym. We keep a low profile here." He looked at Juan. "So, Gonzalez, why do you have to put up with that shit? Don't you have no piece?"

Juan shook his head cautiously. "No, man. I don't wanna shoot no one. I just wanna sell a few drugs."

"You don't have to shoot 'em, man. You just pull it out, so they know you mean business. Then you don't have to fight 'em. I can get you a piece next time you come. Get you a good one, cheap, no serial number, untraceable. Good quality, somethin' you can trust. I can get you a deal: six hundred. I like to make sure my investments are protected, you understand."

Juan lifted a shoulder and said, "Thanks, but that's okay. I got tuition to pay."

Carter's smile vanished. "I gotta insist. You can have it for five, but you're gettin' a piece. Your territory's gonna increase fast when word gets out about the good stuff you have, and you're gonna be protecting some sizable amounts of property in the future. I ain't havin' you comin' back here and saying you can't pay me for the next round 'cause some shithead ripped you off, you got it?"

Juan nodded soberly. "Got it. I'll bring five hundred next week."

"Good. Now, how about this week's money?"

Juan bent and fished it out of his pack, waved it at Carter. "Thirteen hundred for this week's buy."

"You can do better'n that, boy. You sold that last stash quick. You buy fifteen hundred this week. Trust me; you'll sell it."

Juan looked doubtful, but he pulled out his wallet and took out two hundred more.

Carter took the money and hefted himself from the chair. Upright, he towered over Juan; he had to be at least six foot three, with a big frame. "Dee Dee will get you your stuff an' put it in your pack. Dee Dee, get the man twenty-three gees. Now come here, Gonzalez; I want you to look at my computer."

He sat Juan in front of a relatively new but rather dirty desktop in the cluttered dining area and typed on the keyboard, with surprising dexterity. "Now, boy, I want to look at some sites on the web, but I don't want anyone tracin' me. You know how to do that?"

Juan nodded. "First, I set you up with a VPN, a virtual private network. That makes it so no one can trace you; any transaction you make, they can't track it back to your computer. Then I can download TOR. We'll make up a new email for you. Once I do that, you can look at whatever sites you want: regular web, Dark Web, and you'll be anonymous. When I get that far, I'll show you how."

Carter nodded. "How long?"

Juan shrugged. "About an hour or two."

"Okay, go."

Juan set to work. It made the hair stand up on the back of his neck to be working with his head down while the others moved around behind him, but eventually, he got used to it and calmed down. He noticed Dee Dee go out to the kitchen to get his drugs. He could see just a fraction of the room through the doorway, and part of a table, pushed against a wall. Dee Dee reached down into something underneath it and pulled out some plastic bags filled with powder – heroin and fentanyl, Juan assumed – put on a mask and some gloves, turned on an exhaust fan mounted in the wall, and then bent over the table. Juan guessed there must be a scale there and that Dee Dee was measuring.

At length, Dee Dee came into the room with his mask hanging around his neck and put a bag in Juan's pack, and said, "Twenty-three grams, all there."

Carter said, "You got the orders ready for ten and ten-thirty?"

Dee Dee nodded, and Carter switched on the stereo. Rap music thumped into the room, not too loud, and then Carter turned on the television with no sound and put on an MMA fight. He laughed and pointed at the screen. "There's some fighters there. We gonna put you in the ring, boy!"

Juan looked, smiled, and then turned and went back to work.

At just before ten, James and Dee Dee went out to the kitchen, and Juan heard Dee Dee say to James, "This one, here. That other one is for ten-thirty." James picked up a package and went outside through the back door. Juan knew he was making a delivery at the back gate, just like the one he'd taken the other night. Dee Dee came in and sat, and then James came back inside with a small bag, pulled out some cash, and counted it.

"All here," he said.

Carter picked up Juan's cash from the side table and gave it to him, and James added it to the pile and disappeared into a hallway that looked as though it might lead to bedrooms. He came back out without the money. Money in the bedroom, drugs in the kitchen. Juan said, "Hey, Mr. Carter, can I get a glass of water?"

Carter waved a hand. "Go ahead. There's beer in the fridge, if you want, man."

Juan went into the kitchen, glancing to his left without turning his head as he came through the door. There were scales and smaller bags on the kitchen table, along with a sizable bag that Juan suspected contained the drugs for the ten-thirty pickup. Fishing poles and a tackle box were tucked in by the kitchen door, along with a pair of boots, and a white foam cooler sat under the kitchen table, its lid ajar just enough so that Juan could see the bags of white powder inside. It was about a quarter full. He went straight to the sink; there were red plastic cups on the counter, and he took one, filled it with water, and went straight back to the dining room. James had been watching him through the doorway, probably to make sure he didn't go anywhere near the cooler.

There was something about that white foam cooler… Juan racked his brains, trying to remember, but then gave up and forced his mind on his task. Better to get out of there in one piece and think about the cooler later. Finally, he got done what he needed to and called Carter over to the computer. "Okay, you're set up." He had Carter create a new email, opened the TOR browser, showed Carter how to do it, and gave him a few points to navigate the Dark Web. "Go ahead and check stuff out this week, and if you got any questions, call me."

Carter was looking at the screen with interest. "So, if I wanted to set up an online bizness to help sell my stuff around this area, can I do that?"

"You could," said Juan. "You need to be careful who you deal with. Cops look at these sites, too. There was a big site called the Silk Road – sold drugs all over the world. It was high security, and even it got taken down by the cops eventually."

"You know how to set up a web site?"

"Not yet," said Juan, "but I'll be learning in my classes. Maybe I can ask a professor how to do it."

"Okay, you do that. When you gonna be back for your next round?"

Juan scratched his head. "I don't know, for sure. I had some buyers who are like, not regular. You know, I had backed up orders last week, so the stuff went fast, but not all of them buy every week. I might need a week this time."

Carter nodded. "Okay, come back at nine next Monday, unless you run out sooner. Then call me."

Juan nodded, picked up his backpack, and escaped. The door closed, and he could hear the faint thump of the music, which faded as he walked to his car and got in. The ten-thirty pickup was coming down the alley, and he let them pass before he started his car and headed for home.

At his apartment, Jordan took the stairs three at a time. He sent a quick text to DeLuca from his work phone to tell him that he got back okay and that everything went well, and he would report out in the morning. Then Jordan headed straight for his kitchen table and Milt and Marty's reports on Carter. He leafed through them, looking for surveillance photos, and found the one he wanted, along with the surveillance reports on Carter's morning fishing trips. Milt had taken the picture on a hill overlooking the Monongahela, up above a quarry near the Glenwood Bridge. In it, Carter was crossing an open area near the train tracks on his way to his fishing spot.

According to the report, every morning, Carter would show up at dawn and park his car on a dirt road pull-off just before the overpass leading to the Glenwood Bridge, near the quarry. He had a pull wagon, which he loaded with gear, and he pulled it down over the train tracks underneath the Second Street overpass to Duck Hollow Trail, which followed the river's edge. There were always a handful of fishermen there. In one photo, a couple of the other fishermen were visible in the parking area, also on their way down to the river. They all used wagons to cart their fishing supplies.

Jordan peered at the photo. It was too grainy to see well, and so he got online and logged into the secure remote work website and looked for the shared folders on the case. He found them, found the photos, clicked on one, and zoomed in. The picture was still somewhat grainy, but at least it was not distorted by poor printer quality. He could see the contents of the wagon – it included the big tackle box that he had seen by the back door at Carter's house, the rods, sticking up from rod holders mounted at the back of the wagon, and a white foam cooler. It could be filled with ice, waiting for fish, but Jordan had a feeling it wasn't. A quick look at the other fisherman in the picture made him doubt himself. Apparently, foam coolers were what everyone used to keep their catch cold. Maybe the cooler in the kitchen was just a coincidence; maybe Carter had just had an extra one around and used it as a handy place to store his stash under their work table. Then again, perhaps it was significant. It was hard to tell; he'd never fished himself. His father hadn't been the type to take his sons fishing.

He sat and thought for a while. He pulled up online maps and photos of the area and studied them, and looked at a marked-up map that Milt had provided that showed Carter's usual spot on the bank. There was a photo of him fishing in the file, but at that viewpoint, brush started to obscure the surroundings, and although Carter was visible, his wagon was not – the bushes along the edge hid it from view. Still, during multiple rounds of surveillance at the site, no one had approached him. "If they're doing it there, they've got to be doing it at night, when Carter's not there," Jordan muttered to himself.

Research done, Jordan went and changed into dark clothing. The long-sleeved T-shirt he had bought for the Goth case worked nicely. He rummaged through the closet, found some bug spray, doused himself thoroughly, and got his badge and Glock. After putting his work phone on silent, he stuck it in his pocket. He thought for a moment more, jotted a note down and left it on the table, grabbed a bottle of water and his car keys, and took off for the Glenwood Bridge.

It didn't take long to get there; most of the trip was a straight shot down Second Avenue. He turned off on Vespucius Street and parked in the lot of a manufacturing plant that had closed for the night. From there, he trotted across Second Avenue and into the relative anonymity of a sparsely populated residential area. He made a right turn on Gate Lodge Way and took it all the way down until it ended in a loop and passed by the last houses into the trees.

The land on the northeast side of Second Avenue turned into an untamed mass of woods. The other side of Second Avenue was a wide-open space, razed by the quarry. If he were going to make it down to the river unseen, he had to bypass the quarry, stick to the woods on the other side of Second Avenue, and follow the train tracks until he was well east of the bridge. At that point, there were woods on both sides of the rails, which could provide cover. The only time he would be exposed was when he crossed the train tracks themselves, and then again briefly when he crossed Duck Hollow Trail.

It was a warm night, and the growth along the tracks was thick. He had to move up the hill to get through, and although the brush was less dense there, it was steep, and the terrain forced him to scramble along the side of the ridge. It was rough going, and he was panting and sweating by the time he figured he was far enough past Carter's usual fishing area. He made his way down to the growth that fronted the railway and watched and listened for a minute. Then he took a deep breath and ran across the train tracks.

There were four sets of them; the area was wide open, and the moon was bright. He felt exposed and was relieved when he hit the trees on the other side. He paused again, catching his breath, again watching and listening, and crept through the trees until he hit Duck Hollow Trail.

The trail ran in the same direction as the tracks and river, between the two. The Monongahela was one of the few rivers in the country that ran from south to north, coming up from the hills of West Virginia, just west of Pittsburgh. At that point, it turned and ran from west to east towards the city, and Duck Hollow Trail followed that portion of the river. It was a narrow path, but the moonlight illuminated it, and Jordan crossed it, ducking into the shadow of the trees on the other side. He planned to make a big circle and approach the fishing area from the east. There was nothing but the path and lots of woods for a long way. Any fishermen near the quarry would never expect anyone to be coming from that direction at night. There remained one thick but relatively narrow strip of trees between the trail and the river, and before he circled back west along the path, he crept through them down to the river's edge to take a look.

The moonlight shone silver-white over the river, and across and a little bit upstream, he could see Sandcastle Water Park. Jon Hurly's body had been found on the other side of the river, almost directly across from where he was now, two different cases intersecting across an expanse of dark water. Maybe. He might be on a wild goose chase.

There were a couple of boats out; he could see their lights. One was downriver and the other upriver, just coming around the bend. There was no one fishing in this area. The brush was too dense to get a line out, and it was too far from any parking areas, and so he pulled out his phone and chanced a glance at the time. Just after midnight. He pocketed the phone and backed out of the brush and onto the trail, and sticking to the shadows under the tree line, began to move west along the path in the direction he had come – back toward the Glenwood Bridge and Second Avenue – closer to Carter's fishing area along the bank.

He passed a railroad trestle bridge and began to move more slowly, stopping and listening. He could see the Second Avenue overpass up ahead where it turned and became the Glenwood Bridge. The brushy area to his left started to show a few openings now, sparser areas where the fishermen had room to cast. Jordan moved from brush clump to brush clump, peering around them at each clearing to see if there was anyone there before he moved on to the next one. He was about halfway between the railroad trestle bridge and the Glenwood Bridge when he smelled cigarette smoke.

He stopped and ducked and crept forward, bent over, until he saw a man silhouetted against the moonlight on the river. The man was fishing from the bank, his back to the trail. Jordan could see the tip of the cigarette in his mouth flare orange, saw him take it, and flick the ashes from it. It was too dark to identify the man; he could only determine that he was lean, probably around six feet tall, give or take a couple of inches. Jordan had hoped to get within view of the parking area, a little further down, so he could watch it and the fishermen at the same time.

He was near Carter's fishing spot, and it was too risky to go any further with the man so close, so Jordan stayed there. He carefully moved into the brush, as slowly and quietly as possible, finding a place where he could conceal himself yet still have eyes on the man and most of the shoreline. Then he settled down to wait.

It was a long wait. Jordan didn't dare risk looking at his cell phone; the screen would be too bright, but he figured it had been at least two hours, and he was getting discouraged. During that time, he'd realized that there was a second man further down the bank toward the bridge; he'd come up and said something to the first man at one point, and the man had handed him a cigarette. To all appearances, Jordan was merely sitting there watching two men out night fishing. The mosquitos were ferocious; he could hear them buzzing around him and was devoutly thankful he had thought to put on bug spray. His legs were cramping, and he stretched them cautiously, one by one, and was thinking of leaving, when something happened.

A few boats had gone by when he first sat down, but as time wore on, they were fewer and far between. Another one came cruising downstream just then, its lights on, slowing as it approached. A green light appeared on board, then was extinguished. In response, the man on the bank reached down and grabbed a flashlight and flashed it twice, on and off. Jordan sat up, watching intently, but the boat slowly cruised past instead of stopping. He saw a name illuminated on the stern of the vessel: *Lucky Day*. Maybe the flashing lights were just a way of saying hello to a fellow angler. He watched it move downstream with growing frustration, which vanished abruptly when the boat went dark.

Even with its lights out, he could still see it in the moonlight; it was turning around just before the bridge, and as it came back toward them, it pulled in toward the bank, nosing in. One of the men on board tossed a line, and the man on the bank caught it, and the other man appeared, and they both pulled, bringing the bow of the boat toward shore. One of them wrapped the rope around a tree to hold the vessel in place, and they both waded into the water.

The boat was good sized, over thirty feet, and had a small area below deck. A man on the deck was bending over and picking up a foam cooler, obviously handed up to him from someone below. In turn, he handed it over to one of the men in the water, who waded back and put it onshore. The man on the boat handed off a total of six coolers, and the two men handed him a stack of empties, which were taken on board and tossed below. Then one of the fishermen untied the *Lucky Day,* and the other man gave it a push, and the boat backed quietly into the current and then reversed its engines and slowly cruised forward, back the way it had come. Its lights were still out, and they didn't come back on until the boat was well upriver, almost at the bend.

Jordan could feel his heart pounding. The men were picking up the containers, one by one, and distributing them along the river bank, deep in the brush, and one of the men was heading right for him. He tensed and put a black-clad arm over his face; it would shine white if the flashlight caught it. If they found him, he had his gun, but even if he came out of a confrontation alive, a gun battle would be disastrous. Whether he managed to kill his attackers or they fled, someone would realize that they were being watched, the deliveries would cease, and the best opportunity yet for tracking the drug shipments would be gone.

Jordan held his breath as the man approached and stayed motionless as he stopped just eight yards in front of him, at the edge of the brush clump that hid him. The man was close enough now for Jordan to see that he was Caucasian, with a thin face and a dark goatee. The man pulled aside some dead brush, and put the cooler in a hole that had been pre-dug for the purpose, then covered it up with leaves and brush. He worked methodically; his flashlight thankfully set off to the side. Then he rose, grabbed the light, and walked back to the other coolers. Jordan let out a breath.

At length, the two men had hidden four coolers. The first man, the one fishing nearest him, took one of the two remaining coolers and put it on his wagon, and packed up his gear and pulled the cart up on the trail, and headed off for his vehicle. The second man had picked up the last cooler, Jordan surmised, for himself. He walked back with it down the bank, out of sight. Jordan waited for him to come out on the path and head for his car as the first man had, but he didn't leave, so Jordan crept carefully back out of his hiding place and made his way down the trail just a bit further.

The second man was still standing on the bank, fishing; his wagon pulled behind him with a cooler on it. That stack of empty coolers he and his partner had handed off had to be from the previous delivery. There had to be others involved, including Carter, who would come and pick up their stash later in the daytime. The men each came down to the river with one empty container and left with a full one. The boat picked up the empties and delivered the full coolers. No telltale trash left behind. In between pickups, the men hid the four extra coolers in the brush. Jordan suspected that the man he was watching would stay there until morning, until the other fishermen showed up for their 'catches,' and keep an eye on the area, in case a real fisherman showed up. Chances were that anyone else would suspect nothing because the other four coolers were out of sight, but a drug shipment of that size warranted a guard.

Jordan pondered the ramifications of that as he crept carefully backward. Four other coolers would likely mean four other dealers, of which Carter was just one. A total of six drug dealers, including the two who had pulled night duty. Carter by himself had an impressive business going – at least tens of thousands of dollars a day if he got a third of a cooler's worth of merchandise. Multiply that by six, and they could be talking about a hundred thousand dollars' worth of drugs, or more, every day. Every *weekday*, he corrected himself. According to the surveillance reports, Carter went fishing every weekday morning without fail.

He got back down the path without incident and went past the trestle bridge before crossing the trail. Then back through the strip of woods to the train tracks, across them, up the hill, and through the woods on the other side. By the time he got back to his car, he was sweating and worn-out, and his phone read nearly five a.m. In another hour or so, the daytime fishing crew would show up for their catch. He got in his car, got on the road, and called DeLuca.

CHAPTER FOURTEEN

DeLuca said, "What? Wait, wait; slow down, Bell. You aren't making any sense. Go over it again, slowly."

Jordan went back over what he'd found, and then he said, "So if you want to pull off a sting and nab five of the six dealers, you can do it, but you probably have less than an hour if you want to get the guy that's on the bank right now - he'll probably be heading home as soon as the other four show up. Or, you can wait until tonight and pick up the two who take the delivery and get the other four tomorrow morning, and you'll get all six of them. Or, you can leave the dealers alone for a night and follow the boat back up the river to find out where it came from."

"I think I want door number three," said DeLuca. "But I want to go over all of this with Milt and Marty and make sure it jives with what they've seen. Head for home, and I'll pick you up. I'll call them, and we'll meet at the office. I'll bring breakfast."

DeLuca picked up Jordan a half-hour later, and they parked in the lot at work; no need to worry about the press being there and filming at that time of the morning. Milt and Marty pulled in one after the other, almost right behind them. At the office, they made a pot of coffee and set up in the conference room. Marty's face was still flushed with sleep. Milt looked the same as he always did - as if he'd crawled right out of a 1940's detective flick, hair neatly slicked, wearing a light brown suit.

Jordan said, "I went for my meeting with Carter last night, and as James had told me the week before, he wanted me to stay and work on the computer program."

"Start at the beginning," said DeLuca. "What about your drug deal?"

Jordan waved impatiently. He was tired but wired, running on adrenaline. "That went fine. I brought some extra cash with me, and it was a good thing I did because he wanted me to buy a little more. I bought twenty-three grams for fifteen hundred, instead of the twenty that we planned on. I'll probably need that much next week. Oh, and five or six hundred for a gun."

The other three looked at each other. DeLuca said, "A gun?"

"He saw my face, and I told him I got in a fight. He said I need to have a gun if I'm dealing for him – he doesn't want his product stolen. He's going to get me a street piece."

DeLuca said, "Go on."

"Then, Carter brought me over to a desktop computer in the dining area and had me set up a VPN and TOR access for him. I have the information we'll need to track his IP address. That took a while, and while I was doing it, I saw Dee Dee go into the kitchen to a table to measure out my drugs. I wanted to get into the kitchen to see the setup, so I asked to get some water. While I was out there, I got a look. There was measuring equipment on the table, and a foam cooler was sitting underneath it. The lid was ajar, and I could see that it was maybe a third full of bags of white powder. The cooler got me thinking."

Milt and Bear stared at him. Bear said, "You saw a foam cooler in the kitchen, and you came up with their plan just like that."

Jordan shook his head. "No, not right away. I think what made me think of fishing was the fact that Carter also had his tackle box and his rods sitting in the kitchen, over in the corner next to the table. I must have remembered the cooler from your surveillance photos – but I wasn't sure until I saw the pictures again. I figured if they were doing a drop at the river, it had to be at night; we never had any surveillance then because Carter wasn't there. It never occurred to me that there might be more than one of them taking a delivery until I saw what I saw tonight."

DeLuca looked at Bear and Milt. "You guys have anything to add? Does this make sense with what you've seen?"

Milt said thoughtfully, "Yeah, it does. We actually thought of the fishing possibly being a front for a drug drop, but we never saw a drop-off, and Carter never came back up from the river with anything more on his cart than he took down. We never dreamed they were switching out the coolers when he wasn't there. One other thing: Carter never goes down there on weekends, or very rarely. That must mean they stick to weekdays for their deliveries."

"That makes sense," said Bear. "There's less recreational boat traffic on the weekdays, and more police patrols on the water on the weekends, looking out for drunk boaters. The drug dealers probably steer clear of the weekends for both reasons."

DeLuca was frowning. "Funny that the boat had its lights on, other than when it was doing the actual delivery."

"Not really," said Bear, who had his own boat and liked to fish. "If the water patrol saw a boat with its lights out at night, they would flag it down for sure. If our delivery guys are out there with lights on, going slow, and trolling with a couple of poles out, they'd be hiding in plain sight. They'd look like night fishermen."

"It only took them a few minutes to drop off the coolers," said Jordan. "They were in and out, fast. The only weird thing was, I didn't see any money change hands. The coolers that they took on the boat were a stack of empties; it was clear that they were empty by the way they handled them. I didn't see the two men hand them anything else."

"They must be dealing with the money some other way," mused Bear. "It's pretty coordinated – it has to be a big operation."

"Okay," said DeLuca. "This is huge. The big question is, what do we do with it? Do we set up a raid for tonight and tomorrow morning and arrest the dealers? It would take six big dealers off the streets, and we would shut down that delivery system – their suppliers would have to come up with another system and work with new people. It would set them back for weeks, probably. Or option two is we try to track the boat back to where it came from and get to the bigger guys in the food chain."

"I vote for option one," said Milt. "That alone is a bust like this town has never seen before, and it's almost a sure bet. If we try to follow that boat, we might tip them off, and they'd shut the whole thing down. Then we wouldn't even get the dealers. We have enough on Carter to put him away, but the other guys – we've got surveillance photos and can probably figure out who they are, but if we don't catch them with the drugs on them, we'd have no case.

They'll say they were innocent fishermen."

DeLuca said slowly, "We're going to need help on this either way. We'll need help from the PBP, and we need to fill the Feds in on this. It's too big not to."

Bear said flatly, "If you bring the Feds in, you'll know what they'll say. They always want the big fish. They'll want to follow the boat. And I'll tell you right now; there's no way to follow that boat up the river with another boat without them seeing it."

"Unless," said DeLuca, "we track them by land."

Milt frowned. "That's impossible. The roads around the river don't always stay in sight of the water. And they may be coming to the drop area from who knows how far upriver."

"No," said DeLuca, "I said, track them by land, but not by car. We'd station people along the bank every mile or so, hidden. They'd watch for the boat and report in by phone or radio, so the next guy up the river could be watching for it when it gets close. We'd have backup in cars, but they wouldn't need to be right on the river; they'd only need to be nearby. At some point, that boat will need to come to land to get loaded up with drugs, and that's probably at some remote little launch area. There'll have to be a vehicle there to pick up the boat or deliver the drugs to it if they don't take the boat out of the water. At that point, our vehicles could take over, or maybe air surveillance, and they could track the vehicle back to where it came from."

"We'd need a lot of people for that," said Bear. His look of skepticism was fading. "But that might work."

DeLuca looked at Jordan, who had been sitting silently. "You're the guy who broke this open. What do you think?"

"I'm thinking about what Morrissey will say. The whole reason you've been tracking Carter all these months and letting him do his thing is to get to the bigger guys at the top. I think Morrissey is going to tell us to track the boat."

DeLuca nodded. "I think you're right."

And he was. When Morrissey came in, they briefed him over breakfast, and he agreed with Mike's plan to station men along the river to track the boat. He added, "We're going to need to bring the PBP and the Feds in on this – we'll need all the help we can get. But I'm making clear to the Feds that wherever we track them to, as long as it's within the state of Pennsylvania, we keep control of the case and get to call the shots. I'll get on the phone and set up a briefing and tactical session with the PBP and the Feds for this afternoon." He looked at Jordan. "Jordan, I don't need to tell you, this is phenomenal work."

"Bear and Milt did the legwork," Jordan said. "If they hadn't done such detailed surveillance work, I never would have connected the drugs with the fishing expeditions."

"Absolutely," said Morrissey. He looked excited. "This is a great team effort. And now, if you guys will excuse me, I need to make some phone calls. We'll shoot for a briefing at two."

After the meeting, DeLuca pulled Jordan into his office. "Morrissey was right – that was great work. You got yourself into Carter's house and back to where the drugs were, and you made a brilliant leap of logic with that cooler. Unfortunately, that's where the brilliance stopped. There was no way in hell that you should have gone down to that river by yourself last night. I understand that most of your experience has been undercover work, and you have to think for yourself and make decisions on the fly. But last night, after you left Carter's place, you were no longer undercover. You were a cop doing surveillance, and you should have followed procedure and called it in, and waited for some backup. What if they'd found you and shot you down there? You'd be dead, and no one would have known about what you found."

"They'd know," said Jordan. "I left a note concerning where I was going and what I'd found, just in case something happened."

DeLuca shook his head. "So, you thought of that possibility, and you still didn't call it in."

Jordan shrugged. "I didn't think there would be anything. It was a long shot. I'll know better next time."

"Yeah, next time, and next time. You take unnecessary risks, Bell. I want you to go home and think about that and get some sleep before you go to the bar tonight."

"But, the meeting with the PBP and Feds is this afternoon."

"You've already been up for more than twenty-four hours. Go home and get some sleep, and if you feel you must, you can come back for the briefing at two. You did some great work last night, but you need to think about what I said."

Morrissey held the briefing in a larger conference room over on the PBP side of the building. Jordan was back at the office at two, and DeLuca had directed him to stand in the back along the wall; they were trying to keep him under the radar, even from the other law enforcement agencies. He thought he knew why; he saw a familiar face across the room. Jonathan Wilkes, FBI Special Agent in Charge of the New York City office, was there, standing with the FBI SAC of the Pittsburgh field office, Brad Peterson. Jonathan Wilkes had led Jordan's assignment in New York. He was also one of the men who had advised that Jordan be moved to Pittsburgh, to a desk job, for a while. Well, Jordan was in Pittsburgh, but he sure as hell didn't have a desk job.

The room was buzzing. There was a large contingent of PBP officers and detectives, including their Special Deployment Division, the SWAT team, the River Rescue team, and Narcotics, and various other officers from their Investigations branch. There were other law enforcement agencies there, the FBI, the State Police, and an agent from the DEA.

In the morning, Morrissey had met with top players in the PBP and FBI, and they had agreed on a tactical plan. He kicked off the briefing, facing the crowd with Milt and Marty standing behind him. "As many of you know, our PDI agents got a significant lead from a PDI undercover operative last night concerning how large drug shipments are coming into the Pittsburgh area." At this point, there were some glances around the room, looking for the undercover operative. Most of the others were clueless, but a few of the PBP narc guys, the ones stationed in the house behind Carter's, looked at Jordan.

Morrissey outlined the plan for the surveillance mission, informed the group that they would break them into teams with team leaders, and gave a rough description of the task. He talked for several minutes and thanked the PBP for what they had contributed so far but made sure that everyone understood that the PDI was in charge. Jordan had heard most of it already, and when he heard Morrissey conclude, "We're about to make a historic bust, people, let's go do it," he pushed away from the wall and stretched. Enough talking.

There were nods and murmurs of agreement, and people got up and started to move. DeLuca had been sitting in the front row with Jen and Devon, and he stood up and joined Morrissey at the front.

Brad Peterson, Pittsburgh FBI, approached them, with Wilkes by his side. Wilkes said something, and they all looked across the room at Jordan, and then Wilkes motioned. 'Uh, oh,' thought Jordan, and he walked toward them.

As he walked up, Peterson was saying, "Now *this* is an operation. Gentlemen, this is Jonathan Wilkes, FBI SAC from New York City. Jon, this John Morrissey, head of the PDI West, Team Leader Mike DeLuca, and Agents Marty Beran and Milt Walecki." He looked at Jordan. "And this, I take it, is Agent Jordan Bell." Jordan gave him a nod.

Wilkes had dark hair shot with a few strands of silver and piercing dark eyes, and was tall and fit and carried himself like a general. He shook hands all around. "Pleased to meet you all. John, I think we met once in Philly, am I right?"

"Yes, Jon, how are you?"

"Good, thanks." Wilkes inclined his head as he shook Jordan's hand. "Agent Bell. Good to see you again." Jordan saw DeLuca shoot him a sharp glance and wondered if Wilkes knew that they had been using him undercover.

The head of PBP Narcotics, a man named Rick Ferriman, moseyed up, uninvited. He was good at his job but as slick as oil. He reminded Jordan of the used car salesman who had sold him his Impala.

Wilkes said, "I was hoping I'd see you here, Jordan." He said to the others, "Jordan worked for us in New York; I thought I'd heard he came out to work for you guys." Wilkes suspected; he was fishing, Jordan realized, and he was sure that DeLuca and Morrissey grasped that as well, but it went right over Bear's head.

"Yes, he did," said Bear. DeLuca tried to send him a warning look, to no avail; Bear kept talking. "He's the operative John was talking about, the one who broke open the case last night."

Wilkes gave Morrissey a quick sharp glance, but his grin broadened. "It figures that Agent Bell was behind that."

"Yeah, my people have been talking him up," chimed in Ferriman. He looked at Wilkes and Peterson. "Rick Ferriman, PBP Narcotics." As they gave him a nod, he looked at DeLuca and smiled, and it made him look like a snake. "You guys ever want to give Agent Bell a change of scenery, send him my way. He'd be a natural in Narcotics."

DeLuca gave him a nasty look and said, "We'll keep him for a while. He just got here."

Wilkes was studying Ferriman with a smile that barely hid his distaste. He turned to Morrissey and said, "John, do you and Agents Bell and DeLuca have a minute?"

It was a dismissal of the rest of the group. They drifted off, and as Wilkes moved over to a corner of the room, Morrissey and Mike and Jordan exchanged a glance and followed him. Wilkes turned to them and said, "About this case – the reason I'm here is that I do a check on any sizable busts, particularly for narcotics, human trafficking, and illegal weapons sales, and especially in the eastern half of the country. We think there is one outfit behind a large portion of those activities, someone who is in or near New York. We believe that the entity has operations across the country, especially in locations east of the Mississippi. Now, as you know, the opioid epidemic is rampant, and there could be anyone behind this drug delivery system you've uncovered. Still, when we see an operation as big and coordinated as this is, I check it out to see if I can pick up any similarities to other cases and to determine whether it might be connected to our case. If you see any ties to what seems to be a large organization during this investigation – or any other investigation that you pick up – I'd like to know about it. That case, coincidentally, is what Jordan was working on for us in New York."

He cleared his throat. "That brings us to Agent Bell. It was my understanding from David Sutter at NYPD that Agent Bell was to come out here, and the PDI was going to assign him to a desk job." He raised his eyebrows at Morrissey. "That doesn't quite seem to be the case."

'*Well, this is awkward,'* thought Jordan.

Morrissey said smoothly, "Sutter made that suggestion, but he didn't say to keep him at a desk, exclusively. Agent Bell took it on himself to take a look at the prime suspect's residence, was accosted by his lieutenants, and for his protection, pretended to be a street dealer interested in a buy. He made up an alias on the spot, and they took him in. It was too good of an opportunity to pass up."

Wilkes frowned and looked at Jordan. "What alias?"

"Not Moreno. I picked another name," said Jordan. "Juan Gonzalez.'

"And you're okay with all of this?"

"Yes, sir."

Morrissey said, "He's a goddamned pit bull with this stuff. He went off last night on his own to check out a lead. He didn't make us too happy that he did that, but he did, and now we're where we are today, ready to make a bust on a case that we've been following for months. He's not exactly conventional, but he sure makes things happen."

Wilkes said, "You realize that there was a reason we suggested desk duty; he got pretty close to the fire in New York. I'm not going to give out particulars, but we thought that he should stay off the street for a while, for his safety. Sutter didn't pass that on?"

Morrissey and DeLuca looked at each other, and DeLuca said, "Not directly. They made a suggestion but didn't tell us why. We're trying to keep him as low profile as we can."

Jordan spoke up. "It wasn't their fault. I went up to Carter's on my own. And I've been working out of my apartment, mostly, staying out of the limelight and away from the office."

Wilkes nodded. "Okay. I'll trust your judgment – but you need to be careful." He turned to Morrissey. "I've seen only a handful of undercover operatives as good as him over the years. I wouldn't want to see him get compromised."

"Neither would we," Morrissey assured him. "And we'll keep you informed of the results of this investigation; don't worry."

Wilkes nodded and shook hands. "Good to meet you, Agent DeLuca, and good to see you again, John, and Jordan. It looks like you have a first-rate team here. Let me know if I can help in any way." He strode over to SAC Peterson, who was waiting for him, and as they left the room, Morrissey said, "He doesn't know about Jordan's Goth assignment, does he?"

"I don't know how he would."

"Good, let's keep it that way. And tell Marty to quit tossing around Jordan's name."

He strode off and headed over to talk to the Chief of Police. DeLuca looked at Jordan. "Thanks for not throwing us under the bus." He paused. "Let's go back to our conference room and talk."

They went back down to the hallway to the conference room, shut the door, and sat. DeLuca said, "Well, we almost put our foot in it. I had no idea that Wilkes would be here, or even who the hell he was, until today. What's this stuff about keeping you off the streets for your safety?"

Jordan was silent, and DeLuca pressed. "Look, the way things have worked out, I'm for all intents your handler, at least when it comes to undercover assignments. It becomes my job to look after you, and I can't look after you properly if I don't know what I'm supposed to be protecting you from." He paused. "I'll be honest; I checked up on you. I called a buddy of mine who works at NYPD. He didn't know you and wasn't working on the same case, but he asked around. He called me back yesterday. He said there was a joint case between the feds and NYPD, and he thinks it's still going on because he had a hard time getting info. But he said he found out that some bust went bad, and an informant got killed, and right after that, they shipped you off to Pittsburgh. I need to know why."

"I'm not supposed to talk about it."

"I think we just did talk about it, with Wilkes. He said it was for your safety, but there can be more than one reason for that. The first one that comes to mind is someone is looking for you. The second one is that you witnessed or were involved in something bad, and you didn't pass your psych evaluation afterward, so that would make you a danger to yourself or others."

"I passed my psych evaluation," Jordan said. "They would have had to tell you if I didn't; you know that."

"Then, someone is looking for you."

"We don't know for sure."

"Does this person know your name?"

"No. Not my real name. We're reasonably certain that he didn't realize I was a cop, but we couldn't be certain. We don't know how they found the informant out, so we're just not sure."

DeLuca sighed and rubbed his face. "I don't know. Maybe we need to pull you out of these assignments."

"I'm fine," said Jordan. He leaned forward and looked DeLuca in the eye for emphasis. "We're on a roll, at least in the drug case. And I want a chance to find that break in the Goth case. They already pulled me out of New York. Don't do the same thing to me here."

DeLuca studied him. "You weren't singing that tune when I first proposed it. You looked freaked out, which makes me wonder about your mental state. Anyone can pass a psych evaluation if they want to badly enough."

"Yeah, well, I had some doubts, but I got over them. Trust me,

I'm fine."

There was a long silence, and DeLuca finally said, "Okay, but if you see anything off, or you don't feel right, I need you to tell me. I need you to promise me that."

"I promise."

"Okay, if I were you, I'd head back and get a little more sleep before you have to be in the bar tonight."

"But what about the surveillance mission tonight? If you take them down, I want to be in on it."

"No. We've got a freakin' cast of thousands working on this operation, and to be blunt, we don't need you. Where we do need you is in that bar, getting somewhere on the Goth case. Go home and get some rest."

CHAPTER FIFTEEN

Jordan woke at five Tuesday evening, after two more hours of sleep, still exhausted. Those two hours plus the four earlier that day didn't seem quite enough to erase the deficit from the night before. He sat up in bed and yawned and frowned. Yes, he was still tired, tired, and grumpy. No, make that tired and downright pissed off.

He'd just gotten a lead on a drug case that had been going for months – and not just any lead; a huge one, and they had cast him to the curb. He got to set up for the party, but he wouldn't get to attend. Instead, he was being exiled, sent off to Harry's bar. Not that the Goth case wasn't critical, but he wanted to be in on tonight's surveillance. It would be a massive team effort, a big deal, a morale-booster, a rush. And he wouldn't be part of that team; he wouldn't even be sitting on the bench. And damned DeLuca would be the star quarterback, calling the shots, getting all of the glory.

He rose, restless. He'd asked for computer work just days ago, but now he wasn't sure. He had the feeling that he was hanging on the edge of failure and success; if DeLuca decided to pull him out of his undercover work, he would have nothing. He wanted to be in on the hunt.

Well, Jordan thought to himself, he had a job to do tonight, and he'd better get his head back in the game. He'd been concentrating on the drug case so intently that the Goth murders already seemed like a lifetime ago. All of his Goth attire needed cleaning, so Jordan threw it in the washing machine at the end of the hall. He pulled up his computer, his personal computer this time, because he finally had it geared up to search the Dark Web safely, and went out looking.

He landed again on the True Goth site, his eyes running over Sammy Farineau's artwork on the edges of the pages. Scrolls and swirls, groups of lines shaped like waves and leaves, detailed and intricate, done in pen and ink, with color added afterward. Small pictures were interspersed among the designs, pen and ink drawings of random objects: a quill pen, a raven, a cat, an eye, a sword, and other figures dotted the margins. He opened some links in the table of contents and looked at the articles and the comments. Much of it was the same as before. There were a few additional items in the book and the movie sections, and one new music review in the music section. He ran through them and scanned the comments left by the readers. Nothing stood out.

He ended by reviewing the treatise on cutting again. It was the same thing he had read before, and despite the fact it was familiar, it somehow struck him as fresh and significant once again. True Goths cut. The words were bold; the writer was passionate about the subject. Passionate enough to kill? If he did one thing tonight, Jordan thought, it would be to get Sammy Farineau to tell him who was behind the True Goth website.

He threw his clothes in the dryer and microwaved the food that DeLuca's mother had sent home. He almost felt like not eating it on principle because he felt as if DeLuca's seemingly kind gesture on Sunday had been a betrayal of sorts, but he hadn't eaten lunch, and it smelled so good. He ended up wolfing it down, thinking of DeLuca's mother and her questions about Janine, DeLuca's ex-girlfriend. Well, Jordan could clear up those questions pretty quickly. They'd obviously broken up because DeLuca was a self-centered asshole.

The anger worked for him, he realized; there was an element of resentment and disrespect for authority in his Goth punk character. He would put that bad attitude to use tonight. He cleared the dishes, stacked up his work paperwork neatly, and slid it into his backpack. His badge was still sitting on the table, and he tossed it into his bag along with the paperwork. Cleaning the house helped clear out his head. Start anew; no clutter, no preconceptions. He needed some fresh eyes.

He showered and shaved and got dressed: black jeans, the long-sleeved black T-shirt he'd worn the night before, now clean, his black jacket with the chains, black boots. Hair stuck up in clumps with gel, earring back in his ear. The bruise on his face was fading, still there but much diminished in both size and color. And then Jordan Bell, the Goth, got his car keys and his personal cell phone and headed for Harry's. On the way, he stopped and picked up a pack of cigarettes and a lighter.

Suzanne Weir sighed. McCann and his crowd had commandeered the jukebox again, purposely picking songs that rankled. Darkness had fallen, the lights were on, and the place was busy for a Tuesday night; the usual Goth crowd was there, along with a few other Goths, poseurs, not fit to sit at the main table, or at least that's what George Lilt maintained. Everyone was there except the man she wanted.

Jordan had shown up at Harry's the night after the attack in the parking lot, but he'd looked as though he was in pain, uncharacteristically quiet, and beaten down. She was beginning to wonder if the attack had succeeded in scaring him away when there he was. He stepped into the doorway like he owned the place, and everyone looked, even if they didn't want to. They couldn't help it, her especially. He was so good-looking, so dark and dangerous – just her type.

Jordan strode across the floor with a swagger and went straight for the jukebox. He was back to himself, cocky and a little bad, exuding energy and electricity. Every man in that bar wanted to be him, she was sure. And she wanted to be with him.

She waited impatiently for him as he stood at the jukebox and put in his credit card, and picked out several songs. McCann's crowd gave him a sour look, but he ignored them and walked over to the table, and she pulled out a chair for him.

"There is still one of their songs in the queue, but then we'll get some real music," he said.

"Thank God," said Peter. "You look better."

Jordan smiled brilliantly. "I feel great. What's happening?"

"Not much," said Victoria, smiling. "Just hanging." She'd given up on him, Suzanne could tell. Victoria knew she was interested in him, and she was letting her have him – or at least make a try for him. Victoria was a good friend – she knew what Suzanne had gone through with Will McCann.

Suzanne just smiled at Jordan, and he smiled back at her. The night had just gotten a lot more interesting.

Jordan sat and observed for a while. Everyone in the crowd seemed upbeat, except for Sammy, who still seemed to be in a funk. Jordan started up a conversation with Suzanne, and she was flirting in a big way. He was intensely attracted to her himself and kept losing his focus, staring into her eyes, trying to decide if they were brown with gold flecks or hazel. He had to tear himself away to get his head back on straight and went up to the bar for drinks: soft drinks for both of them.

He leaned over the bar, watching Harry pour them, with McCann in the corner of his vision. Harry put the drinks on the bar, and as usual, Jordan gave him a more-than-generous tip. "How ya' feelin'?" asked Harry as he swabbed the bar with a towel.

"A lot better, thanks," said Jordan. He took a drink and said, with a jerk of his head toward McCann, "You've probably known him a long time. What's with him?"

"Will?" asked Harry. He paused in mid-swab. "He's pretty headstrong, but he's not all that bad. He's just got a short trigger, that's all, and I think you rub him the wrong way." He lowered his voice. "It was good of you not to press charges, although I'm not sayin' he didn't deserve it."

Jordan shrugged. "I'm not sure it was him. It happened pretty fast, and it was dark."

Harry gave him a smile that said he didn't believe one word he was saying. "He's pretty territorial about this place. I think it's all he has. Those friends of his like to act tough and make trouble; they aren't the type to stick by you when you're down."

Jordan raised an eyebrow. "I'll say he's territorial. He calls it 'his bar.'"

Harry lifted a shoulder. "Well, he's been coming here for a long time. He was the one who got the Goth group started coming here, back in the days when he was Goth."

"Why did he stop? Being Goth, I mean."

Harry shook his head. "I'm not real sure. I think he was living at home, and his parents read him the riot act and told him if he straightened up, they'd send him to college, and if not, he was out on the street. I'm not sure dropping the Goth stuff was part of the agreement, but it could have been."

Jordan glanced at McCann. He had a feeling that the 'going to college' bit wasn't going to work out well for him. McCann was only taking a course or two at a time and spending nearly every night in a bar. But he said, "That had to be pretty rough. Goth is a way of life if you're truly Goth. And then his Goth friends probably disowned him."

"Yeah, that happened. I think McCann still thought of this bar as his home away from home. He brought the Goth group here, after all, and they forgot that, looked at the bar as their place, not his anymore. It pissed him off, sure. So, he gathered up some of his college friends and kept coming here."

"And then Suzanne broke up with him."

Harry shook his head. "Not the way he tells it. He says he dumped her when he stopped being Goth."

Jordan frowned. That didn't jive with what Suzanne had told him, although his money was on Suzanne. He'd seen the way McCann looked at her. The statement about the bar being his was just a convenient excuse to stalk her. McCann probably circulated the story that he dumped her to assuage his hurt ego.

Harry said, "You were the straw that broke the camel's back if you ask me. Another Goth, and you walked in and acted like you owned the place, your first night here. I felt bad that you got beat up; that's not right in any book. But you are kind of a shit-disturber, aren't you? You pushed his buttons on purpose."

"Yeah," said Jordan, "maybe I did. I'll try to cool it, Harry. I don't want to cause you any trouble."

"Too late for that anyway," said Harry, shaking his head sadly. "Those poor kids who were murdered," his voice trailed off. He sighed. "I don't think I'll ever look at this place the same." He sighed. "A man's gotta live, though, and this place is all I've got. Me and Will; this is all we got."

Jordan thought that over as he walked back to the table. Even if Will had dumped Suzanne, which he thought was highly unlikely, he still had a reason for hating the Goth group; they'd made him an outcast. Reason enough to kill? How deep was his hatred? Undoubtedly, his future was looking bleak. According to Harry, Will was facing life on the street if college didn't work out. Complete ruin was lurking, and desperation could deepen his sense of injury. He could be taking that anger and fear out on the Goth community, the community that had dumped him when he went mainstream.

He set a soda down in front of Suzanne, and they sat and talked for a while. On the other side of him, Victoria talked with Sammy off and on. Peter and George had their eyes on the room, trading a short comment now and then. The music was loud, and it was hard to talk and impossible to hear anyone across the table unless they shouted. Even when seated right next to each other, he and Suzanne had to lean over and speak in the other's ear when they wanted to say something, and every time they did, she moved a little closer until finally, they were touching. She leaned over to say something once more, and this time put her hand on his thigh, and Jordan felt a current of electricity run through him. He'd never felt this aroused, this entranced by a woman.

He somehow noticed that Sammy was getting up from the table, feeling in his pocket for his cigarette pack. That was his cue. He excused himself, letting Suzanne think he was going to the men's room and followed Sammy to the back of the bar.

When he got back there, the rear door was settling into place against the rock used to prop it ajar, and Jordan carefully opened it and stepped out. Sammy was lighting a cigarette and glanced sharply sideways, but when he saw who it was, he relaxed and leaned back against the wall, his face forward. Not antagonistic, but not necessarily welcoming, either.

Jordan pulled out a cigarette and lit it, carefully inhaling so that he didn't choke. He looked forward out into the back lot, like Sammy, and blew out the smoke, and it made a wispy silver plume, illuminated by the faint glow of the street light.

Sammy said, "I didn't know you smoked."

Jordan shrugged. "I'm trying to quit. Sometimes I'll have one when I'm out, still. I get in the mood sometimes, you know?"

Silence descended. Sammy was holding his cigarette pinched between his thumb and his forefinger, and he took a drag. He glanced sideways and said, "Thanks for – uh – not hitting on Victoria."

Jordan shook his head and smiled. "You don't have to thank me. It was pretty obvious she's into you."

"Aw, c'mon." Sammy paused, flushing. "All the girls look at you.

You look like a rock star."

"No, they don't. And so what?" said Jordan. "That's shallow. You're an artist, which is beyond cool. Victoria's smart enough to see what matters."

Sammy averted his eyes again, but he was smiling. Jordan paused, took a hit. "I was on that True Goth site again, and I checked out your artwork. Awesome. It's so detailed; that had to take a long time to do."

Sammy inhaled, shrugged. "Kinda. It's not so bad."

"You said you helped put that site together?"

"Well, not really. Two other people run it. I just did some web pages, did the artwork, and helped set up some links."

"Two people?" Jordan frowned. "I thought there was someone called Darkness who runs it."

"Yeah, Darkness is one. The other person goes by Death. They put Darkness out there as the contact and the site owner. Death is more behind the scenes, does more of the technical stuff. The whole thing was Darkness' idea, but Death helped pull it all together." He looked troubled and spoke as if he wanted to dodge the subject. There was a noise behind them, inside in the hallway, and Sammy darted a glance backward, keeping silent until they heard the thump of one of the bathroom doors shutting.

"What is it, man?" said Jordan. "You seem uptight."

"It's just -," Sammy broke off, and Jordan waited. Silence often goaded people into talking to fill the void. Sammy took another drag of his cigarette and shook his head, distress in his face.

"There are these links in the artwork," he said finally. "Death and Darkness had me set them up. You click on some of the little pictures, and they take you to other sites. It's kind of secret. If someone writes in and wants more information on something, Darkness will respond, usually privately, and tell them which link to select. It makes the users feel like they're in a special inner group."

"That doesn't sound that bad."

"No, it's not," Sammy agreed. "But one of the links on the cutting page is a picture of a knife. For a while, it took you to a site on how to commit suicide." He looked at Jordan, his face somber. "The site proposed this one method: slitting the wrists lengthwise, deep cuts from the elbow down to the wrist. Word is going around that that was how Poppy and Jon died." He looked away and absently flicked ashes from his cigarette. "They took the page down, right before the murders started."

Jordan stared at him. Before the murders? "Do you think someone read that and got ideas from it?"

"Maybe," said Sammy slowly. "Or maybe it was one of them."

"Death or Darkness? Why do you think that?"

"I don't know," Sammy said miserably. "It's just a feeling, and some things that Death has said, off and on."

"You should report this to the police, man."

"Yeah, I keep thinking that, but if I'm wrong, I'll be screwing an innocent person."

"So, you know who they are."

Sammy nodded. "Yeah."

"Is it someone we know?"

"Yes."

"Who?"

"I can't tell you, man."

"Look, Sammy, I can't tell you what to do, but you should report this. If they didn't do it, there wouldn't be any proof, and if they did, well, they deserve what they get, right? You can tell the cops to not let on who told them. If Death and Darkness did this and you don't say anything, you'll be letting murderers off the hook. Maybe even causing someone else's death."

Sammy was silent, then he said, "I'm not sure it's both of them. I think it's only one."

"Okay, murderer, then. Look, man, I'll go with you if you want."

"That's okay. I know what you're saying. I'll go." He stubbed out the butt of his cigarette against the brick wall and tossed it into a plastic bucket filled with sand. Jordan, glad to be rid of his smoke, did the same, and they turned to go inside.

"I'm with you, man," said Jordan. "You want some moral support, just let me know." Sammy nodded, head down.

As they opened the door, they had to wait for others crossing paths in the small hallway. Peter was coming out of the bathroom, and George Lilt was going in. Either one could have been standing in the back hallway at some point during the conversation. Jordan tensed, wondering if they had heard anything, but their faces were bland, completely expressionless. It was loud inside, as well; it would have been difficult to listen to a conversation outside; a person would have to stand right next to the door with their ear close to the crack. They followed Peter's bulk back out into the bar, and Jordan sat down and forced a smile at Suzanne. Things were opening up, little by little. He had been hoping to get names himself, but if Sammy went to the police with them, they would be just as far ahead. One thing was sure; he couldn't push it anymore tonight. If Sammy didn't go in tomorrow, he could work on him tomorrow night.

Suzanne smiled at him and grabbed their empty glasses. "My turn," she said. "I'm having a real drink; you want one?"

Jordan raised his eyebrows. "I thought you didn't drink."

She shrugged. "I've been careful lately with what's been going on. And I don't drink a lot, anyway, because I have to drive home. But yeah, I drink." She smiled at him, teasing. "Come on, live a little."

Jordan hesitated and then shrugged. "Okay. Vodka and tonic."

He sat there and used the opportunity to observe George Lilt, who was coming back to his seat from the restroom, and Peter Martin. Neither of them looked out of the ordinary; they both wore a bored scowl most of the time, and those expressions hadn't changed. Jordan was reasonably sure that if the murderer was one of them, they hadn't heard Sammy's confession. He rolled the question around in his head and looked around the bar. Who was Death, and who was Darkness? Were they even in the room?

Suzanne came back with the drinks, and Jordan took a sip; it tasted strong. He wanted to ask her if she'd ever heard of True Goth, but he didn't want to bring the subject up at the table. When Suzanne suggested that they get out of there and go somewhere they could talk, he saw an opportunity. They finished their drinks, and as they walked out together, Jordan could feel the eyes of everyone in the bar on them.

Out in the lot, he glanced around, taking note of their surroundings. It was a beautiful summer night, and he felt a little buzzy, the combination of the cigarette and the drink. He smiled at Suzanne. "Where do you want to go?"

"Not a bar," she said. "And my place is kind of far, and it's not the greatest." She toyed with the chains on his jacket. "How about your place? Are you close?"

Jordan hedged. He was supposed to be backing off as far as Suzanne was concerned, and it sounded like she was trying to move things along. "I'm close, but my place isn't that great, either. It's apartment housing geared toward students."

She cocked her head. "I thought you worked. Peter said you did something with computers for the city."

"The state. I do, but I'm taking some more computer courses at Pitt. My fall class starts in two weeks."

She smiled at him. "Your place sounds fine. We can both drive. I can go home from there. I need to work tomorrow."

He smiled back – he couldn't help it, and said, "Okay. I live just over the Birmingham Bridge in Oakland. Follow me."

Once in his car and away from her intoxicating presence, his head took over, and he wondered how on earth he was going to handle it if she came on to him. Once this case was over, there was a chance that they could have a relationship, but not if he took her to bed tonight and lied to her about who he was. When she found out later that he was a cop, and worse yet, not Goth, she would feel betrayed, used. And, as DeLuca had pointed out, sleeping with a person close to the case wasn't professional behavior and could compromise the investigation itself.

His thoughts went to his apartment, trying to remember if anything incriminating was in sight. Thank God he'd put away his case notes and his badge. His gun was in the bedroom on the nightstand. He'd need to hide it, too, not because they would end up in there, he told himself firmly, but because she might need to use the bathroom, and the only access to it was through the bedroom.

They pulled into the parking lot and got out of their cars, and he smiled at her. She smiled back at him and slipped an arm around his waist as they walked to his apartment, and he thought, "Oh boy, here we go."

CHAPTER SIXTEEN

Jordan glanced around quickly as Suzanne came through his apartment door. No work files, no badge. They were in his backpack, which was on the floor over by the living room wall. Nothing in the room said 'cop.' He took in a breath.

Suzanne was looking around and said, "Okay, I think my place is actually better." He flushed, and she smiled at him teasingly. "Oh, it's okay."

Jordan pretended to be offended. "Just okay?" Then he grinned. "I know, it kind of sucks. I can afford better, but it's close to school, and I like to live below my means."

"Spoken like a wise man," said Suzanne.

He offered her a drink, and she asked for bottled water, which was fortunate because that was all he had, other than coffee. As soon as he got it for her, he excused himself and went back into his bedroom and hid his Glock in his nightstand drawer. Then he pretended to use the bathroom, flushed the toilet, and washed his hands.

When he came back into the living room, she was sitting on the sofa, and he sat down near her but not quite next to her. That didn't work; she bounced up and moved over to his side, and leaned against him, sighing. "This is much more comfortable. And we can even hear each other."

He put an arm around her shoulders, not wanting to seem stiff. "Yeah, this is much better."

"So, we were talking about books the other night. What's your favorite?"

"Hmm, I'm not sure I have just one. I find authors I like, and then I read whatever they've written. I like Poe; I like Dickens. Herman Melville. What about you?"

"I like the classic Gothic romances, but I prefer the newer Goth writers." She sighed contentedly. "I like books in general. Working in a library is my dream job. Except for the pay, maybe."

They talked about books and music for a while, then Jordan jumped up, grabbed his laptop, and returned to the sofa. "Here, I found something the other day." He brought up the True Goth site and turned the screen so that she could see it. "Have you ever seen this before?"

She frowned thoughtfully. "Maybe. I think Peter or George brought their laptop to the bar and had it up one day, or something like it. I've never been on it myself." She cocked her head. "It looks interesting; can I see?"

He handed her the laptop, and she clicked through the web pages. "Wow, there's some serious stuff in here. How do you get to this?"

Jordan hadn't realized he was holding his breath and let it out quietly with a surge of relief. Suzanne couldn't be Death or Darkness; she barely recognized the site. "It's actually on the Deep Web," he said. "You need a special browser to get there."

"Oh, right, the computer guy," she smiled. "Well, maybe if you come to my place sometime, you can hook me up to that browser. I would like to look at this."

They were close, and she looked up at him, her face right in his, and he stared into her eyes as she leaned forward and kissed him. It was a gentle kiss, her lips were soft and warm, and he couldn't help himself; he closed his eyes and deepened the kiss, threading his fingers through her hair, the silkiness of it another sensory revelation. He knew he shouldn't be doing this, but she was like a drug…

Eventually, he managed to pull away.

"What's wrong?" she asked.

"Nothing – it's good – it's too good. I don't want to ruin anything by moving too fast."

She flushed to the roots of her hair and put a hand over her face. "Oh, my God, this is embarrassing. I'm sorry, I just thought," she broke off, flustered.

He pulled her hand down gently and kissed her. "You thought

what I thought. It's just; well, I think we have potential. Maybe we should ease into this. It will make it more special when it does happen."

She put a hand up and stroked his face, and murmured, "*You* are dangerous." She leaned forward and gave him another kiss, soft, quick, almost chaste. "Okay," she said. "I agree. Let's take it slow."

Jordan nodded, disappointment and relief both fighting for dominance. He reached out and touched her face, thumbed her jawline gently. "I would hate to mess this up."

"Me too. So, I'm going to head home. Plus, we both have to work tomorrow." She smiled when she said it, but he could sense that she was upset. Damn it.

He walked her out to her car and leaned on the door as she got in. "See you tomorrow night. Be careful going home."

"I will. Good night."

He leaned down, kissed her, shut the door, and then stood there and watched her drive away.

Death was up early the next morning. He had followed Jordan Bell home from the bar the night before and found out where he lived, noting with disapproval that Suzanne Weir was with him. He watched for a while. Weir had brought her car and hadn't stayed long. Now, Death was again parked down the street, waiting. At around seven, his patience was rewarded. A ride pulled up, and he saw Bell come out and get in the car. They drove off, and Death followed at a safe distance. Down I-376 to I-279 and over the Fort Duquesne Bridge, into North Side.

By this time, his suspicion was becoming a conviction, and he followed the driver to Western Avenue. The man dropped Bell off at a side entrance of the Pittsburgh Bureau of Police headquarters, and Bell ducked inside. Death couldn't be sure why he chose that entrance, but he had an idea. He was now convinced that Jordan Bell was an undercover cop. It would make sense that Bell didn't want to use his vehicle or go into the PBP headquarters via the main entrance.

He called Darkness on the way home. "Yeah, he's a cop. I saw him go into the Pittsburgh Police headquarters this morning."

"We need to take care of Sammy as soon as possible. You heard them last night. Bell was trying to talk him into going to the cops.

We can't let Sammy do that."

"Okay," said Death. "Here's what we'll do."

Jordan had decided that morning to come into the office to report out in person. He had some important news – that was his excuse – but more than that, he wanted to remind DeLuca that he was part of his team. He was intensely curious as to how the surveillance had played out, and he wanted a face-to-face with DeLuca, both to get an update on the drug case and to deliver his latest report.

The office was empty, and the PBP offices had looked sparser than usual that morning, but then Jordan remembered that it had been a late-night operation, and many of them were probably making a late start. He kicked himself for not thinking of that but then reminded himself that it was just as well. It was best to get in early enough to beat any press that might decide to show. He made some coffee and had a cup, and plugged his laptop into its docking station to type up a report for the evening before.

His work cell rang at 7:40, and DeLuca was on the line. "Where's my report, Bell? Did you sleep in this morning?"

"I'm at the office," said Bell, coolly. "Waiting for you."

There was a split-second pause, and DeLuca said, "Okay, I'm about ten minutes out. We'll meet when I get in."

Fifteen minutes later, DeLuca strode into the office with a quick nod. He plugged in his laptop and got a cup of coffee, and called to Jordan, "Okay, come on in."

Jordan rose, grabbed a pad of paper and a pen, walked over, entered the cubicle, and sat.

"Why don't you grab a cup of coffee?" suggested Mike.

"Already had one, thanks." Jordan kept his words short and sat up straight in his chair. He wanted the man to know that he was still angry about being left out yesterday. "How did it go last night?"

DeLuca logged into his laptop, typing, and said, "You didn't miss much." He glanced at his screen, then at Jordan, and sat back and sighed. "It was a long night."

"Why, what happened?"

"Well, we're still not sure how they're getting the drugs on the boat. We picked it up early – an officer saw them putting in down at Monongahela, sometime after eleven, about twenty-two miles south of the drop spot. We watched them come up the river, and sure enough, at around 2:20 a.m., they made their drug drop at the place that you saw, near the bridge. Then the boat went back downriver and pulled out. They had used an SUV with a boat trailer to put in and had just parked them while they were gone. After they pushed off, the officer went over to the vehicle and got the plates and the VIN number; it's registered to a Gerard Mote. When the men on the boat got back, the vehicle support guys tracked them back to a small house on the outskirts of Monongahela, and the suspects just parked the SUV and the boat in the driveway and went inside. It turns out that Gerard Mote is renting the house."

"What's the plan? Raid the house?"

DeLuca shook his head. "We're going to watch it. We still need to see how they're getting the drugs; we didn't see them pick anything up on the way up. The owner of the house is cooperating. We'll get him a warrant today, and he'll give us a key. Tonight, when they go out on the boat, we're going to get inside and see if we can find anything. If not, we'll get back out, and they shouldn't be the wiser."

"There's one other thing," he continued. "We timed them between watchers, and there were several slow-downs, which we attributed to them either fishing or pretending to fish or maybe crossing the locks. There was one slow-down that was a lot longer, though, right around Elrama, about seven miles into their trip, and there's no lock there. We're going to get some eyes on that stretch tonight."

Jordan eyed him thoughtfully. "You think that they might be picking up the drugs en route."

DeLuca nodded. "Maybe they just fished there longer, but it's a possibility, yes. The alternative is that someone is delivering the drugs to the house, and Mote and his guys are loading the boat before they hit the river. We have people stationed out by the house, watching it today, and tonight we'll have a high-altitude drone overhead, as well, courtesy of our friends at the FBI, one that can fly high enough that they won't see it. One way or another, we're going to find out."

"Well, that's something," said Jordan. "That you found the house."

"Yeah, it was," said DeLuca. "How did your night go?"

"Interesting. I got Sammy to open up about the people who run the True Goth site."

"People. As in plural."

"Yes - but here's the thing. Sammy is suspicious of one of them."

DeLuca sat up in his chair. "Suspicious? Concerning the murders?"

"Yes. The True Goth website only calls out one moderator, who goes by the online name of Darkness, but Sammy said another person does much of the behind-the-scenes work, who goes by the name of Death. He told me that there were some special links in the artwork on the pages that lead to other sites, and he was disturbed by one of them. It was a page on how to commit suicide, and the recommended method sounds like the murder M.O. It described making deep cuts along the length of the forearms. The odder thing was, the page was taken down right before the murders started."

"*Before* they started," repeated DeLuca, considering the implications of that.

"Right. If Death and Darkness are the murderers, that would mean they were getting rid of incriminating evidence before they started killing. It's possible someone else entirely saw it, and it gave that person ideas, but the timing of its removal is suspicious."

"Does he know the names of these people?"

"Yes. Sammy wouldn't give me the names of either of them, but I'm still trying to talk him into it. I also told him to go to the police. He said he would, but he may have just been trying to shut me up. Sammy said he thinks it's only one of them, based on some comments that the person told him, but I'm also pretty sure it's someone in the group at the bar."

"It seems as though there might be more than one. If the murderer transported each victim in the victim's vehicle to the body drop points, he'd need someone to pick him up after he left the body and the car."

"Maybe. Or maybe the killer hiked away from the drop point and then called for a ride."

"Okay, I guess I could buy that."

Jordan said, "Anyway, I asked Sammy if Death and Darkness were anyone we know, and he said yes."

"So, Death and Darkness are part of the Goth group, and he thinks one of those two is the murderer."

"Maybe part of the Goth group, or maybe not. He just said yes when I asked if it was someone we know, and that could include

McCann. McCann is a long shot, but he was Goth at one time. I talked to Harry, the bartender, last night, and he thinks McCann gave up his Goth beliefs under duress from his parents. They threatened to kick him out on the street if he didn't shape up and go back to school. It's possible that he could be Death or Darkness and is operating the site as a secret outlet for his Goth beliefs."

"Yeah, that does sound like a long shot," said DeLuca.

"Yes, it does, but we can't forget motive. Of all of them, McCann seems to carry around the most hatred. Harry thought that McCann felt abandoned by the Goth group and was pissed off because he had discovered the bar, and they took it over. And, of course, there's the breakup with Suzanne Weir. But even putting that aside, he is obsessed with that bar. He calls it 'his bar,' and there is no disguising the fact that he hates that Goth group."

"Sounds unstable."

"That thought occurred to me, too. I didn't want to rule out that McCann might be one of the two, Death or Darkness. The only problem with that is the fact that McCann hates the Goth group, so would he want to partner with one to run True Goth?"

"Maybe he's established a truce with one person. Maybe they started the site together before he went mainstream."

"Yes, possibly. The other possibility is that it's not McCann at all, and both of them are part of the Goth group. Peter Martin and George Lilt would be the most likely suspects in that scenario."

"It could be one of them and one of the women," mused DeLuca. "If, as Sammy thinks, only one of them is the killer, the other could be innocent."

"Yes, but I don't think it's one of the women. True Goth espouses cutting – self-harm – and I think every one of them cuts except Victoria. I don't see her as a moderator of the site. She's not a deep thinker. I don't see her writing any of the articles. And I don't think it's Suzanne because I showed her the site on my laptop last night, and she didn't seem familiar with it. Suzanne said she thought she had seen something like it on George or Peter's laptop, but she wasn't sure. And she didn't know how to get to it; it didn't sound like she even had a way to browse the Deep Web, so Suzanne couldn't access it if she wanted to. However, even if one of the girls was the other moderator of the site, the evidence doesn't indicate that they were the murderer. For one, they're physically too small to pull it off, and for another, at the river where they dumped Jon Hurly's body, there was a footprint down at the water's edge that forensics thought was a man's print, roughly size eleven."

DeLuca pursed his lips. "And how did Suzanne come to be looking at something on your laptop?"

Jordan tried not to look defensive. "Because she came to my apartment last night."

"I thought we talked about this."

"We did, and relax, we didn't sleep together, if that's what you're implying," Jordan shot back.

He told DeLuca about Suzanne's suggestion that they go somewhere to talk, and her request to go to the apartment, and the fact that they chatted for a while and she left. DeLuca watched his face as he explained, but he didn't push the issue. Instead, he said, "Okay, so we're down to three that we consider the most likely, right? In what order would you put them?"

"George Lilt, first," said Jordan. "He's a Goth snob. He's arrogant and judgmental, he's a deep thinker, and the guy is obsessed with Goth culture. He's also big enough to pull off the killings." He paused, considering. "I guess I'd put Peter second, just because it would be a lot more likely that he's working with George, and he's big enough physically, and I know for sure he's a cutter. He strikes me as lazy, though. Not motivated, and he doesn't seem to be as much of a snob about Goth stuff as George, so of the two, if only one of them were the murderer, I'd pick George. And third would be McCann, for the reasons we've already discussed."

"Mmm. You're heading back to the bar tonight?"

"Yes, unless you have something else for me to do."

It was a not-so-veiled suggestion that he wanted in on the drug case. DeLuca sat and thought for a minute. "Maybe. We need Sammy to cough up those names. If you can get that information from him in time, you could probably come along with us tonight."

"I'd like that."

"We're doing some planning sessions today; you might as well sit in on them since you're here. They're going to start at ten, and we're breaking at two and sending everyone who will be out tonight home for some rest."

He paused and threw Jordan a bone. "That was good work last night, Bell. We're making some progress. Make sure you get your report to Jen and Devon, so they can get up to speed." Jordan nodded and rose to go, and DeLuca said, "Bell, what I did yesterday wasn't just to punish you for going against procedure. Part of it was for your protection. We're trying to keep you low-profile."

Jordan looked back at him and paused for just a split second. "I understand," he said, "I appreciate it," even though he wasn't sure that he did.

CHAPTER SEVENTEEN

Jordan microwaved his dinner and tried to get his head in order.

He had met Devon and Jen in the morning after meeting with DeLuca and updated them on what he had found the night before. The Goth case was their case, after all, just as the drug case belonged to Marty and Milt. None of the investigations belonged to him. He was just the guy who went out, took all the risks, and came in with all the information. He was in name DeLuca's partner, but in reality, he was just his lackey. He was nobody.

He had stayed for the meetings on the drug case that day, sitting in the back with Devon and Jen. DeLuca ran the sessions and made all of the decisions, although he consulted with the Feds, Chief Goodman, and Milt and Marty, who were up at the front with him. The star quarterback, having his moment, tossing a few scraps to the others. As Jordan watched him, however, he had to admit to grudging admiration. DeLuca was a natural leader. He managed the discussions calmly, listened to all of the inputs, and then made a decision, quietly but firmly defending it against any objections, and then moved on to the next topic without giving ground. Although Jordan was still disgruntled, he realized after watching DeLuca that the man didn't treat him any differently than he treated the Chief of Police, the FBI SACs, or anyone else. DeLuca didn't have much patience for negativity or excuses, but Jordan had to admit, he was fair. Unfortunately, that meant that as much Jordan hated to admit it, DeLuca had likely made what he considered a reasonable decision when he sidelined him the evening before.

The group meeting was much smaller than the day before, with mainly the top brass and the team leaders, which was why DeLuca had probably allowed him to attend. Jordan stayed in the back and kept his mouth shut, like a good rookie.

He did talk to Jonathan Wilkes, SAC from New York, during one of the breaks. The man seemed glad to see him and asked several questions; Jordan got the impression Wilkes was testing him, somehow. He liked Wilkes, though, and at least the man had shown an interest in him. For some reason, however, the encounter made Jordan uncomfortable. Of course, anything that reminded him of New York had that effect. He had gone home that afternoon feeling unsettled. DeLuca had put him in his place, which had been a blow to his self-confidence, and he could feel the old familiar anxiety that he associated with New York starting to percolate. Jordan the Goth was not anxious or insecure; he was cocky and self-possessed. He needed to get into character before he went to the bar.

He got dressed, and the visual change helped him put on a little attitude, but as he drove to the bar, he still felt uneasy. He tried to shrug the rest of his funk off as he walked into the bar at around eight that night.

"Hey," he greeted the Goth crowd as he pulled up a chair. Everyone was there except Sammy. They looked somber, he realized, and Victoria looked near tears. "What's wrong?"

Suzanne looked at him, pale and subdued. "No one can reach Sammy. Not since at least five this evening."

"What?" He looked around the table as if expecting one of them to tell him differently.

Peter said, "Victoria tried to call him at five to see if he wanted to go out to dinner before hitting Harry's. He hasn't called her back. We've all tried to text him. Victoria went to his place and knocked on his door, but he didn't answer, and his car wasn't there."

Jordan could feel his stomach twist. If something had happened to Sammy because he'd confided in him… he thought back to the evening before when he and Sammy had emerged from the rear parking lot into the hallway. Peter and George had both been in the hall, one coming out of the restroom and one going in. And there had been a noise in the hallway even before that. One of them, or maybe someone else, could have overheard them. Had the conversation put Sammy in jeopardy? He said, "Maybe he lost his phone. It happens."

"That's what I said," said Suzanne, laying a comforting hand on Victoria's arm. "He may have lost his phone and is out shopping for a new one. We're going to wait until eight-thirty. A lot of nights, Sammy didn't get here until then. Then Victoria's going to call his mother and see if she has heard from him."

Victoria had her hands on the table, twisting and untwisting them. "It's just that with everything that's happened lately…," she stopped, blinking back tears. "And people can borrow a phone – I can't believe he wouldn't use someone's phone to call one of us; let us know he's okay." Her voice broke on the last word.

Suzanne put her head down and rubbed at her temple, surreptitiously wiping away a tear, trying not to let Victoria see her.

"I don't think we should wait," said George, giving voice to Jordan's thoughts. "I think we should call the cops."

"I wonder if Harry has a number," said Jordan. "Maybe he has a card from one of the investigators or something. I could go ask him who we should call."

"Would you?" asked Victoria, her voice quavering.

Jordan was on his feet. "Sure. You said you tried Sammy around five?"

"I texted him at four-thirty," said Peter. "He didn't answer that, either."

"I know he did freelance artwork, but does he have any other job? Would he be at work?"

Victoria shook her head. "He works from home, mostly."

"Okay," said Jordan. "I'll be right back."

He stopped at the bar first and told Harry what was happening, and asked Harry if the cops had given him a number to call for emergencies or questions. Harry gave him a card, as Jordan thought he might, and he held it up for the others to see, pulling out his cell phone as he walked outside to make the call. The card was Jen's. As he walked past the bar area, Jordan noticed that McCann was nowhere in sight. Sometimes McCann didn't get there until later, but his absence prompted questions.

Outside, Jordan hesitated. He wanted to call DeLuca, but he

knew DeLuca was still in planning sessions and doing readiness checks with their support teams. He glanced around to make sure there were no eavesdroppers and called Jen. "Jen, it's Jordan."

"Yeah, Jordan, what's going on?"

"I'm at the bar -,"

Her voice cut in anxiously. "Are you okay?"

"Yes, yes, I'm fine, but we've got an issue. Sammy Farineau is missing, and he's been out of contact with his friends since at least 4:30 this afternoon."

"Oh, not good."

"That's what I thought. Can you get someone over to Sammy's house to do a welfare check? And maybe get out a BOLO for his vehicle?"

"Yes, right on it. We'll also ping his cell phone. I'll call Devon, and we'll come into the office and get it rolling. Let us know if he shows up, and I want you to check back with one of us when you leave."

"Okay. Victoria Jensen has his mom's number – she's going to call her. I'll let you know if we come up with any info on this end."

"All right – and Jordan, be careful. If something happened to Sammy because someone heard you and him talking last night, you could be a target, too."

"Yeah, I'll be careful." That thought hadn't occurred to him until she said it, and he realized that maybe he should have brought his gun. He didn't feel afraid, though, not for himself. He felt ill. If Sammy died because of him, it would be like Lucaya all over again.

He went back inside, gave the card back to Harry, and walked over to the back table. Victoria was on her phone, standing in the back hallway.

Suzanne said, "She's talking with Sammy's mom. His mom is freaking out – she hasn't heard from him for two days. Victoria told her that he was here last night, but that's the last time anyone here has seen him."

"Harry had a card from one of the cops," said Jordan. "Agent Sandberg. I called her, and she said they were going to send someone over to Sammy's place and put an alert out for his car. The agent seemed like she was taking it pretty seriously. She said she'd get this going right away."

Victoria came back and told them what they already knew, that Sammy's mother hadn't heard from him, and Jordan let her know that the police were out looking for him. Then they settled in to wait, no one even caring that the college kids had commandeered the jukebox again.

It was a grim hour before Victoria finally cracked. During that time, Jordan went over the night before in his head. He even pretended to go out back for a smoke to get a feel for how well he could sense someone on the other side of the door. He propped it open, and before stepping outside, put an ear to the crack himself. It was possible, he decided. Someone could have heard their conversation without actually putting themselves in view. As Jordan stood outside and pretended to smoke, another horrible thought came to him. Suzanne had gone home with him last night. If his conversation with Sammy had put him in jeopardy, what about Suzanne? Was she a target now?

When he came in, everyone at the table was standing. Victoria was tearfully telling the group that she had to go home, and please call her if they heard anything. As Peter and George stepped over to hug her, Suzanne stepped aside to Jordan. "I'm going home with her," she said. "She shouldn't be alone. I'm going to drive her car and leave mine here and get a ride back to pick up my car later." Her eyes were misting, and she tried to blink back the tears. "This is so scary."

Jordan put an arm around her. "I'm going to go with you to make sure you get there all right. I'll drive your car, so you have it with you. I can get a ride back here. I'll wait here with George and Peter. Don't drive home alone tonight; stay with Victoria."

"Okay, I will," she said. "I can go home in the morning. I don't need to work until the afternoon tomorrow."

She gave Jordan her car keys and Victoria's address, a residence on the border of Dormont and Greentree, in case Jordan lost them on the way there. Victoria lived at her parents' home, but they were traveling, and the house was dark when they pulled up. Suzanne parked the car in front of the house, and she and Victoria got out, and Jordan parked Suzanne's car right behind Victoria's. He went inside the house first, checked it thoroughly, and then called for a ride. Suzanne came out on the front stoop to wait for it with him.

He put an arm around her and planted a gentle chaste kiss on her forehead. "Hopefully, everything is okay," he said, even though it was becoming more apparent, as time went on, that it was not. "Stay inside and lock the doors. If you see or hear anything that bothers you, don't try to check it out. Call 911 right away."

She looked up at him, her eyes wide. "You're scaring me."

Jordan shook his head. "We don't know what's going on here. Just be on the safe side. If you want, I'll stay here tonight and sleep on the sofa."

She hesitated, then shook her head. "That's nice of you, but we can manage. We'll lock the doors and stay inside, and keep our phones close."

He hugged her and handed over her car keys as his ride pulled up. "Okay. I'm going back to the bar. Call or text if you need me or if you can't sleep and want to talk. If we don't talk again tonight, send me a text when you get home tomorrow."

He was back at the bar before ten and went inside to let George and Peter know that the girls were safe at Victoria's house. McCann had arrived and treated Jordan to his usual scowl. Jordan looked around the bar, taking all three of them in. George Lilt, Peter Martin, and Will McCann. One of them, he was sure, was the murderer. He felt useless sitting there. Was it too late to get in on the raid?

He walked outside and got DeLuca on the phone. "I'm out," he said. "Can I still get in on tonight?"

There was a hesitation, then DeLuca said, "We're just heading out now. We'll meet you at your place with your gear."

DeLuca drove, Bear sat shotgun, and Jordan piled into the back with Milt. It took a while to get down to Monongahela, and on the drive down, Jordan filled them in on Sammy's disappearance and let them know that Jen and Devon were following any developments. They received the news with grim faces, and their expressions did nothing to make Jordan feel better.

A little over an hour later, he crouched in the brush at the end of a field along with DeLuca and Milt and Bear, plus two PBP narcotics people, watching the rental house. It was getting close to eleven-thirty. The lights were on inside the house, the porch lamp was on outside, and there was activity.

The dwelling was a small two-story with white siding that sat on a dead-end road on the outskirts of Monongahela, out by Mingo Creek County Park. The rental property was one of three homes, spread well apart, maybe a quarter of a mile between each of them. It was the last house on the street. Not great if the drug dealers needed to make a quick getaway, but private.

There was a light on, illuminating the gravel driveway, and the men, three of them, were outside now, throwing a few things in the SUV – small coolers maybe, the kind that could hold a six-pack or sandwiches, or maybe bait. No big white foam coolers. The house had been staked out by PBP narcotics all day, and there had been no one coming and going. The only delivery had been from a guy dropping off two pizzas at about seven. The two evening-shift narcotics cops had come on around then, replacing their daytime counterparts, and their watch lasted until 3:00 a.m.

Getting in there hadn't been easy, and all four of them were sweating; the night was warm and humid. When they'd gotten as close as they could by vehicle, DeLuca had parked his SUV off Route 88, and they'd hiked in through the woods. They couldn't get any closer than about a hundred and fifty yards away because there was an open field between them and the house.

"It looks like they're all outside," said DeLuca, watching through his field glasses, as the last man exited the house. One light had been left on, inside. "One, two, three. They're all in the vehicle."

The SUV pulled out slowly, bumping and bouncing on the gravel driveway, with the boat bobbing behind on its trailer. They watched the red taillights go down the road and gave them a good fifteen minutes before they jogged across the field, leaving the two narc guys behind to keep eyes on the area. They were all in dark PDI jackets, and they were dripping by the time they reached the house. DeLuca felt for the key in his pocket. They had served the warrant to the owner earlier in the day, a former cop who was more than happy to cooperate.

"Shit," panted Bear. "Why'd we have to do this in August?"

They paused a minute to catch their breath, and DeLuca said, "I'll go through the front with the key; Milt, you cover me as we enter. Bear and Bell, watch the back, just in case there's someone else in there. I'll let you in after we're clear. Milt, you go up the right side, and I'll go up the left, and look in the windows and check out what you can as you go. If either of us sees anyone in there, we abort.

Everyone clear?"

They nodded, and DeLuca and Milt split up. Bear took a position at one back corner, and Jordan took a post at the other, and he watched DeLuca traverse the left side of the house. DeLuca kept his head down, raising it quickly as he reached each window to check inside. There was a light on in the kitchen, and some of it filtered through to the rooms in the front of the house. Then DeLuca disappeared around the corner, and a few minutes later, they saw him in the kitchen. The back door opened, and DeLuca waved them inside.

They went through the house room by room, splitting up, taking their time. They paid particular attention to the basement, looking for evidence of any modifications to the walls; there were none. Also, to the attic, Jordan, the lightest of them, got that job; they hoisted him up through the small trap door in the hallway. He reported that no one had been up there in months. There was nothing up there but some old junk, and the only footprints in the dust were his.

The owner had assured them there were no false walls or hidden closets in the house, so what they saw was what they got. And what they got was nothing. There was no sign of drugs, nothing incriminating in any paperwork lying around, which showed that Gerard Mote paid all of his utility bills. The only mind-altering substances they could find were a twelve-pack of beer in the refrigerator and a half bottle each of whiskey and tequila on the kitchen counter. The house was surprisingly neat; the renters weren't even guilty of poor housekeeping.

After an hour, DeLuca called it off. They walked around checking to make sure they hadn't left any signs, and Bear and Jordan went out the back, and Milt locked the door behind them. DeLuca and Milt went back out the front, the way they had come, and DeLuca locked the front door on the way out. They stumped back to the surveillance point, and DeLuca called the command vehicle on his radio, which was parked well upriver, closer to the drop point, and tonight, it was staffed by the two FBI SACs, Peterson and Wilkes, and Chief of Police Goodman.

Deluca spoke into his phone, putting it on speaker. "DeLuca, reporting in. We got nothing out here. The house was clean as a whistle. I think they must do Bible study for entertainment every night."

Goodman answered back. "Roger that. We think we found out why. Our guys across the river from Elrama are getting some activity."

They exchanged glances. The most protracted slowdown the night before had occurred at Elrama. Goodman continued, "There's a gravel road off Bunola River Road that cuts across the tracks and goes down to the river, just north of Raccoon Run. There's a place where the bank is low, and the river is shallow enough that a boat can put in. Our guys spotted a truck there; it pulled in about a half-hour before the boat showed up. They're loading the boat out of that truck right now."

"Do we have vehicle teams in place?"

"Affirmative. Ready to go – but we've got the FBI drone, too. We're relying on that, and the vehicles will keep their distance."

"Okay, roger that. I think we can call off the next team scheduled to watch the house. We'll get out of here and try to follow. Out."

DeLuca looked at the narcotics team. "It doesn't look like you guys are going to see anything here, but we'll keep surveillance on for your shift. Stay until it looks like they're in for the night. We'll call the next team off. Thanks, guys." Then to Milt and Bear and Jordan, he said, "Let's go. If we hurry, maybe we can pick up the back end of the tail."

They set off at a trot through the woods and stopped to rest once, and DeLuca called the house owner on his cell phone. "It looks like your renters are clean, in more ways than one. Not only did we not find drugs, but they're doing a nice job keeping your house up. Do us a favor, though. They are still persons of interest in this case, so we need you to keep quiet on this. We'll let you know if we need to take action against them."

"You mean *when* we need to take action against them," muttered Bear, mopping his brow, as DeLuca ended the call. "I can't wait to nab them and our merry band of drug dealers up in town."

"I can't wait to see where that damn truck is going," said Milt.

DeLuca set off again at a trot. "Well, we better move. We've gotta get out on the road and find the quickest way across the river."

As it turned out, they didn't end up that far behind. Back out on 88, DeLuca called in again, and Goodman informed him that the truck was headed south along the river on the other side, on Route

136. DeLuca took 88 back toward the river and through town, coming out on Route 837, which also ran south along the river, only on their side. They could look across and see taillights on Route 136.

"Maybe one of our pursuit vehicles," offered Milt.

Between Monongahela and Donora, the river took a big bend, and they made up some time because they were on the inner loop of the curve. They were nearing the Donora Monessen Bridge, which DeLuca had planned to cross to get to the other side - and so, apparently, were the people on the other side.

"I'll bet they're headed for 70," said Jordan.

DeLuca called in on the radio. "DeLuca here. We're on the road, getting ready to cross the Donora Monessen Bridge. We need the positions of the pursuit team and the truck and a description of the truck."

A voice came on. "Copy that. This is FBI Agent Rhodes. We're right across the river from you on 906. The truck just made a left on the Vance Dei Cas Highway. We've got two vehicles here, one Taurus and one Impala; you're going to fall in behind us as you come across the bridge. The truck is an Isuzu NPR box truck, medium-sized, PA plates. Black cab, and painting on the vehicle's side that says 'Miller's Amish Furniture.' We're keeping back – the drone's got eyes on it." He instructed the drone operator to patch in DeLuca's radio to give him updates, and they crossed the bridge and fell in behind the pursuit vehicles.

As pursuits went, it was an easy one; the drone did all of the work. The truck took the Vance Dei Cas Highway to Interstate 70 and headed east, and they kept well back, nearly out of sight. At New Stanton, the drone operator informed them that the truck had switched over to Interstate 76 east, the Pennsylvania Turnpike. Then Jen called DeLuca's cell phone, and, frowning, DeLuca hit call and put the phone on speaker. "Hi Jen, it's Mike. You're on speaker, and we're on the road; I've got Milt and Bear and Bell in here."

"Hi, guys. I'm not going to hold you up. I imagine that Jordan has already told you that Sammy Farineau is missing. No one's seen him since he left the bar last night. I want to let you know, we've got a BOLO out on Farineau's vehicle, and we had someone go to his house and check it out. He wasn't there, and neither was his car; no sign of foul play. The last place that his phone pinged was his house, at about noon. His parents haven't seen him since Sunday."

Bear shook his head. "That's not good."

"Agreed. We're still hoping that Farineau will turn up, but it's concerning. Devon and I have been monitoring this from the office, but we may head home soon. I told the PBP to call me immediately on my cell phone if they find anything. I'll call you with any updates."

"Okay, thanks for the info."

DeLuca disconnected the call, and Bear shook his head. "I don't like the sound of that." He looked at Jordan. "You're going to need to watch yourself. We have to assume that someone overheard your conversation with him. If they went after him, they might be after you, too."

DeLuca said, "The funny thing is, Sammy didn't cough up the names. We still don't know who he suspected."

"Maybe the murderer doesn't know that," said Milt, hunched forward in the back seat. "He might have heard part of the conversation, but not all of it."

Bear said, "On the other hand, they may know that he hasn't talked yet, but they're afraid he might."

"Good points," said DeLuca, but then the radio cut in and informed them that the truck had exited the highway at Somerset and had gone north on Route 281.

Agent Rhodes came on and said, "Advise caution ahead. We're dropping back after we get through Somerset. It gets pretty sparsely populated in a hurry."

A few minutes out of Somerset, the drone operator reported that the truck had pulled off on a gravel side road. They were not too far from the Flight 93 Memorial, constructed to honor the flight that had gone down in the September 11 attacks, and they had crossed the Flight 93 Memorial Highway when Agent Rhodes came on the radio again. "We're going to drive up just short of that gravel road and send a team in by foot to take a look."

"We'll go in," said DeLuca. "We're already geared up."

They pulled the vehicles over on a nearby side road to get out of sight and reconnoitered with Rhodes. The drone operator came on the radio. "They pulled down a dead-end gravel road on the other side of 281 from you, about two klicks down; the road is maybe three-quarters of a mile long. It drops down in a small valley, and there's a large corrugated metal building there. If you stick to the right of that road on the way in, there are plenty of trees; you'd be hiking in cover the whole way. However, I'd recommend cutting across 281 directly opposite from where you're at and going straight in through the woods. You'll end up on a hill; you might get a better look, with less chance of detection."

"Roger that," said DeLuca. "Out." And to Bear and Milt and Jordan: "Let's go."

Another three-quarter-mile brisk hike through the woods, and they arrived panting and sweating at the top of a hill, looking down on what appeared to be a small furniture manufacturing outfit. DeLuca scanned the area with his field glasses. The building had corrugated metal walls and was flanked by the gravel road and a gravel parking lot, and sat in the middle of a small depression, surrounded by hills. There was a light on one corner of the roof, illuminating the lot. There was only cover on the south side, the side they were on, which was forested. The other hills were mostly clear, fields of grass that glimmered in the moonlight, dotted here and there by small stands of trees. There were four trucks parked in the lot, and yellow light spilled out from a door on the building's east side. As they watched, another delivery truck came trundling down the road, another late-night delivery.

Milt clapped a hand on Jordan's shoulder. "Kid," he said, "I think you just hit the jackpot."

CHAPTER EIGHTEEN

They found Sammy Farineau the next day.

His car was discovered in the lot of a small municipal park just south of the Pittsburgh International Airport. Local police called in the plates after noticing the car at about eight in the morning and deciding that someone must have parked it there overnight, against park regulations. That tied them into the BOLO notification, and they alerted the PBP, who called Jen.

DeLuca called Jordan into the office and tore himself away from the drug investigation long enough to ride out with Jordan, Jen, and Devon. The drug team was in the middle of planning a complicated raid that they intended to carry out that evening, and they would need to catch up when they got back. A third Goth murder, however, merited all of their attention.

Devon drove, and the ME van followed them. Jordan was quiet on the trip. He spoke briefly at the beginning of the ride, detailing his time at the bar the night before, but then lapsed into silence. He felt tired, dragged out.

They pulled into the parking lot, surrounded by lush green trees and invisible from the road. The local police were waiting for them there, the trunk of Sammy's Honda already pried open.

Farineau was lying on his side in the trunk, in a fetal position. His right shoulder was facing up, and his left forearm was extended, revealing his wrist. His long sleeves were pulled up to his elbows, and they could see the cuts on his left arm – old crosswise cuts, most of them healed scars, with maybe one or two new marks – and fresh long deep slices from the elbow to the wrist. As with the other murders, there was a conspicuous lack of blood. Jordan took one look and then stepped back and let the rest of them in. He walked over and leaned against Devon's car, close enough to hear the conversation, but he looked away, across the parking lot.

The rest of them glanced at him, and then Devon said, "No attempt to hide the body this time, other than temporarily."

Jen said, "Jordan thought that the first two victims were meant to be found. I think I agree with him." Jordan could see her shoot him a glance out of the corner of his eye, encouraging him to get involved in the conversation, but he ignored her.

"Yeah, but this is different," said Devon. "He didn't even attempt to make it look like someone was trying to hide the body."

DeLuca said, "He was in a hurry. He didn't have time to plan this out; he had to get to Sammy before he decided to go to the police." He bent and looked at Sammy's arms. "No ligature marks this time. He must have knocked him out and cut him while he was unconscious. He still wants us to understand that he did it, though, because he stuck to the same kill method."

"The question is," mused Jen, "why would the names of who ran the Goth site be incriminating? I mean, there was the fact that the subsite described the murder method, but that in itself wasn't incriminating. By itself, it wouldn't hold up in court."

"Maybe it's not the method that they wanted to hide. Maybe it's motive," said DeLuca. "If we zeroed in on who Sammy suspected and started digging, would we find another motive hidden under there? I need you guys to do the same in-depth research that you did for McCann, for George Lilt and Peter Martin. Track their cell phone records the nights of the murders -,"

"Already done," said Devon. "We got warrants and did that yesterday after Jordan gave us his theory that they were among the most likely suspects. Each night of the murder, they went straight home from the bar, and their cell phone records showed they stayed there, or at least their phones did. We ran it on the girls, too, to be thorough. None of their cell phones moved around after they got home, and they all reached home before the times of the murders."

DeLuca shook his head. "I guess we may be barking up the wrong tree, and it's someone else entirely. But I don't think so. The fact that someone took down the True Goth subsite before the murders and that Sammy was killed while he was considering turning in the real names of the people behind True Goth ties it into that website somehow. It may be that the killer is smart enough not to take his cell phone to a murder scene. I want you to keep digging; get us some background on Martin and Lilt. And maybe we'll get lucky with forensics."

Dr. Angela Washington, the ME, had approached during their conversation, working her hands into gloves. "If you've finished viewing the victim, I should get started," she said.

They stepped back, DeLuca nodding at her, and he glanced back over his shoulder at Jordan. "Give me a minute," he said quietly to Jen and Devon.

Jordan leaned against Devon's car, hands in his pockets, staring off into the trees as DeLuca approached. He didn't acknowledge DeLuca, who said, "You okay?"

Jordan kept his voice flat. "Yeah."

"It's not your fault, Bell."

Jordan's only response was to squint at the trees and shake his head, his jaw working. DeLuca turned and looked back at Jen and Devon and gave his head a jerk toward the vehicle.

On the way back, DeLuca got a phone call from Morrissey and filled him in. "Yeah, it was Farineau, all right, looked like the same M.O. Drug the victim, and cut them, although this time the victim wasn't restrained, so we think he was still unconscious while he was murdered. I think the killer was in a hurry – I think Farineau's death wasn't part of his original plan." He listened for a moment. "Yeah, okay. Will do."

He hung up and said, "Morrissey wants all of you in the planning sessions for the drug raid today. He wants the whole team there when it goes down."

Devon said, "He wants to make sure the PDI gets the credit for it on the news. The more people running around with PDI jackets on when the cameras are rolling, the better. Oops, my bad, did I say that?"

"Well, it isn't going to hurt his chances for re-appointment, that's for sure," said DeLuca. "It won't hurt the governor any either. And by extension, it also doesn't hurt any of us. And don't complain; busts this big don't come along that often. This takedown is one you'll look back on."

"I'm not complaining, trust me," said Devon. "Bring it on."

Jordan didn't acknowledge the conversation; he just stared out of the window at the morning traffic. He'd been itching to be a part of the drug bust, but now, even though DeLuca had explicitly invited him, it didn't seem as important as it had been. Not when Sammy Farineau was lying dead in the trunk of a car.

Tactical sessions for the raids took up the rest of the day. Jordan tried to concentrate on the planning sessions as best he could, but he was fighting anxiety again, almost as bad as the day DeLuca had proposed he go undercover at the bar. He could feel a panic attack creeping around the edges of his consciousness, waiting for an opportunity to pounce. It had happened again; he had used someone, he had pulled him in and caused him to become a target, and the man had died because of it. First, Lucaya, and now Sammy.

The planning sessions gradually piqued his interest, however, and as the day wore on, he got more absorbed; they were a welcome diversion. The top planners, DeLuca, Morrissey, Chief Goodman, and the two FBI men, Peterson and Wilkes, discussed the sequence of events. If they took down the furniture warehouse too early before the truck left for the evening, the men on the boat wouldn't get the night's shipment. They would know something was up and would probably notify the dealers at the fishing hole, who would be expecting a delivery. That would impair the chances to pull off a bust at the fishing hole, the drug drop site.

If, on the other hand, they hit the fishing hole first, if they didn't subdue the men on the boat and the men on the bank immediately, one of them could call while the bust was proceeding and warn the people at the warehouse.

"There's no way around it," said DeLuca. "It has to happen simultaneously. We'll have the PBP manage the bust at the fishing hole, with some FBI assistance if they want it, and as soon as the bust starts to go down, they can contact the team at the warehouse, and we'll hit it at the same time."

Wilkes said, "Maybe I can help here. I might be able to get my hands on some equipment to jam cell phone signals at the warehouse."

"Who is calling the shots at the warehouse?" asked Peterson.

"We are, of course," said Morrissey. "This is a PDI case. The warehouse is in Pennsylvania, so we still have jurisdiction. We will welcome help and suggestions from the FBI, and we will also need some local and state police assistance. I also have offers of help from the U.S. Marshal's office and the DEA."

Peterson didn't look entirely happy with that, but he didn't have an argument; the Bureau had agreed in advance that this would remain a PDI case as long it didn't cross state borders. The group decided that Peterson and Goodman would handle the bust at the river drop, and DeLuca would helm the raid on the warehouse, with Wilkes' assistance.

Morrissey looked at Chief Goodman and said, "You might be able to pull off a second bust in the morning when the four daytime dealers show up for their haul, provided the word doesn't get out first. We have one request: we want to keep Drayvon Carter on the loose."

Wilkes, Peterson, and Goodman all frowned, and Peterson said, "Why?"

Morrissey looked across the room at Jordan. "He's why. Agent Bell still has an in with Carter. After the dust settles on this raid, the people behind it will try to re-establish drug deliveries via another method. If Bell is on the inside, he can help us understand any new plans. Also, as big as this bust is, it's only half of the puzzle. The money is the other half. It's not going back on the boat. We still have no idea how the money gets back to the provider of the drugs. It has to be a completely different delivery system, and we need to know what it is. A guy on the inside doesn't come along often – we don't want to throw away this opportunity."

Peterson nodded thoughtfully. "I can see that."

Jordan was sitting with Jen and Devon; he felt them staring at him, along with the rest of the group. DeLuca and Wilkes were both studying him; eyes narrowed speculatively. He fought the urge to shift uncomfortably and returned their gaze.

"Okay," said Goodman. "We'll hit Carter for a traffic violation on the way there. It'll hold him up long enough that we'll have the others in custody before he gets there. Then he won't wonder why all the others got arrested and he didn't. He'll simply think that he got lucky."

Morrissey nodded approvingly. "Good plan. Okay, let's split up, two groups: one working the bust here in Pittsburgh, and the other at the furniture warehouse. Get your plans together, and we'll meet back here in two hours, so both groups understand each other's plans. Then we need to get the troops in here and give them their assignments. We've got roughly twelve hours before we need to pull this off."

After the meeting, DeLuca grabbed Jordan, pulling him aside before the detailed raid discussions started. "You're coming along with me tonight, but you'll need to go into the bar for a while first. I have the feeling that they'll all gather there once the news gets out about Farineau. It would look odd if you weren't there. If, for some reason, they aren't there, then go ahead and leave and get some rest. I want you to head back home now until you have to go out. You look fried."

Jordan frowned. "What about my assignment in the raid? How will I find out what I need to do?"

"You're still a rookie, Bell. Your assignment in the raid is to stay back with me while I command the field and to watch and observe how the tactical teams carry it out."

Jordan shook his head. "I'm capable of participating. I'm not going to sit there like the team mascot."

DeLuca leaned in close, his eyes on Jordan's, and said, "How many times have you been to the firing range since you started here, Bell? Not counting the day that I took you for testing?"

DeLuca had him. Jordan said quietly, "None. But I have been going to martial arts training every week."

"That's commendable, but it's not enough. Our opponents won't be inviting you to a wrestling match; they're going to have guns. Your performance on the range that day was marginal, and I doubt it's improved since then. You will stay back with me, and I'll give you the details on the way out there. Be back here tonight promptly at 11:30, and you'll be issued your gear for the raid."

Jordan set his jaw, but he kept his face neutral.

"And Bell," said DeLuca, "one more thing. I need your head in the game for both of these assignments tonight. If it's not, I don't want you out there, either at the bar or at the raid. It's not safe for you or anyone else. I want you to tell me right now if you think there's a reason you shouldn't go to either assignment."

Jordan's chin came up, and he looked Mike directly in the eye. "No reason. I'm fine. I'll proceed as ordered, sir."

DeLuca nodded. "Good. See you tonight."

Jordan planned to get to the bar early that night because he intended to leave early to get downtown for the raid. He got dressed, thinking that all black was never more appropriate. He was heading down to his car at around six when he got a text from Suzanne.

"We got word on Sammy. He's gone. We're all meeting at Victoria's house tonight, instead of the bar," it read. "See you there."

He picked up food on the way, sub sandwiches, because his mother had taught him that was what people did when they went to a wake. The group might be hungry. It wasn't as if they could order bar food at Victoria's house.

When he got there, he found that others had had similar ideas. He put his sandwiches down on the kitchen counter next to a green salad, a macaroni salad, two pizzas, and four large bottles of soda and went to hug Victoria.

Her face was blotchy, and her eyes red from crying. She looked much younger without the elaborate eyeliner, dark lipstick, and caked-on mascara, and Jordan thought, prettier, despite the swollen eyes. "I'm sorry," he whispered in her ear and thought to himself how she would hate him if she knew he was the reason for Sammy's death.

They all sat and talked for a while, and the others told stories about Sammy. Jordan didn't have that history, didn't have much to contribute along those lines, and he eventually went into the kitchen and got the girls something to drink and then went back and got one for himself. Suzanne followed him and went straight to him, and he put the soda down on the counter and held her for a long minute. His back was against the countertop, and she pressed into him, almost every inch of her body plastered against his. He ran a hand down her hair, and when they parted, there was a wet spot on his shirt, and Suzanne wiped at it with one hand while she wiped her eyes with the other. "Sorry," she said, her voice trembling.

He placed a gentle kiss on her forehead. "It's okay," he said softly.

She said, "The other deaths were bad; they were sad, too, and scary, but Sammy's been with us from the start. He was one of Will's friends back in the day. It was him, Will, and George, who started coming to the bar first. Then Peter. Then Sammy met Victoria and invited her, and she invited me. Jon Hurly came later, and none of us knew Poppy that well. But Sammy…we've all known Sammy for so long, and that makes it hard for the rest of us. And Victoria, well, she and Sammy dated, off and on, for probably three years. I can't imagine how bad this is for her. It's just never going to be the same."

Jordan thought about that. The initial three Goths at the bar had been Will McCann, Sammy, and George. Could they have started the True Goth website? As unlikely as it seemed for Will to be involved in it, he could still be running it with George, pretending to be mainstream on the outside and sticking firm to his Goth beliefs on the inside. True Goth…

Suzanne was saying, "Maybe I'll take some of this food out there, so they'll eat," and Jordan came out of his thoughts and went to help her. She carried the sandwich tray and headed for the living room, and as he picked up the pizza boxes, the edge of one of them caught his plastic cup, upending it on the countertop. Luckily it clattered into the sink, and most of the mess went down the drain. He grabbed a paper towel and mopped up the rest, tossed the cup, and then just stood there for a moment, leaning on the counter with both hands. He felt clumsy, out of sorts, overwhelmed; the anxiety and fatigue were getting to him.

On the way back out to the living room, he glanced at George Lilt, whose typically sour face was a deeper shade of bitter today. If George or Peter or McCann were running the True Goth site, which of them would be the likeliest to be a murderer? On the surface, with all of his anger issues, it would seem to be McCann. But maybe there was another motive there, somewhere. Something that would tie in someone else.

He sat with them for a while longer, and at around nine, he made his apologies for leaving, mumbling something about needing to go in early the next day. He had a raid to get to.

CHAPTER NINETEEN

The area around Somerset was beautiful; Jordan had been there before in the daylight. The green rolling hills made an idyllic scene, and the nearby Flight 93 Memorial gave it the aura of a shrine, elevating the area to something otherworldly. God's country. And in the middle of it squatted a front for a big drug trafficking operation, like a tumor, a blot on the landscape.

In the nighttime, the grass on the hills glowed silver in the moonlight, and the stands of trees looked black by comparison. Jordan had ridden out with Wilkes, DeLuca, Marty, and Milt. They had met at a spot about ten miles away with the entire team; everyone outfitted in dark-colored regulation clothing, flak jackets and helmets, and weapons ranging from service handguns to automatic weapons. Jordan had his Glock but had strict orders from DeLuca not to use it except in an emergency. It was his first time in a bulletproof vest. It felt odd: stiff and bulky.

The group was organized into teams and included local law enforcement, state patrol members, DEA agents, and a couple of U.S. marshals. All of the PDI group was there, and Jordan thought to himself how strange they all looked in their gear, and Milt looked the most different of all. Take him out of his old-fashioned suit and cover his slicked-back hair with a helmet, and he looked younger somehow, mean and hard. They all looked hard and dangerous, even Jen. Jordan felt like a novice, a fish out of water.

They went over final assignments and the method of approach. There would be two groups, one stationed on the forested south ridge that DeLuca, Jordan, Marty, and Milt had reconnoitered the night before. Milt and Marty would command that team. The other group, led by DeLuca, would be stationed directly across the small valley, on the north ridge, which was even higher in elevation but primarily covered with grass, except for a small stand of trees near the top. Wilkes would stay nearby on the side road with the vehicles and another FBI agent, and they would manage the cell phone jamming equipment and coordinate the drone support. More local police waited in nearby towns with transport vehicles and ambulances in discreet locations but at the ready.

"About the cell signal jammer," said Wilkes, addressing the team, "It has a one-mile radius. We'll be working with radios exclusively because of it. And if you get a runner, you need to make sure they are stopped. If they escape and get outside the one-mile radius, they'll be able to use their phone. If they get word out, it won't affect the bust going on at the drug drop tonight because that will already be underway, but we may lose our ability to carry out that morning bust of the drug dealers and maybe other possible busts that we may determine once we get inside this warehouse. You need to be sure to keep everyone contained within that one-mile radius until we have them in custody and confiscate their phones."

DeLuca went over some last instructions. "It's going to take those of us on the north side longer to get in place, but there will be a wait involved for both teams. I need to get the signal from Pittsburgh that their raid is about to begin. Agent Wilkes will activate the cell jammer at that point, and then we will move in. For those of you stationed on the south side, you know your chain of command; Agent Walecki is in charge, seconded by Agent Beran, both of them reporting through me. On the north side, I will be in charge, along with Agent Amery, from the DEA. Agent Wilkes will be using our radio frequency to keep us updated on the drone reports. Is everyone clear on their assignments?"

He looked around at nods. "Okay, the drone operator is going to make sure it's clear for us to come in on 281. The south team will pull off just before the road to the warehouse and hike across from there. The north team will proceed to another pull-off down the road to go in from the other side. Make sure all vehicles are parked so that they are out of sight from anyone traveling on 281. Team, good luck. Let's go."

Even though the drone operator had called all-clear, the drive there on Route 281 was tense; if a truck left the warehouse, it would come across their convoy and would likely ruin the element of surprise. There was a sense of relief as the vehicles reached their hiding places and they parked, but Jordan felt tension ramping up again as they jogged across Route 281 and through a tree line into an area of grassy hills. The north team had to climb three of them, heading south, until they reached the incline next to the warehouse. They gathered on the north side of it just below the crest, out of sight of the warehouse itself, and the team spread out across the hilltop and took their positions. Jordan followed DeLuca the rest of the way up the hill to set up the command post in the small stand of trees at the top.

From there, they could see the warehouse below. There were trucks in the lot, and light spilled out of a large garage door. There were no windows in the building, and the only exits were on the east and west sides of the building. The plan was for the teams to move down the hills on the north and south sides. They would then swing around toward the entrances and shut them down, with the bulk of the teams pouring through the garage door on the east side. There was a single man door on the other side of the building, and a smaller second group would take up positions on the western corners to cover it.

All team members were to advance on command, all except DeLuca, who would oversee the operation from his vantage point on the hill, and Jordan, who would, well, watch. There was no doubt, being there was better than being left behind, but the assignment was humiliating. He had felt eyes on them as they were going up the hill; it was a walk of shame, and he was glad when they reached the cover of the trees, and they were out of sight of the rest of the team. As they waited, Jordan's anxiety increased, and as the reason for it hit him, his discomfort amplified; the raid reminded him of the police takedown of the warehouse in New York. Then, he had been on the inside instead of outside, but the situation was similar. Just as in New York, he was standing by, a non-participant, waiting for the raid to start.

The teams were in position by one in the morning, and a minute or so before two o'clock, DeLuca and Wilkes got cell phone messages that the bust was going down at the river drop point. Wilkes and an assisting agent familiar with the equipment, both of them stationed across Route 281 near the vehicles, immediately started the jam of the cell phone signals, and DeLuca got on the radio and said, "This is the command post. The raid is a go. Repeat, the raid is a go. Teams, start your advance."

Jordan stood by DeLuca's side in the trees and watched, sweat beading on his forehead in the summer night, as the teams crept down the grassy slope, dark blobs against the moonlit landscape. The north team reached the bottom, and across the way on the south side, Jordan could see figures emerging from the trees, faint and ghostly in the moonlight. They were converging on the building, the penetration team collecting near the east entrance. In seconds, they would be ready to go in. And at that moment, the unexpected happened.

The teams were still moving when the man-door opened on the west side of the building, and a man stepped out and lit a cigarette. The teams meant to cover the west side of the building were not quite in place yet and couldn't see him, but the drone operator and DeLuca could, and DeLuca said into the radio, quietly, "Man out on the west side of the building."

They weren't sure if the man heard the crackle of the radios carried by the men or footsteps as the west team hurried their advance to get around the corner, but suddenly his head came up. The man pounded on the door and shouted something before running straight ahead into a small group of trees. There were shouts inside the building, and the large door on the east side slowly began to shut. "Go in, breach, now!" yelled DeLuca into the radio.

The closest team members on the east side ran in, ducking under the closing door and yelling commands to the people inside, directing them to put their hands up. The door started going up again almost immediately as one of the team members found the control, and then shots rang out. On the west side, a few team members had followed the man who had fled into the brush. The others on that side of the building instinctively ducked as bullets pierced the corrugated metal walls from the inside out.

DeLuca's attention was riveted on the action below, listening to the feed on the radio, and didn't see the man break from the cover of the trees and dodge to another clump closer to the north slope. From his vantage point, Jordan could see the men searching for him; they moved through the trees in the other direction, southwest, toward the gravel road. He glanced again at the warehouse; the shots had quieted, but there were still shouts inside as the men tried to get the people inside to stand down and drop their weapons. Jordan had a sudden flashback of New York: the shooting, the horrific noise, the support team pouring in from the exits, and Lucaya lying there on the floor. He shook his head to rid himself of the image, and the man in the clump of trees emerged again, making a break for it up the hill, about sixty yards to their right.

"Mike!" said Jordan urgently. If the man made it to the top of the hill, he'd have a considerable head start and possibly a good chance of getting away and outside of the range of the cell phone jammer before they caught him.

DeLuca held up a hand, ignoring him, listening intently to the radio. "Okay, roger that. Any casualties? Okay, great job. We'll get some medical support."

Jordan edged away as DeLuca talked, still watching as the man scrambled up the steep slope. The searchers were far below, moving along the gravel road; Jordan and DeLuca were now the only ones in a position to apprehend him. The man was halfway up, and Jordan knew that they couldn't wait any longer. He took off along the face of the slope, trying to head off the man before he reached the top. Behind him, he heard DeLuca shout his name. The man heard it, too, and his head whipped around. Jordan pulled his Glock. In the moonlight, he could see dark hair, possibly Hispanic features. He yelled, in English and then in Spanish, "Halt! Freeze right there, or I'll shoot!"

The man stopped and whirled toward him, and behind Jordan, DeLuca yelled, "Gun! Bell, get down!" At that moment, another flashback of the warehouse crashed into Jordan's head, the vision more real than the hillside he stood upon, and he stumbled to a halt, shaking his head again, fighting for clarity as bullets whizzed around him. He blinked hard, and reality returned. The man began to move, but he got off another shot as he did so. Jordan heard a sound behind him, a half grunt of pain, half exclamation, and whirling back around again; he saw DeLuca go down.

"Bell, get down!" DeLuca roared, and Jordan finally dropped to the ground, and as he got his gun in front of him to shoot, the man swiveled and fired again. There was the sound of bullets smacking the dirt to his right, and then the sharp cracks of DeLuca's gunshots behind him, and the man tumbled and rolled to a stop. Jordan jumped to his feet and ran over to him, and as he got closer, he slowed, moving cautiously, gun extended. The man was on his side, eyes closed, moaning and clutching his thigh, a dark stain blooming on his light-colored jeans. His weapon had landed two feet from his hand, and Jordan picked it up and ran back to check on DeLuca.

The enormity of what had just happened was beginning to dawn on Jordan as he reached him, and he landed on his knees next to DeLuca, who was sitting up, wincing, his right hand on his upper left arm, blood seeping out between his fingers. "I'm sorry," stammered Jordan. "Are you okay? He was going to get away -,"

"Shut up, Bell." Others were running up the hill now, drawn by the sound of gunfire. "I'm fine. It's just a scratch." Marty Beran, despite his bulk, got there first.

"Aw, shit," he said. "Boss, you're hit. Let me see." He pushed in between them, and Jordan stood up, out of the way. Bear bent over and looked at the wound. "Okay, not too bad. You've got a nice gash, and there's a good amount of blood, but it's skin deep; nothing a few stitches won't fix."

"Yeah, I don't think the other guy's so lucky," said DeLuca. His voice was tight with pain, but he was as calm and controlled as ever. "Bell, does the man need help?"

"Yes," managed Jordan. "He was hit in the leg; his thigh." He stood by helplessly, feeling like an idiot, as DEA Agent Amery pulled out a first aid kit and handed some bandages to Bear, who began to bind up DeLuca's arm. Agent Amery grabbed the bag and trotted over to the wounded man. Jordan still had both guns in his hands, the man's handgun and his own Glock, and Milt reached over and gently pried the other man's weapon from Jordan's hand.

Milt said, "That's your Glock, right? Whose gun is this?" He held up the handgun.

Jordan looked at his Glock as if he'd never seen it before and put it back in its holster. He hadn't fired it, not once. Instead, he had frozen, like a deer in the headlights. He flushed. "It belongs to the suspect. I went over and made sure to disarm him."

Milt nodded, not unkindly. "Good thinking. Okay, this is a justified shoot; we'll need this for evidence."

It then occurred to Jordan that DeLuca could have been killed; it was a matter of inches, and the bullet would have hit his head instead of his arm. Even a substantial wound to an arm or a leg would be bad news way out here, especially if the bullet hit an artery. His knees went wobbly, and he went over to a fallen log and sat down.

DeLuca was eyeing him sharply. "You okay, Bell? You didn't get hit, did you?"

"No, I wasn't hit."

DeLuca looked at Milt. "You should get back down there."

Milt nodded. "I will. Everything's under control down there. I put Jen in charge while we came up here. It ended up being pretty easy. One idiot started shooting, and he got one in the shoulder and quit. The rest of them gave it up almost immediately. At least a third of them were sleeping when we hit it. You guys got more action up here than we did. There are about a dozen of them. They're already sitting along the wall with their hands cuffed behind them, waiting for transport." He grinned, his teeth gleaming in the darkness. "There's a shitload of stuff down there, boss. I guess a big truckload came in today. I've never seen anything like it. It's downright insane."

"Okay, we're coming down."

Milt nodded. "We've got medics on the way in. They'll take care of the two wounded men. We'll get one to look at your arm when you get down there."

He took off at a trot back down the slope. Agent Amery stayed with the wounded man, and Bear accompanied DeLuca on the way down, walking alongside and keeping an eye on him. Jordan trailed behind like the hired help, carrying DeLuca's radio gear, humiliation in every step.

A yellow pool of light spilled out of the big garage bay doors as they approached, and as they entered, the scene was almost enough to put the incident out of Jordan's mind. He stood, staring, with the rest of them.

"Damn," DeLuca said aloud, and Bear grinned.

"I know," said Bear. "It's something else."

Jordan watched the news feed of the bust from his apartment the next morning. Morrissey had made sure that his team stuck around for the cameras that showed up in the morning – that is, all of them except Jordan. Wilkes and DeLuca insisted that Jordan be out of the area before then to avoid the risk of being seen on the national news.

He had caught a ride back home at about four in the morning with Jonathan Wilkes and an FBI agent and had somehow managed four hours of sleep before a dream, vague and disturbing, woke him. Once Jordan was awake again, there was no going back to sleep; the events from the night before made sure of that. He got up and made coffee and watched as the cameras panned the warehouse, picking up his team members and the stacks of heroin bricks on tables behind them.

Mike DeLuca was the hottest thing on the national news. Every news station wanted an exclusive interview, but DeLuca only agreed to one for use by all networks. The agreement was that the story would not run until after eight a.m. to avoid jeopardizing the one remaining piece of the bust, apprehending the morning fisherman. That had happened four hours ago now, at six a.m., and the operation had been successful. Chief Goodman's team had wrapped up the bust of the boat crew and the night fisherman the night before, and that morning they had gotten all three of the morning fishermen, all of them caught with their coolers of drugs.

DeLuca's interview came up yet again; the story was running as part of the morning news cycle and came on every half hour on at least one of the channels. Mike DeLuca's good looks, commanding presence, the bandage on his arm, stoically ignored by him, of course, and his status as the officer in charge of the successfully-executed bust – all of it made him irresistible to the press. He was excellent on camera, too, fielding questions in an intelligent, matter-of-fact manner. Between DeLuca's magnetism and the size of the haul – nearly a million dollars in heroin, plus some smaller amounts of cocaine, fentanyl, and meth – the drug bust was the top story on the national news. There was a mention of the detective work that had tipped them off to the river drop, but DeLuca didn't comment on who had done that work. He cited Milt Walecki and Marty Beran as the lead officers on the case, and DeLuca let the media assume they were behind it all.

The second top story on the national news was the Goth murders, catapulted there by the third murder, and by the fact that the same team that had carried out the drug bust was investigating the Goth case, as well. DeLuca had to field questions on that case, too; the reporters brought it up at the end of the interview. DeLuca didn't provide them much information concerning their progress on the murders; he didn't have much to give, Jordan knew.

Jordan had to admit, he felt low because they hadn't included him in the accolades, but he understood why. Plus, he hadn't earned the right to celebrate, not by a long shot. Jordan hadn't physically participated in the raid itself, and it was his fault that DeLuca was wounded. The last thing he wanted now was attention from anyone; he felt like crawling into a hole somewhere. He was responsible for nearly getting his partner killed, and he *had* succeeded in getting Sammy Farineau killed. He was a walking disaster.

Aside from those mistakes, or on top of them, was whatever was going on in his head. He had frozen the night before, only for seconds, but they were crucial seconds. Worse yet, there was no guarantee it wouldn't happen again. It was something else to worry about, stew over, and heap on top of the growing pile of anxiety. He needed to get his mind on something else. He sighed and looked around his apartment and decided that the place needed some necessary cleaning. He did that and went down to get his mail, which he hadn't bothered to do for a few days.

When he came back up, his personal cell phone was ringing. Peter Martin was on the line.

"Hey Jordan," he said. "I hate to call you at work, but I was hoping I'd catch you on your lunch hour. Are you coming out tonight?"

"Yeah, I was planning on it."

"Oh, good. I didn't want to sit around at home – my parents are driving me freakin' nuts – but no one else will be at the bar. Victoria is staying home, and Suzanne is going over to her house to keep her company. George said he was doing something else tonight."

"Okay, meet you at Harry's?"

"No, let's go somewhere else for a change. It's just going to be us two, and I'm tired of dealing with McCann and his band of assholes – plus, I'm not sure that Harry's is a safe place for anyone Goth to be anymore, especially since there would be only two of us tonight. Someone told me about a new bar and grill up on Mount Washington. You wanna go there?"

"Okay, sounds good."

Peter gave Jordan the name and address and said, "Meet you up there at nine."

Jordan signed off with an 'okay' and sat there for a moment, thinking. Then he picked up his work phone and dialed DeLuca.

CHAPTER TWENTY

When Jordan reached DeLuca; he was finally on his way back to town with the rest of the PDI team minus one. Milt had been left in charge of the warehouse personnel documenting and cataloging the contraband. Jordan recounted his conversation with Peter Martin, and DeLuca said, "Do you think this is legit?"

"I don't have any reason not to. It's a public place; it's as safe as Harry's."

"But you're not sure."

"It's not a big deal. I just figured someone should know that I'm going to meet Peter tonight."

"Okay." DeLuca sounded dog tired. "We're going to be at the office in an hour. Meet us there, and we'll talk about it. Make sure you go in by the side entrance."

Max Weinberg was home, watching the television, when the call came. Derek hissed into the phone, "Did you see the news? What in the hell is going on? That warehouse was ours!"

"I know, I know," said Max. "I'm working on it. It came from out of nowhere. They cracked our delivery system somehow."

"How?"

"I don't know. It was pretty tight. If anything, I would have expected a bust on the river, maybe a random raid by the river patrol. But of course, that would have been a blip on the radar. One boatload was nothing in terms of losing inventory. The warehouse is a whole other thing. We've got multiple big-time dealers who are going to be out of product next week, and not just the ones they nabbed in Pittsburgh."

"We had six guys at that boat drop. The news said they only got five. What happened to the other guy?"

"Some other cops stopped Drayvon Carter for running a stop sign before he got to the pickup, so he was running late. He got down there, saw the bust going down, turned around, and headed back home. He's going to pick up the other guys' dealers, and we're going to try to get him product some other way so he can supply them. We need a temporary delivery method, and then we need to set up something more long term again."

"That sure as hell works out good for Carter. He's going to pick up everyone else's dealers. His territory is going to explode. And whenever someone makes out, it makes me suspicious."

"Yeah, I thought of that, but Carter's going to take a huge financial hit from this before he starts making money again. Ryman talked to him directly, and Carter was pissed. He seemed genuinely freaked out by getting stopped by the cops. No, I think they figured out the drop at the river, and Carter just got lucky. The cops had to track the boat to the truck and the truck to the warehouse. That's the only way they could have made those busts at the river and the warehouse."

"This is unacceptable."

"There is one good thing."

"What? What can be good about this?"

"The police still don't have a line on the money. If they did, that would be a lot more worrisome."

"Yeah, well, they're never going to get that far because we're going to find out how they pulled this off, so they don't get this close again."

"I know, trust me, I'm working on it."

The phone clicked, and Max grimaced. They could deal with the little daily busts by the cops, the small dealers going down. They could even handle losing a big dealer here or there. But this raid had hit hard. It had wiped out all of their big dealers in Pittsburgh except one and crippled delivery to many of the rest of them in that region. Delays in supply could cause them to lose territories permanently. There were plenty of others who would move in with a new pipeline to fill the gap. The Russians, in particular, were breathing down their necks.

He'd let Derek down, and worse yet, Max didn't even know how. But he was sure as hell going to find out.

Jordan snuck in the side entrance of the PBP headquarters and trudged through the hallways. There was a celebratory mood in the air; groups of officers and detectives were standing around, still talking about the busts the night before. As he made his way down the hallway, he heard someone from behind him call his name. He turned; Rick Ferriman, head of the PBP Narcotics division, was striding toward him. He came up, threw an arm over Jordan's shoulders, and pumped his hand. "Agent Bell," he said. "I just wanted to congratulate you. None of that would have happened last night if it weren't for you; outstanding work."

Jordan flushed. "Thanks."

"I know it's tough when you're undercover. You bring in the goods, and you get none of the praise because no one's supposed to know about you. We in Narcotics know that feeling too well. You'd be a natural fit with us. I want you to know that if you ever want a change, I'd take you into my group immediately. It might be good to be with a team that understands and appreciates what you do."

Jordan nodded. "Thanks, I'll keep that in mind."

"You do that." Ferriman slapped him on the back and strode off. As Jordan turned and continued down the hallway, he saw DeLuca standing at the end of it, waiting for him.

He had a look of disapproval on his face. "What did he want?"

"To give me a job."

"What?"

"Relax," said Jordan as he turned and fell in beside him, and they began walking down to their corner of the building. "I'm not going anywhere. I haven't figured out how to do this job right yet." He tried to keep his tone light, but he couldn't quite keep the self-disgust out of his voice.

DeLuca looked at him. They were passing their conference room, and he pulled open the door. "Come in here for a minute."

They stepped inside, and Jordan stood, stone-faced, waiting for the lecture that he knew was coming. DeLuca said, "What's on your mind?"

Jordan stared at him. "On my mind? You mean other than my

epic failure last night?"

DeLuca shook his head. "It wasn't an epic failure; we're both still standing here, and we took the shooter down. We both could have done some things differently, myself included. For starters, I could have listened to you when you were trying to alert me. If I'd done that, I could have given you some quick instructions, and we could have both gone after him and addressed the situation. I wouldn't have ended up in a bad spot, in the line of fire, and unable to fire back."

Jordan shook his head. "That was stupid of me. I didn't think of that. And then I got out there, and I – I don't know what happened. I froze for a second."

"That been known to happen to rookies the first time they face a shooter. Even seasoned cops, sometimes. Some freeze and don't shoot, and others shoot too fast; it's a tough situation. You went after the guy. That was the right instinct because we didn't want him to get outside the perimeter. And you recovered well. As soon as he was down, you got his weapon and neutralized the situation. Plus, it was an unexpected development; it wasn't as if we planned for that. The unexpected always amplifies the adrenaline rush, which affects your reactions."

Jordan grimaced. "You could have been killed."

DeLuca shrugged. "You could have, too. It wasn't a good situation to find ourselves in, but as I said, we're still standing here. So, we learn from the situation and move on. There's one other thing I want to tell you, and that is to say thank you and congratulations on your great work on the drug case. That bust wouldn't have happened last night if it hadn't been for your heads-up work. I know it stinks that you don't get any public recognition for that, but you can bet Morrissey will find a way to thank you. Okay?"

Jordan nodded. He appreciated DeLuca's attempt, but the praise was somehow embarrassing. DeLuca was trying to reassure him, and tough guys didn't need reassurance. He was grateful, though; DeLuca could have kicked his ass for his shortcomings last night, and he hadn't. He'd even shouldered some of the blame himself. He glanced at DeLuca's arm. "Are you okay?"

"Fine," said DeLuca. "I got stitched up right on the site, and they put on a new bandage. It was just a scratch. Now let's go and round up the others and talk about Peter Martin."

They met in the conference room with Jen and Devon, Bear, and Morrissey. They looked tired, and they were all in need of showers, except for Jordan. Even Morrissey had spent the night in his office and looked rumpled and unshaven. They listened as Jordan recounted the phone call. Jen was the first one to speak.

"I don't like it," she said. "If we think that the murderer killed Sammy Farineau because he was afraid Sammy had spilled the names of the True Goth site to Jordan, then it would follow that Jordan is at risk, too. This meeting could be a set-up."

Devon was frowning. "Not necessarily. Maybe the murderer heard enough to know that Sammy didn't give Jordan the names. He killed Sammy to keep him from giving them up. Then he'd be in the clear with no reason to go after Jordan."

"Unless he doesn't know for sure," said Bear. He looked at Jordan. "He might not be sure about you; maybe you know, and maybe you don't. Maybe he wants to find out how much you do know."

"Okay, but if Peter Martin isn't the murderer, he might not know about the conversation between Sammy and me at all, and whether or not I know the names of the True Goth founders wouldn't matter," said Jordan. "This could just be a night out and maybe a chance to find out something more."

"It *is* a public place," said Morrissey, "I think we need to send Jordan out. The more contact with the prime suspects, the better. The alternative is that he sits at home and does nothing because none of the rest of them will be out tonight. We can't afford to do nothing. We have three dead people and nothing but a handful of theories."

"Okay, but if Bell is going to meet with him, we need a plan," said DeLuca. "If it turns out that Martin is the murderer and this is a set-up, then we need some safeguards."

Morrissey looked at him. "What did you have in mind?"

"Milt is still out at the raid site, but all of the rest of us, me and Bear, Jen and Devon, will be on the street nearby, in two vehicles as backup."

"Sounds like overkill," said Jordan. "Going and sitting in a bar with Peter Martin isn't anything different than I've been doing for the past couple of weeks."

DeLuca said, "Except for the fact that he invited you out specifically, one on one, and he's one of our prime suspects."

Morrissey said to DeLuca, "You'd have to stay out of sight."

"I know. Bell would get a GPS tracker. We can stay back out of sight and still know exactly where he is."

Jordan shrugged. It seemed like a lot of fuss, and after the events of the previous evening, he had an aversion to attention. But he wasn't going to argue with DeLuca, not after what had happened.

"Okay," said Morrissey. "Everyone needs to get home and get some sleep before tonight, then, so you all should bug out of here and go home. But before you leave, I have to tell you, that was some first-class work on the drug case those last few days, all of you. The governor has sent his thanks. Now let's see if we can clean up this murder investigation."

Before Jordan left, Mike pulled him into his office. "You're sure you're up for this?"

Jordan eyed him. He knew what DeLuca meant, and he still felt rattled, but he had to redeem himself. "Why wouldn't I be?"

DeLuca didn't push it. "Okay, then, I want you to take this." He handed Jordan a small GPS device about the size of a quarter. "Put this somewhere inconspicuous, like in the toe of your shoe. It has a sticky pad on it. Just peel off the backing."

"If you need to track me, why not just use my cell phone?"

DeLuca said, "Because that would require communicating with the cell phone tower people, and this GPS has a portable monitor. We can track you in real-time, right in the vehicle. The department spent the money on it; we might as well use it."

"Okay. I think you and Morrissey are reading too much into this meeting. I hope you don't end up disappointed."

DeLuca shrugged. "If that's the case, that's fine. It's just best to be on the safe side. You should bring your gun, too. Go home and get some sleep; I know I'm going to."

That night, Jordan swung the Impala into the parking lot of the bar at the top of Mount Washington at a few minutes before nine and pulled out his personal phone; he had gotten a text while he'd been driving. The message was from Peter: "Park down at Station Square and take the incline up the hill. We can go down to S.S. later." Jordan shook his head. Too late for that; he was already up there.

He pulled out his work phone and sent DeLuca a text so that he understood that they would be going down to Station Square later, and then he stuck his work phone in the glove box and put his personal cell phone in his jacket pocket. He had opted not to bring his gun, and the leather jacket was the reason for that. It was too short and too snug, and the gun's bulk was decidedly visible underneath it. He had four agents for backup, and they all had guns, and it was unlikely anyone was going to need one.

Peter was inside the bar, nursing a mug of beer that was already nearly gone, and Jordan slid into the booth across from him. "What's up?"

Peter shrugged. "Life sucks."

"It's better than the alternative."

"Yeah, I hear that. Sorry, I don't mean to complain. I mean, we could be Sammy, right? It's just - " he gestured vaguely, "all of this shit just stinks."

The waitress came over, and Jordan ordered a beer, too, and Peter ordered a second. "I didn't know you drank," Jordan said.

Peter shrugged. "Most nights at Harry's, I don't. That crowd doesn't drink much, and I have to drive home afterward. Tonight, well, I'll leave my car and get a ride home if I have to. I thought we could get something to eat here, and then go down and try out that new bar in Station Square."

They talked for a while and ordered hamburgers and more beer. Jordan was feeling his drinks; they were craft beers, and they were twice as strong as a regular beer. Halfway through the second one, he slowed his drinking to a crawl. Peter was well through his third and starting to slur his words. He was more sullen than usual and was fidgeting with things: his cell phone, his silverware, his napkin. Something was on his mind. Jordan didn't push; they had all night.

They finished their meal, and Peter said, "Let's get out of here. I feel like walking. Let's see what other bars are up here."

They walked around, circling a few blocks, and ended up on Grandview Avenue. They strolled along the sidewalk next to a wrought iron fence, taking in the view of the rivers and the city below. Peter was acting strangely, talking too much, rambling on about Pittsburgh Pirates players and their stats, and eventually, they stopped at the Monongahela Incline. The incline was a cable car track that ran up and down Mount Washington's steep slope and connected the summit with the riverfront. There was a collection of hotels, shops, bars, and restaurants on the river at the hill's base, called Station Square. Peter had used the incline to come up; he already had a round trip ticket and started forward to board the car, but Jordan said, "Hold on, I need to pay my fare. I got your message too late. My car is up here, and I didn't get a ticket yet. I'll just come back up on the incline when we're done."

Peter looked at the empty cable car getting ready to leave and looked back at Jordan impatiently, but he said nothing. By the time Jordan had his ticket, the next car was there, and a family with three young children had joined them. They all got in and sat. The children stared at them, the mother pursed her lips with disapproval, and the father looked positively hostile. They had gotten looks in the bar, as well. Two young men, all in black, with piercings in their ears and chains on their clothing, were quite obviously not desirable clientele.

Peter was silent on the way down the incline; he had stopped his incessant rambling, but he looked preoccupied. They got off at the bottom of the hill and found themselves on West Carson Street. They had to wait for traffic to cross to Station Square, and by the time they got to the other side, Jordan glanced to his right and caught a glimpse of DeLuca's SUV and Devon's car coming down the hill and then turning, pulling into the parking lot a block down. It was the main lot, and Jordan surmised that Peter's car would be there as well. The team would undoubtedly set up so that they could see it. He had to admit; he felt relief at the sight of them; the tracker was working, then.

Peter had noticed none of that; he was concentrating on his footing, but when they got to the bar that he had suggested, he asked for another craft beer. Jordan, who was feeling his first beer and a half, ordered a light beer and pretended to drink it. It was a beautiful night. They sat at an outside table, watching the city lights sparkle on the river, and listened to the house band. Peter shook his head and ran a hand over his face.

Jordan frowned. "What's with you? You've been tripping about something all night."

"Just – shit," Peter slurred, miserably. "Sammy, George, all of it."

Jordan leaned closer. "George? What about George?"

Peter looked around and swallowed the rest of his beer. "Let's walk."

He was staggering now and tripped once or twice on the cobblestone walk as they headed toward the parking lot. They crossed the street to the lot and stopped on the corner. Peter looked around the lot, swaying, making sure they were alone. "I think it's freakin' George, man," he slurred.

Jordan stared at him. "What do you mean?"

"I think maybe George did it. Killed them. I don't know for sure, but I saw him going out of the parking lot at Harry's place a couple of nights ago, and he didn't turn the right way to go home. So, I got curious, and I followed him. He went out to this place; it's this big old house for sale, right on the river, south of here. But the house is old, run-down, and back among the trees, and it didn't look like anyone was living there."

Jordan shook his head. "So why do you think he did it? Just because he went to some old house?"

Peter ran a hand over his face. "That's the thing. I guess I'm not sure. But it's a freakin' creepy old house – why would he go to a place like that? I did think it could be like, drugs or something. He used to do a little pot; maybe he still does. Maybe it's a drug house, or he hooks up with a dealer there or something. That's why I wasn't sure if I should go to the cops or not. We've been friends for a long time. I'd hate to have them bust him if it was just some weed or something."

Jordan frowned. "Are you sure he didn't see you?"

"I don't think he did. I saw him turn in, and I just kept going past on the road, along with a couple of other cars. By the time I drove back past it, I couldn't even see his car; he must have driven back in on the driveway. The drive went back into the trees."

"Which night was it?"

"Tuesday."

Jordan processed that. Tuesday night was the night he had talked to Sammy in the rear parking lot, the last night he was seen alive, although the theory was that he had been taken at noon at his apartment on Wednesday because that was when his cell phone had stopped pinging. It didn't quite fit, but he said, "We should check it out. If it's nothing, we can keep our mouths shut. Can you show me where it is?"

"I don't think I can drive right now."

"I can drive your car. We can look at it, and I'll drop you off at home and get a ride back to my place. Tomorrow's Saturday. I can get my car anytime."

Peter looked miserable. "I don't know, man."

"Come on, you know we've got to do this. What if George did do it? How far is it?"

"Maybe a half hour. It's down by West Mifflin."

"That's not bad. Come on, Peter. You're right, it's probably nothing, but if it is, we owe it to Sammy, man. And the others. Not to mention, one of us could be next."

Peter sighed, a big gusty miserable sigh. "Okay." He dug in his pocket for his keys and held them out, swiveling around to look for his car. Jordan took the keys from him. Peter was swaying badly. "It's over there," he pointed, and as Peter turned to head toward it, he tripped over a curb. He flailed, and Jordan grabbed him, and he grabbed Jordan, and they both almost went down. Peter was hefty, a good three inches taller than Jordan, and about seventy pounds heavier. Jordan managed to keep him on his feet and grabbed his arm to steady him as he lumbered over the curb. "Okay, man, you've got it."

"Sorry, I'm not used to drinking this much. I'm just so screwed up over this shit."

"It's okay," said Jordan. "It's gonna be okay."

They got in Peter's car and took off, and Jordan saw DeLuca's vehicle pull out well behind them, at least three cars back. Jordan drove south, past Harry's and through Southside. He cut through the town of West Mifflin, and Peter directed him back onto Route 837, along the river. They were getting close. Jordan wanted to pull over and text DeLuca to tell him what was going on, but he couldn't come up with a plausible excuse to stop, so he kept his hands on the wheel. DeLuca and the team had dropped out of sight.

Jordan was starting to get a bad feeling, but even if this was a trap, they still had the advantage because Peter didn't know that there was a backup team following. And maybe Peter had been telling the truth, but it was a lame story, and Jordan didn't think so. He wished now that he'd brought his gun. He would have to stall when they got there and give DeLuca and the team time to catch up. He shot a glance in the rearview mirror. The sun was setting; the evening was coming on, and all he could see was headlights. They were still back there, Jordan told himself; they had to be.

That section of Route 837 was called Duquesne Road, and it ran alongside the train tracks right along the Monongahela River, which was on their left. To their right was a dense section of trees, and eventually, Peter pointed to a gravel drive, with a For Sale by Owner sign at the corner. Set back in the trees was a large older two-story home; they could glimpse a portion of it in the headlights. Jordan pulled slowly onto the gravel road and bumped along, taking his time.

He stopped well short of the end of the drive, leaving his car visible from the road, and they just sat there for a moment, looking up at the house, which lay to the left of the driveway. Closer up, it was evident that it was badly in need of repair. They were far enough inside the surrounding trees to see other buildings now; off to the right was a rusting corrugated metal shed, barely visible in the waning light. At the end of the drive, there was a two-car garage, separated from the house and just as run-down. There were no other cars in sight.

"You're right," said Jordan. "I can't figure out why George would come out here."

"Yeah, it's weird, right?" Peter looked around them, his eyes dark in the gloom. "This creeps me out. Let's get this over with."

Jordan shut off the car and slowly climbed out and headed for the house, keeping some distance between himself and Peter. He stepped up onto brick steps and crumbling mortar choked with weeds and tried the front door, standing sideways so he wouldn't have to turn his back. "It's locked."

He looked at Peter, who loomed at the foot of the steps. Jordan tensed, waiting for a charge, but Peter just shrugged and backed up. Jordan came down the steps. "Let's try the first-floor windows. I'll go left, you go right, and we'll meet in the back."

Peter nodded and obediently took off to his right, and Jordan watched him go, speculatively. If Peter was going to make a move, he sure wasn't acting that way. Jordan glanced around, looking for signs of drug paraphernalia. There were none, the windows were intact, and the weeds were thick enough that it was evident that there was little traffic over the front steps. It didn't appear to be a drug house. He went to the left, checking the windows, and came around to the back of the place to find Peter already standing there.

"My windows were all locked up," said Peter. "And I already tried the back door, and it's locked."

Jordan scanned the back of the house. "Well, we know he's not getting in there unless he has a key. But there are so many weeds on the front porch that it doesn't look like anyone's been going in and out. The back doesn't look much better."

Peter was walking, boots crunching on the gravel drive, back toward the garage. He wiped at a pane in a side window and peered inside. "It's pretty dark, but it looks empty."

That left the shed, and they hiked across the gravel driveway toward it. The driveway gave way to a narrow gravel path, nearly overgrown with bushes and weeds. Jordan reached it first, started down it, and then stopped, keenly aware that he'd made a mistake; he should have kept Peter in front of him. He began to turn when he was abruptly jerked back by the collar, and a big arm came around his neck. He reacted, his martial arts training kicking in, and instead of arching his back, he curled inward, and at the same time, he put a foot between Peter's legs and bent over, pulling down hard. Peter lost his balance, and Jordan crouched further, pulling him up onto his back and right over his head, flipping him hard onto his back. Peter grunted, momentarily stunned, and Jordan moved quickly to an arm bar, pulling Peter's arm out straight across his body, pinning him helplessly on the ground.

Peter tried to make a move toward him but yelped in pain as his arm protested. He lay there panting, his face dark with anger. "What in the hell are you doing, man?" He scrabbled his feet on the gravel, but he couldn't turn his upper body.

"I could ask you the same thing," said Jordan, through gritted teeth. "It wasn't George who came out here at all, was it? It was you all along. You might as well talk. You aren't going anywhere. I can hold you like this all night -,"

And then he felt a whoosh of air and something crashed into the back of his head, and his vision went white, and then black.

CHAPTER TWENTY-ONE

Jordan came to a few moments later. He was in a small dark building made of corrugated metal. A lantern turned down low illuminated rusting metal walls and old wooden support beams, and a crumbling concrete floor. His head was pounding, and he blinked as forms shifted around him: an old wooden table, a rusting utility sink. They were moving or seemed to be, and he closed his eyes, trying to tamp down rising nausea. He heard movement and felt a sensation at his ankle, and he opened his eyes again, fighting to make sense of the situation. Peter. Peter Martin was tying his ankle to a chair. He was in the shed. Peter had attacked him. Or had he attacked Peter? He couldn't remember. And beyond Peter, someone lay on the floor, dead or unconscious. A jolt of recognition ran through Jordan. Will McCann.

He shook his head, grunting at the pain that shot through it, and tried to flex his limbs. He was sitting in an old wooden chair, with one elbow and both ankles tied tightly to it; his right hand still free. Peter had taped his left wrist to the arm of the chair with duct tape, which held his lower left forearm in place with the inside facing up. His face felt stiff; Peter had taped his mouth as well, he realized, as bit by bit, clarity returned. How long had he been there? Where was DeLuca? Peter Martin stood up with a roll of duct tape in his hand, and Jordan tensed as he felt a hand come from behind him and run gently down his cheek.

He craned his neck sideways as Suzanne Weir strolled around him and into view. "The dashing Mr. Bell," she purred. "You woke up for the party." Jordan stared at her stupidly. She crossed in front of Peter and bent to look into Jordan's eyes. Suzanne was smiling, her beautiful face alight with sick anticipation. "It's too bad it turned out this way," she said. "I really did want you, you know. But you lied to me. And even then, even when I found out you were a cop, I still wanted you, but you told me no." Her expression hardened. "And those are two things that no one does to me, ever."

Behind her, Peter was scowling, shifting uncomfortably. Suzanne continued. "So, we adjusted our plan. Congratulations; you just became a part of it." She licked her lips and flicked open a blade, thin and razor-sharp, her voice cold. "Don't just stand there. Tape his other arm."

Peter moved around her to Jordan's right side, stripping off another section of tape, and Jordan closed his eyes and bowed his head and went limp, pretending to go out again. As he felt Peter adjust his arm, he jerked it out of his grip and punched upward, landing a nasty backhand on Peter's nose. Peter bellowed and stepped back, Suzanne skittering out of his way, and then the door banged open, and DeLuca's voice rapped out, "Don't move! Put your hands on your head, now!"

Bear and Jen and Devon flowed through the doorway around DeLuca, weapons extended. The wicked-looking knife went clattering to the concrete floor, and Suzanne Weir cried out, "Oh, thank God! Help us; he was going to kill us all!" She was cowering in the corner, shying away from Peter Martin. Jordan wanted to tell them that she was part of it but couldn't, with the duct tape on his mouth, but DeLuca looked as though he wasn't buying her story anyway.

Martin stumbled backward away from Bell, blood trickling from his nose, and stared at her, gaping incredulously. "You bitch!" was all he could manage, and he glared at her as Bear moved behind him to cuff him.

Weir protested as Jen cuffed her hands behind her. "This is a mistake. I'm a victim!" She continued to protest, her voice shrill with panic, but DeLuca tuned her out and bent over Jordan. DeLuca's face bobbed and darkened, and Jordan's eyes felt heavy.

Nausea was rising, thick and hot, and DeLuca stepped forward and stripped the duct tape from his mouth as gently as he could. He bent down and looked into Jordan's eyes, concern on his face. "It's okay, Bell," he said. "We'll get you out of this."

Bear and Jen unceremoniously moved their captives to separate walls and sat them down, hard. Devon was checking Will McCann for a pulse. "He's alive," he said. "He's just out."

DeLuca got on the phone and requested police backup, including forensics and two ambulances, and they started working on the tape and ropes around Jordan's left wrist and ankles. Jordan's head was bobbing, and the room was revolving again. They were asking him questions, but each query slipped away before he could formulate an answer. He could feel blood oozing down the back of his head and trickling onto his neck. He gagged once or twice during the process; part of it was due to the smell. The chair he was in sat over a drain in the floor, once probably under the rusting sink. There was dried blood spattered around it on either side under the arms of the chair, and blood caked thick on either side where it ran into the drain. Deeper down in the pipe sat quarts of putrefying blood, he was sure. And he was just as sure that in that drain, they would find the DNA of Poppy Jankovic, Jon Hurly, and Sammy Farineau.

Suzanne Weir ended her babbling by demanding a lawyer and sat with her head down on her knees. Jordan looked toward her once, and his addled head didn't seem to process the sight correctly; he felt sadness and a surge of pity. Then reason intruded, and he looked away. Peter Martin glowered at Weir from across the room, sweating with fear and with pure hatred on his face. There were the sirens of local ambulances and police, and more sirens in the distance; backup from the PBP central organizations, including forensics. Will McCann went into the first ambulance because no one was entirely sure what was wrong with him, and then DeLuca and Bear were standing in front of him.

They grabbed him by the arms and helped him up, and then the room spun and went hazy, and Jordan's head rolled, and his legs gave way. They sat him back down in the chair, and he slumped, and then everything went black for a while.

He awoke outside on a gurney, his head pounding, feeling as if he was floating. As he tried to tamp down nausea, he could hear DeLuca telling Jen that he wanted her to ride with him in the ambulance.

To the medics, DeLuca said, "Where would a Pittsburgh neurosurgeon be based? What hospital?"

They looked at each other. "Probably UPMC Presbyterian," said one of them. "But there are others that are closer."

DeLuca shook his head. "UPMC Presbyterian has a first-class trauma center. Take him there." He looked at Jen and said, "Call the hospital and have them call his dad. He's a neurosurgeon."

Jen looked surprised. "No shit."

Jordan frowned; he didn't want that, but for some reason, he couldn't speak. The technicians lifted the gurney, and the motion set the world to whirling around him again.

Devon and Bear had both suspects on their feet and were steering them toward the door. Suzanne Weir came out first. She had regained her composure and looked haughtily at DeLuca. "I want a lawyer as soon as I get there. And you'll be facing a lawsuit." DeLuca looked as if he wanted to punch her.

Peter Martin came out next, with Bear behind him. He was saying something quietly to DeLuca, but they were loading Jordan into the ambulance, and he couldn't hear because it was dark in there, so dark and quiet…

Jordan regained consciousness in the ambulance, and this time, his thoughts seemed sharper. His head was still pounding, and the nausea was just as bad, but at least he could focus. The vehicle was moving. He scowled up at the medic. "Where am I going?"

"UPMC Presbyterian."

"No," Jordan said flatly. "I don't want to go."

Jen's voice came from the other side of the ambulance. "Too bad, kid. Boss' orders."

Jordan swiveled his head, carefully, to look at her. He could only turn it so far; they had put on a neck support. "What happened?"

"You don't remember?"

He closed his eyes briefly. "Peter told me about this house. He said he tracked George to it the other night. We were checking it out, and he grabbed me from behind." He frowned. "I got him down... I threw him and did an armbar."

Jen's eyebrows rose, and she smiled. "Impressive."

Jordan frowned again, concentrating. "Then, I blacked out or something."

"You were hit in the back of the head, probably by Suzanne."

He processed that for a moment. "Then I woke up in the chair." He closed his eyes, trying to remember. "Peter was there and Suzanne. Will McCann was on the floor." He opened his eyes and looked at her. "Was he dead?"

"No, just unconscious. He's on his way to the hospital too. Do you remember if they said anything?"

Jordan's head was pounding, and the memories were hazy, like half-remembered dreams. Pieces of what Suzanne had said floated through his mind, and he felt his nausea increase. "Not really." The light was bothering him. He squinted.

The medic looked at Jen and put his finger to his lips, and she nodded, and Jordan closed his eyes.

Everett Rowland Bell was just on his way home from the hospital and a late-night emergency surgery when the call came through that his son was on his way in with a concussion, and he turned around and drove back to UPMC. He couldn't get any particulars over the phone, other than it sounded like someone had hit Jordan in the head, and he wondered if it had been a mugging.

He parked and strode into the trauma unit and checked at the nurses' station. "Hi, Sue. Jordan – what unit is he in?" he demanded.

"Hello, Dr. Bell. He's in 5G. He's conscious. They took him for a head X-ray; radiology is bringing the results down now."

He started to turn away, but her next words stopped him in his tracks. "I didn't know he was with the PDI."

"PDI?"

"Yes – the police – they're the ones that just made that big drug bust, right? The bust that was on the national news yesterday? One of the medics said that a suspect hit your son. He must be working on that Goth murder case that's been on the news, by the looks of him. He seems so young – I was surprised."

Everett stared at her and finally found his voice. "Yes, well, he's twenty-three."

He strode down the hallway, lips tightening.

Jordan must have drifted out again because an orderly was wheeling him into a trauma unit at the hospital when he woke next. He wasn't there long before they took him to X-ray. Then back to the exam room, where they took off the neck brace, and the motion finally got to him, and he vomited, more than he thought humanly possible. After that, though, he felt a little better and was able to sit up while a trauma center doctor stitched the back of his head.

Jen stepped into the room, smiling as she saw him sitting up. "You're looking better." She stepped forward and gently laid his cell phone next to him. "I've got your cell phone. Peter Martin pulled it out of your pocket in the parking lot at Station Square when you were helping to hold him up. Devon and I stopped to pick it up. It was a good thing you had the GPS on you."

He tried a smile and failed. His thoughts were becoming a little more organized, and memory was returning, and Suzanne Weir monopolized most of both. He had utterly misjudged her – Jordan Bell, the supposed master of human observation, had been entirely taken in. He barely heard Jen say that she was going, that Bear was going to pick her up and to rest well, but Jordan was devoutly glad she went. He didn't have the will or the strength to talk.

The doctor finished stitching his head, and he said, "Your X-rays should be back any minute, but we're going to admit you. From what your partner said, and from my observations, you have a moderate concussion. She also said you were in an altercation several days ago that involved blows to your face and head. We're going to do a CT scan and some cognitive tests and keep you for observation for a while."

"I don't want to stay."

"And I think you should," said the doctor. "Plan to stay the night, anyway, and we'll take another look at you in the morning. Besides, I hear your dad is coming in – he'd have my job if I released you. I'll be back shortly."

He stepped out, and Jordan groaned. He heard voices out in the hallway, and he tensed, waiting. The door flew open, and Everett Rowland Bell stepped into the doorway, one hand holding the door and the other some charts. His mouth opened, and he shut it and looked Jordan up and down, taking in the black clothing, the boots, the chains, the earring, the unruly spiked hair, disapproval growing on his face.

"Dad -," began Jordan, but his father turned abruptly and walked out, handing the charts to the trauma doctor in the doorway. "This one's yours," he said. "I want nothing to do with this."

They took him for a CT scan, and Jordan endured it; he didn't have much choice. It took two hours before he could walk, but as soon as he could, he shuffled down the hallway to the nurses' station and told the nurse on duty that he was going home. She protested and threatened to call the doctor, but his curt, "I'm fine," stopped her. She watched him dubiously as he pecked at his phone and ordered a ride, but she let him go.

Now at home, he sat on his sofa, in a fog of hurt and exhaustion. It was as far as he could make it, once he had pulled himself up the agonizing three flights of stairs. His head was pounding, and his stomach was rolling again. The physical effort hadn't helped his mental clarity; disjointed thoughts ran through his head like a bad horror movie. Memories of the warehouse in New York, of the gun battle the night before, of the shed, and Suzanne's beautiful cold smile kept popping into his head in a crazy carousel, sometimes more real than his shabby apartment. He needed relief from his own mind, badly. If only he could move, he could get in his bed and sleep.

He must have dozed off, sitting there. His head jerked up at the bang of gunfire. No – it was someone pounding on the door. It had been going on for a while, he realized. He heard DeLuca's voice outside. "It's Mike; open the door!"

He rose from the sofa, swayed for a minute, and started forward and made it to the door. Someone down the hall stuck his head of his door out to yell at DeLuca just as the door finally opened, and when DeLuca saw Jordan, he looked relieved and then concerned. He was carrying some papers and a six-pack of beer, and Jordan stared at it. "I don't want any beer."

"It's not for you; it's for me," said DeLuca. "Let me in."

Jordan shuffled aside and opened the door, moving like a zombie, and DeLuca stepped in and closed the door. "I stopped at the hospital to see how you were. Why did you leave? They told you to stay."

Jordan lifted a shoulder in a half-shrug and shuffled again, shutting the door. He turned and hobbled into the room; he wasn't moving very well. "I didn't want to be there."

DeLuca waved the papers at him and set them on the kitchen table. "You forgot these. Discharge instructions. I picked them up from the hospital. Someone's supposed to stay with you tonight and check on you."

"Yeah, they told me that."

"Well, if you had to leave, why'd you come here?"

Jordan blinked at him. "Where else would I go?"

"Well, somewhere that someone could monitor you. Your parent's house, for starters. Your dad's going to be upset to find out that you left the hospital."

Jordan let out a bitter snort. Words came out that he didn't intend to say; it was as if he was drunk. "My dad doesn't care. He hates me. He always has. They called him in to treat me at the hospital – not that I wanted that – and he took one look at me and walked away. So, no, I couldn't go to my parent's house." He turned away and shuffled over to the sofa and sat, trying to look like it didn't matter, but his head wasn't working right, and his face was an open book.

DeLuca just stood there, and Jordan could see his face change, see understanding flit into it, and then pity. His eyes wandered around the pathetic little apartment, and Jordan could tell what he was thinking - that Jordan was alone, abandoned, like an unwanted mutt. Jordan didn't want that pity, but it would take too much effort to deny it. He was spent; he had nothing left.

Mike straightened, pulled a kitchen chair over, sat and opened a beer, and changed the subject. "Well, we got them, kid. As we speak, Peter Martin is downtown with Devon, Morrissey, and the D.A., telling all, in exchange for not being charged with murder.

He's already given a preliminary statement. He admitted that he and Suzanne Weir ran True Goth. The website was her idea, but Peter set it up with some help from Sammy Farineau. Martin said she was obsessed with cutting, that she was sick and got off on the murders, which is part of the reason they picked that M.O., but the other reason was that they wanted a noticeable murder method. Weir's end game all along was to take revenge on Will McCann for dumping her. Martin said she was a little off that way – she would get unreasonably angry at anyone who slighted her and had an irrational fear of rejection, and McCann's rejection was the ultimate slight. She planned to make it look like a serial killer was killing off Goths, and in the end, to pin it on McCann. They had a suicide note written to make it look like McCann killed himself at the murder site. She had originally only planned to kill Poppy and Jon Hurly – Peter said she despised them because she thought they were poseurs, and they had the gall to argue with her, so she hated them. But then, Sammy became a threat, so they had to get rid of him. And you pissed her off, and they thought that Sammy had told you too much, so in the end, they pulled you into the plan."

Jordan's forehead furrowed, and he looked at the ceiling as if remembering. "She knew I was a cop, somehow. She said I lied to her about it."

Mike nodded and took a drink of beer. "Peter said that in his statement. You ended up next in line on her hate list, after Will. The night she came over to your apartment, Peter said you left the room for a few minutes, and Suzanne went through your backpack. She saw your badge in it. Then she still, uh, wanted -,"

Jordan felt sick. "To go to bed with me."

"Yeah. You were already on Suzanne's bad list, but she still wanted to use you – and when you turned her down, you really ticked her off. That fear of rejection thing and all. Peter saw her afterward, and he said she went ballistic. 'Rage' was the word he used. So, you ended up as part of the final plot." He paused. "I'm sorry. I know you liked her."

Jordan looked away. "No, I didn't. I hardly knew her." He steered the subject back. "So, what was their final plot?"

"Well, Peter thought that the final plan was to kill you and make all of it look like Will McCann had done it. They had gotten to McCann earlier in the evening – Suzanne had met him at Harry's and spiked his drink, and then lured him out to the parking lot to talk before it took effect – much like they'd done to Poppy Jankovic. Peter was waiting out there. They got him into his car, and by then, he was passing out, and they turned off his phone at the bar and ditched it in the river, which was pretty much how they handled all of the cell phones of the victims, and drove him down to the abandoned house and parked his car in the garage."

Jordan knit his brow, thinking. "We checked out the buildings when we got there. Peter checked the garage before I could walk over there. He said it was empty."

Mike nodded. "That would make sense. He wouldn't want you to see the cars inside. They had dropped Will's car off there earlier. Suzanne then drove Peter back to Station Square, where he'd left his car. Then she drove back to the shed to keep an eye on Will and to wait for you and Peter to get there." He took another drink of beer, waiting for Jordan to catch up – he was taking extra time to process information. "That shed was an old fish cleaning house. The old sink used to sit over the drain. Forensics will get samples out of that drain – we should be able to get DNA on the three murder victims. Peter said they murdered all three of them there. Or rather, Suzanne did. Peter maintains that he helped her obtain her victims, but she did the actual cutting."

He finished his beer, crumpled the can, and continued. "Anyway, Peter was wrong about the final plan. Suzanne had a gun in her backpack, along with a different suicide note. Suzanne planned to shoot both Will and Peter after taking care of you, making it look like a murder-suicide. The letter had Will confessing that he and Peter ran True Goth, and together they committed the Goth murders. A check of Peter's computer would have borne that out - he did set up the True Goth site. She would have had her revenge on Will, and with no loose ends.

"We already know they got Poppy at the bar. They decided that location was somewhat risky and changed their plans for the next two victims. They got to both Jon Hurly and Sammy right at their homes – for Hurly, Peter showed up with two iced coffee drinks, supposedly to hang out. Hurly's mom was at work the night they took him; he was alone. They laced one of the coffees with Rohypnol. Suzanne came along and stayed hidden out in Peter's car until Hurly was unconscious, and then she drove Peter's car, and he drove Hurly in Hurly's car to the shed.

"They were careful to leave their cell phones at home. As for Farineau, Peter had overheard some of your conversation with him. They knew that Sammy was suspicious of one of them and probably rightly surmised that it was Peter, so in that case, Suzanne went in with the drinks and drugged Sammy. The night they kidnapped Poppy, Peter took Poppy, unconscious in the trunk of her car, to his house first to drop off his phone, and then took her to the murder site, to make it look as though he had gone home from the bar, and was at home at the time of the murder. Peter admitted the cell phone tricks were his idea. He's more technically savvy than he seems."

Mike paused. "They tried to get to you last night, too, when you went over to Victoria's house. Peter said that you were in the kitchen, helping bring food or drinks out to the other room, and Suzanne went into the kitchen with you and spiked your drink. She was going to get you to go outside with her to talk before it started taking effect and then talk you into getting into your car. Suzanne was going to drive it around the corner, leave you after you passed out, and then come in and tell the others you left. Then she and Peter would leave twenty minutes later or so, and one of them would have driven you and your car to the murder site. But Peter said you never drank the spiked drink. He said you came out of the kitchen without it; they weren't sure why."

Jordan looked at the floor, then back up. "I spilled it. I knocked it into the sink, and then I never got another one."

Mike said, "So then they tried your apartment later in the evening. Suzanne came up and knocked on your door – again with drinks, iced tea. But by that time, you were out on the drug raid and weren't home." It got quiet for a moment as they both processed what might have been, and Mike tried to lighten the mood.

He grinned at Jordan. "So, the next time I ask you to wear a GPS tracker in your shoe, I guess you won't give me any trouble."

Jordan tried to muster a smile but failed miserably. "I know," he said. "Thanks for having my back."

Mike said briskly, "There's more, but it can wait until tomorrow. You should be getting to bed. Your discharge instructions say you should be getting a lot of rest."

Jordan raised an eyebrow, and finally, his mouth quirked in a smile. "Yeah. I've been waiting for you to shut up and leave."

"Oh, no," said Mike. "I'm not leaving. I'm going to have another beer or two and sleep on your sofa, and wake your ass up every two hours."

Jordan groaned and rolled his eyes, and Mike rose and stepped over and pulled him up, tightening his grip as Jordan swayed on his feet. "You look like shit. Get to bed."

Jordan gave a faint nod and drifted off toward his bedroom. He crawled into bed and laid on his side, and somehow, he felt a little better. He was drifting off when he heard Mike tiptoe into the bathroom to use it, and then he was out.

CHAPTER TWENTY-TWO

Jordan slept through the night, except for DeLuca's brief checks every couple of hours, at least one of which startled him into sitting bolt upright. His last hazy recollection was of the shower running – DeLuca helping himself to his bathroom facilities – and one final gentle prod awake before DeLuca left for the day. Jordan had mumbled something about calling him later and had gone back to sleep.

He woke after nine, feeling only marginally better physically, and, mentally, well, he had to admit, he felt pretty bad. Worse than he'd imagined. He was depressed, on edge, and felt lost, emotionally brutalized. He got up and moved slowly into the living room, and sat on the sofa. The discharge instructions were sitting there, and he read the common symptoms of concussion, which included possible depression or anxiety, among others. 'Well, that explains it,' he told himself. 'What you're going through is perfectly normal.' It made him feel a little better, but not much – he still felt awful – sad, jumpy, with an impending sense of doom.

His head still hurt, but he was more lucid this morning, and his nausea had receded. He had no appetite, but at least he didn't feel the constant urge to be sick. He just felt – down. Crushed. He had an almost irresistible urge to ride over to see his mother, to apologize for lying to her, to get a hug, to make sure that the one person in his life that had cared about him still did.

He pursed his lips in annoyance at himself at his moment of weakness, grabbed the remote, and flicked the television on, only to find that Mike DeLuca was on the national news again. This time Mike was in the background, standing with Jen and Devon behind Morrissey and the mayor as the two men gave statements at a press conference on the solving of the Goth murder case. The camera panned past Morrissey and zeroed in on Mike during the press question and answer session. The commentator gave an aside to the audience, informing them that yes, Mike DeLuca was the same man who had helmed the drug bust two days ago. Mike looked none the worse for wear, handsome and professional in a suit and tie; he must have had extra clothing somewhere, thought Jordan, as a foggy memory of the running shower came to him. Maybe at the office, perhaps in his car. Of course, he did. He was Superman.

Somehow, he didn't mind the attention that Mike was getting, not anymore. He had no desire for recognition himself at the moment, far from it, and Mike deserved it. The man was demanding, but he also brought out the best in people. Jordan had to admit that he had a secret desire to please him, to measure up to those high standards. Hero worship? No. Well, maybe a little. Sometimes, when Mike wasn't acting like a jerk. Strangely, Mike had been a lot less of one lately.

The picture changed abruptly, and Jordan's nausea was back. Suzanne Weir's mug shot had popped up on the screen. He turned the television off and thought that maybe he would go into the office on Monday and ask Mike and Morrissey to remove him from his undercover work with Drayvon Carter. He knew they were counting on him, but he'd done enough in the last two weeks, more, he knew, than any rookie on the planet. And he was stretched beyond his limit; he had nothing left. He closed his eyes and leaned back on the sofa, and then jumped as someone pounded on the door.

The surge of adrenaline on top of his disarranged thought processes completely derailed him. He recovered quickly but found himself standing, tense and disoriented. Someone was still knocking. He rubbed his forehead and tried to gather his faculties as he moved toward the door.

As soon as he unlocked it, a man pushed in, and Jordan balled a fist, ready to strike until he recognized his brother, Marcus. Marcus kept coming, and Jordan backed up.

"What in the hell's wrong with you!" Marcus exploded. His face was red and angry; spittle flew from his lips. "Mom's been crying all night. First, she was crying because you were hurt and because you lied to her, but then Mrs. Martin called her and reamed her out. She said you came to their party a couple of weeks ago intending to entrap Peter, and she accused Mom and Dad of knowing about it. She's threatening a lawsuit, and she called Mom all kinds of names."

For a moment, Jordan was at a loss; he'd screwed up again, somehow, and had managed to hurt his mother, but then something in him snapped. He'd be damned if he was going to take the rap for this. "That sounds like Mrs. Martin's problem," he said coldly. "For the record, I didn't go there to entrap Peter. And no, I'm not going to take the blame for their precious son's decision to go on a killing spree. Or did the Martins forget about that?"

"What you did was dirty, and you know it."

"It was nothing of the sort. It's called undercover work."

"Oh, is that your excuse for your getup last night? Dad said that you looked like a drug addict. He told me to tell you to stay away from the house, especially when he's not there. He said if you do show up, he'll arrest you for trespassing. Mom is done, too. She doesn't want to see you again. Do what you want with your life, but keep them out of it." He turned and opened the door and flung over his shoulder, "Have a nice life, freak." He slammed the door on the way out.

Jordan stood there for a moment and then went and sat on the sofa again. He sat there for a long time, an hour or more. Then he got his phone and called Jonathan Wilkes.

"Hi, Agent Wilkes?"

"Jordan! Call me Jon. Congratulations on solving your murder case. I'm back in New York, but I saw the news this morning. Two big cases in one week; that's quite the accomplishment. What can I do for you?"

"I was wondering, did you see any connection between your case and the drug bust?"

"Nothing explicit, but it had all the hallmarks of a big organized operation, like the one we're looking for. We think our man might be behind it, but we have no evidence yet. We're still interviewing the people that we rounded up. SAC Peterson is handling most of that questioning, along with your Agents Walecki and Beran."

"Okay, I'll have to catch up with them. I've been, uh, busy with the murder case lately."

"Do you mind me asking why you want to know?"

"No particular reason, other than catching the man you want. I thought that we could help on this end."

"What might help is if we could figure out the money trail. It would eventually lead back to him."

"Good point. I know that's the next angle Morrissey wants us to work. Okay, thanks for the info."

"Any time, Jordan."

He hung up and sat, thinking. Although he was no longer working on the assignment in New York, it felt like unfinished business. He had the notion that until they found the man that he had seen on the mezzanine in the warehouse, he would never really get his life back. But on the other hand, he'd moved on to a new job and new prospects, and so, undoubtedly had his foe. Taking down the drug dealers in Pittsburgh and the distribution point at the Amish warehouse had been a big deal. It was more than many law enforcement officers ever got to do. He should be satisfied. And he was still in with Carter; maybe he would make some progress in the future. If they were lucky, they'd at least make some more local busts. That was as good as it was probably going to get. More than likely that would have to be enough.

Then he thought about Lucaya. He went to the kitchen table, got his laptop, and plunked down on his sofa. He went in through TOR and got into the Dark Web and started nosing around. Looking for what, he wasn't sure; maybe disruptions in some of the drug sites because of the big bust. Looking for anything that might be a connection to that man he had seen. He might never get anywhere, but he would never stop looking.

Mike DeLuca knocked on Jordan Bell's apartment door the next day, Sunday, at noon. DeLuca looked taken aback when the door opened; Jordan had talked to him twice on Saturday and assured him he felt much better. He must not have looked outstanding, though, judging by Mike's reaction. And when Jordan thought about it, in the mirror that morning, he had looked zombie-like, thin and exhausted and dragged out. At the very least, he needed a shower and shave.

Mike said, "Why don't you go in and clean up? We're going to go get some normal."

Jordan looked at him. "Normal?"

"Yeah. The DeLuca family Sunday dinner. More normal than a person has a right to. Or maybe it's not normal, but what the hell. You have to admit, the food is good."

"I don't know," said Jordan, doubtfully.

"I do," said Mike firmly. "Go clean yourself up; I can wait."

Another look in the bathroom mirror a little while later told him that he looked a lot better cleaned up, and that made him feel a bit more human, but he was quiet on the way there; he didn't feel like talking. Mike let the silence be, but it was comfortable somehow. A lot less strained than it had been a few weeks ago.

Everyone was there when they got there; the living room was packed, and Jordan perked up as he entered the room, feeding off the energy. Everyone gathered around them, and Bobby boomed out, "How about that crack agent, Mike DeLuca? Two ginormous cases in one week!" Mike looked uncomfortable and shot a glance at Jordan.

They were slapping Mike on the back, and his brother Joey said, "Nice going, man. You're a freakin' national hero!"

"Jordan's the hero," said Mike firmly. He sounded almost irritated, and Jordan looked at him.

"Right," Joey said, smiling, with barely a glance at Jordan.

"No, I mean it," snapped Mike. "We wouldn't have solved either case without him."

His sharp tone made the room go quiet, and Joey said, "Sorry, man, I meant Jordan, too."

Their father stepped in and pushed his way through to Jordan. "Let me shake your hand, young man," he said, pumping Jordan's hand vigorously and giving him a solid DeLuca slap on the arm. "That was a hell of a job!"

"Damn straight," said Bobby, and the rest of them clapped Jordan on the back, and the women hugged him, and Jordan almost blushed, and laughter and voices filled the room again.

"You look like you need a good dinner," said Mike's mother, putting an arm around him. "Come out to the kitchen. Your face looks better – the bruise is gone. You need to be careful on that bike. Oh, and Sissy's got a real nice girl for you to meet…"

Later that night, Mike dropped Jordan off, well-fed and feeling more relaxed. It had been good to get out, but as they approached the apartment, Jordan fell quiet. He wasn't looking forward to going back inside.

Mike said, "Stay home tomorrow; get some more rest. Your instructions from the hospital said you shouldn't drive for a week. If you get bored, catch up on your reports."

"Okay," said Jordan. "Good night, and thanks for dinner."

He didn't say a word about his appointment with Drayvon Carter the next night, and neither did Mike.

He trudged up the stairs to his apartment, and inside, he paced for a little while and finally sat. He sat and thought for hours, it seemed, processing everything that had happened in the last several weeks, in both Pittsburgh and New York. He turned every event over in his head and then filed each one away. Not all of them were easy to deal with, but when he finished, he felt better. Stronger, in control again. Less anxious. Maybe his head injury was healing, and his symptoms were subsiding. But somehow, he didn't think that was all of it.

The next morning, Mike DeLuca stepped up to Morrissey's office, knocked, stepped in, and closed the door.

"Mornin'," said Morrissey, leaning back and picking up his coffee cup. He looked relaxed, content. "It was nice coming in this morning, for a change. No more press – they're all hanging out at the courthouse. The arraignments for the drug dealers are today. You here to talk agenda for the staff meeting?"

"Yeah, I do want to talk about the staff meeting," said Mike. "But first, I want to be clear on what we're going to do with Jordan. I'm a little concerned about him.

Morrissey raised an eyebrow. "Go ahead."

He told Morrissey about finding out about the kid's lack of

support system and his general air over the weekend: quiet, depressed, tense.

"And the night I stayed at his house, I found anti-anxiety meds in his medicine cabinet. They'd been prescribed by a doctor in New York, probably after whatever went down there that got him shipped here."

Morrissey frowned. "Any idea how many he's taking?"

"Well, that's the thing. None, as far as I can tell. It was a single prescription, no refills, and I counted them; Jordan hasn't taken any of them."

Morrissey's face cleared. "So then, what's the problem?"

"The problem is that the shrink who prescribed them thought that they were necessary at the time. Jordan must have been showing some signs of stress then, enough to get the doctor to write the prescription. And then there was the incident on the hill at the raid the other night when he froze. And what the kid went through at the shed, with Martin and Weir. And the way he's been this weekend, I can't put my finger on it, exactly, but I get the feeling he's at the end of his rope. I want to pull him out of the Drayvon Carter thing, at least for a while."

Morrissey's eyes flickered over his shoulder, and he inclined his head. "Maybe we should ask him what he thinks about it."

Mike turned. Jordan Bell was striding into the office, neatly groomed and in a suit, and he slung his backpack onto his desk as if it was just another day at the office. He greeted Bear and Milt with a grin, and Jen and Devon got up and walked over to him. Jordan was smiling and conversing easily with the group, and Devon offered to buy him a coffee, and they walked over to the pot, chatting as though the last few days had never happened.

Mike swung back around, defensively. "You can't go by that. You know what an actor he is. He's not even supposed to be here; he's still on medical leave. He should not go out to Carter's tonight."

Morrissey shrugged. "Okay, I get your point, but let's see how he does in the staff meeting. We'll catch everyone up on the latest concerning our cases. We still have a lot of paperwork to file. I have information on the various charges for both cases from the D.A. – and we'll talk about where to go next with the drug investigation."

It felt good to be in the office again, thought Jordan. Even the routine of staff meeting felt welcome. Normal, predictable. The world was righting on its axis. They went over some details and paperwork needed to wrap up the Goth case and then turned to Drayvon Carter.

"So that brings us to where-from-here, in the drug case," said Morrissey.

Mike looked at Jordan pointedly. "Jordan, you're still technically on medical leave. I think you should take tonight off. Reschedule with Carter."

Strangely, Bear grinned at that statement, and so did Jen and Devon and Milt. Jordan felt as though he'd missed a joke. He said, "I don't think tonight will be a big deal. All I'm doing is picking up an order and the gun."

"Maybe not," said Mike, "but Carter's going to be preoccupied with other stuff, like how to get his pipeline going again. He won't take notice if a small-time dealer asks for a delay. We can afford to blow him off for a week."

"And on the other hand, it would probably be good to see how he's reacting to this," said Jordan. "It'll be quick, in and out." He relaxed his hand; he was holding his pen tightly enough to snap it.

Morrissey jumped in, with a sharp look at Mike. "I think Jordan is right. One quick visit, and he'll be clear for the week. Let him get in there and see how Carter is handling this."

After the meeting, Mike headed straight for his desk, obviously irritated at being overruled. Behind him, Bear looked at Jordan with mock astonishment and said, "Jordan? Jordan?? Really?"

Jordan looked confused, and Jen said, "Mike called you by your first name."

Devon called out, loudly enough for Mike to hear, "That ain't right. It took me two years to get 'Devon.'" But he was smiling, and so were the others.

"Yeah, and Jordan just crammed months' worth of detective work into three weeks, unlike you clowns," Mike shot back, although, from his face, it was evident that he hadn't realized his slip until that moment.

Milt clapped Jordan on the back and said, "Welcome to the team, kid."

And Jordan, a little surprised himself, thought, '*Well, I guess that works both ways.*' Sometime during the last few days, he realized he'd started thinking of DeLuca as 'Mike.'

Jordan sat outside at the back gate at nine that night, waiting for James, and turned on Juan Gonzalez. It was a little more challenging than usual, getting that attitude: the lazy, insolent street punk. It didn't help that James hadn't shown and that he'd been sitting at the gate for ten minutes. He fussed with the hair on the back of his head, pulling it around the spot the doctors had shaved to stitch it up, and then put a baseball cap on backward to hide it.

Jordan had called Carter that day and confirmed his nine o'clock appointment, even though Carter had told him a week ago to come at that time on the next Monday night. It seemed like so long ago, much longer than a week, with everything that had happened in between. Carter had sounded distracted but told him to show up. Now here he was, and no James. The clock dragged on, ten more long minutes.

He debated leaving, but he didn't want to make Carter angry by making the appointment and not showing up for it, so he pulled the car around to the side and parked in the alley, where he had parked the week before. He grabbed his backpack with the money: the payment for this week's drugs, plus five hundred for the gun that Carter had said he would get him. And some extra in his pack, just in case.

He walked up to the front door, glancing around, and shook himself as he got there. 'Get your head in the game,' he thought. He gave himself a second or two more to get into character, and he knocked.

A shadow appeared at the peephole in the door, and then it opened, and James said suspiciously, "Gonzalez. What you want?"

"I was s'posed to get a delivery at the gate, man, at nine," said Juan.

The door shut, and there were voices, and then it opened again, and James said, "Come in then. Make it quick."

Juan stepped inside. They had pulled the leaves out on the table in the dining room and had pushed the computer monitor off to one side, and papers lay next to it. Drayvon Carter and Dee Dee were standing over by the computer; the men had been doing some planning or assessment. A map was up on the printer monitor; it looked as though they had it zoomed in on a portion of the country. Pennsylvania, Ohio, West Virginia. Drayvon Carter looked angry, impatient. Tension hung in the air.

"You got my money?" said Carter.

"Yeah. Five hundred for the piece, and I got fifteen hundred again for this week."

Carter stepped over. "I need seven-hundred for the piece. It ended up being more expensive than I thought. I can't give you no twenty-three grams this week. Supply is a little short."

Juan frowned up at him as he handed him the money. "What do you mean?"

Carter said, irritably, "I said, I can't give you no drugs this week."

Juan would complain, thought Jordan, so he did. "What am I supposed to tell my buyers?" he whined. "I just got 'em lined, up, and -,"

Carter grabbed him by the shirtfront and slammed him into the wall, and Juan's heart went into his throat. He'd pushed too hard. Carter looked ready to crack. He loomed over him, his big fist smashing into Juan's chest. He looked furious, at the breaking point. "Don't question me, you little punk! When I say somethin', I mean it! You listen to the news at all?"

"Y-yes," stammered Juan. *Okay, breathe. It's okay to look scared, Juan would be.*

"You see the big drug bust this week?" Another little shake.

"Yeah."

"That was my pipeline, man – all of it." He released Juan's shirt and stepped back. The brim of Juan's ball cap had hit the wall, and Juan righted the hat on his head. "Now, we're workin' on a new one, but it takes some time. You come back this time next week, and I'll have something. Maybe not as much as you were gettin', but I'll have something."

Juan nodded. "Okay, sorry, man." He looked over at the table and the computer. "Maybe I can help. Anything you need me to do?"

Carter looked a little mollified and seemed to consider that but said, "Not yet. I'll think about it; let you know." He jerked his head at Dee Dee. "Get him his piece."

Dee Dee went back into the bedroom and came out with a Smith and Wesson nine-millimeter with the serial number filed off. "Here," he said gruffly, as the gun and money exchanged hands. "Seven hundred is a deal on this; it goes for a lot more on the street. It's loaded, but if you need more ammo, tell us, we'll get it for a good price. Now get outta here, punk."

Juan tucked the gun in his back waistband and slipped out of the door. The night air smelled clean and fresh. He got into his Impala and headed out.

He made it home, got inside, and sent a text message to Mike to tell him he was back and that it went as expected, except that Carter didn't have any drugs. When he put the phone down, he realized that his hands were trembling. He swore softly and shook them hard.

He thought for a minute, headed back to the bathroom, took out his medicine, and let one pill fall into his hand. He stared at it for a long moment, then put it back into the bottle. Not now. Maybe at bedtime. He could hold off until later. And if he could hold off until then, he might not need it. Then he went back out in the living room and sat down. He had to figure out how to handle this; he'd be damned if he let it get him down.

His work cell phone rang, and he answered it.

"Hi," said Mike. "So, it went okay, huh? No problems?"

"No, no problems," said Jordan. "I paid Carter for the gun, and he told me to come back next week, and he would have some more drugs. He had his computer up, with a map of several states from New York to Michigan, and he was working on something with James and Dee Dee: working so hard that they forgot to do the drop at the gate. I had to go to the door."

"You were inside? What was his mood?"

"Tense. Irritable. I offered to help, and Carter said he'd think about it."

"Okay. You doing okay?"

"Yeah," said Jordan. "I'm fine."

And suddenly, the realization hit him; he *was* fine. He'd just walked into a den of vipers; Carter was in as bad of a mood as he probably ever would be again, until the day they took him down. And Jordan had rolled with it, went with a tense situation, just like he always had. It made him think of the anxiety he'd experienced before his high school plays. Jordan had always thought of that feeling as something positive, something that kept his performances sharp. '*Stagefright*,' he said to himself, and he almost smiled at the thought. All the nerves were merely a case of stage fright.

They ended the call, and Jordan sat and reflected. Tomorrow would be relatively stress-free. Go into the office, write reports, and go to class; fall classes started the next day. No undercover work at all. No undercover work for a whole week. He could do this.

He turned off the living room lamp, took a deep breath, walked into the bathroom, and looked at himself in the mirror. He looked tired, a little older, but somehow tougher than he had a few weeks ago. He felt a surge of confidence rush through him again, like a wave: refreshing, uplifting. He'd come through the fire, and he was still here. He pulled out the pill bottle once more. He stared at it for a long moment and thought about Drayvon Carter, and New York, and the Goth case. Then he held the bottle over the trash can and slowly released it, and let it land with a thump.

BOOKS IN THE CHAMELEON SERIES

SOUTHSIDE GOTHIC
DOWNTOWN DANCE
RAMPAGE IN THE HILLS
BRIDGE GAME

Made in the USA
Middletown, DE
17 July 2022

69591654R00129